PRETTY SHATTERED HEART

ROBBI RENEE

SYNOPSIS

Heart can be defined as the central or innermost part of something. But when that core function is broken, shattered into pieces at the hands of the ones you love most–the distress, suffering, and anguish—can be debilitating.

Sexy, savvy, unbossed, and unbothered, Symphony James is always in control. As for her situationships with men, she dictates who, when, and more importantly, how. Secretly crippled by a tumultuous past, love, relationships, and family were never the desires of her heart. The savage sweetpea only experienced love with conditions until she met *him.*

Unlike most men, Tyus Okoro wasn't intimidated by the hard-care, incorrigible, yet stunningly beautiful Symphony James. Her boss chick behavior was nothing but motivation for him to dismantle her complications—layer by layer. But would he finally meet his match?

DEDICATION

My Life's Trinity - Grace. Grind. Gratitude

Dedicated to my favorite person and biggest fan - my mother.
Thank you for your continued love, encouragement and support.
You've celebrated my wins and losses, making no goal ever out of
reach.
Your prayers sustain me in more ways than you know.
I love you, Momma.

#alwaysyourbabygirl

Note from the Publisher: This is a work of fiction. Any resemblance to actual persons living or dead or references to locations, persons, events, or locations is purely coincidental. The characters, circumstances, and events are imaginative and not intended to reflect real events.

LOVE NOTES

BY ROBBI RENEE

1

"I need to make a grocery list - almond milk, eggs, oatmeal, turkey bacon." Symphony paused her mental shopping list as Calvin heavily breathed against her ear.

"Ah, shit. Damn, Symphony. You feel so good, baby." He grunted against her lifeless, uninterested frame. "You feel me deep in your shit, dollface?"

Symphony rolled her eyes, bored as fuck because she didn't feel a thing. Calvin was pumping, grinding, and gyrating - making all that damn noise - and all Symphony could think about was what she needed to order from the grocery store. *Maybe I'll make some salmon. Add salmon and brown rice to the list.*

"Oh yes Cal, it's great." She lied. Humdrumly responding, hoping Calvin would hurry the hell up. This was the third time she had sex with Calvin, and the third time she had to fake an orgasm. Symphony felt like she was in that scene from *Waiting to Exhale* when Lela Rochon's character faked orgasms with her overweight lover Michael. *Literally like watching paint dry.*

"Oh my God. Symphony. Baby. Baby. Shit! Ooohh." Calvin's old ass literally howled like a wolf. His minute-man moan echoed against the fifty year old walls of Symphony's master bedroom. "Whew! Shit." He kissed her forehead, breath bated. His body unpleasantly heavy against her delicacy. "Did I take care of you, dollface?" Calvin peeled off of her, panting, sweating, and exhausted.

But why? He ain't do shit. She pondered.

Symphony met Calvin Amos at his car dealership, Amos Audi, almost a year ago. Although Calvin owned the place, as soon he saw the beautifully stunning Symphony walk through the doors, he wanted her. She became his personal customer and was given the VIP plus treatment. Some shit he made up in the moment. Symphony walked out of the dealership with a sparkling brand new black Audi A5 Coupe for well under the sticker price and a dinner invitation to Lamar's, an upscale Italian restaurant downtown.

Calvin was 52 years old and probably a real ladies' man for fifty year old ladies. He was handsome, in pretty good shape, wealthy, a widow with grown children almost as old as Symphony. He treated her like a queen and Symphony actually enjoyed spending non-sexual time with Calvin. Based on her situationship rules, he was a perfect match for the woman who did not want kids, or a man with young kids, or baby mama ex-wifey drama.

Symphony typically preferred candidates for her situationships way too young but legal, or way too old but wealthy to avoid any issues. In Symphony's words, *"I can have a lil boy toy to come through and take care of my needs when the old man river can't. But that old dick can run me that American Express."* At 33 years old, Symphony really didn't require a *sugar daddy* type of man because she earned a decent living as the recently promoted Assistant Director of Nursing at St. Gabriel Hospital. But she never rejected fancy dinners, designer bags, and lavish trips and Calvin provided just that.

"You hear me, baby? Did daddy take care of you?" Calvin whispered, staring at the ceiling of Symphony's bedroom, still breathless. "Symphony, I asked you a question. Where are you going, baby?"

Symphony rolled out of the bed, reaching into the night-stand drawer, sifting through a medium-sized glass box. Calvin's voice echoed in the background, but Symphony was focused on finding what she needed while mumbling, *"he wasting my damn time."*

Her face brightened as she slowly revealed a purple and gold, ten inches, girthy, bedside boyfriend, delicately positioned between her fingers as if it was a glistening trophy.

"Cal, I'm sorry to say, but no - daddy in fact *did not* take care of me." Symphony bluntly proclaimed, checking the battery life on her vibrating friend.

"What the hell is that Symphony?" Calvin shouted as he eyed the girthy instrument that put him to shame. He repositioned in the bed to get a good look at this shit, wondering what the hell she's about to do with it.

"Well, my Bedroom Kandi consultant calls him *Your Highness*, but I call him *Purple Rain*." She squealed, as she massaged the length of the silicone shaft.

"Are you really about to use a damn vibrator when we just fucked?" Calvin was now out of the bed and footed across the room to join her with his softened dick dangling.

"No Calvin, *you* just fucked. I just laid there making my damn grocery list." Symphony padded her naked curvy physique past him, attempting to get to the bathroom when he grabbed her wrist.

"You can be a real bitch sometimes, Symphony. How the fuck you think that shit makes me feel?" Calvin yelled, his peanut butter brown skin and dark brown eyes grew fiery as he tightened his grip. "Your ass ain't never said this shit before." His ego was defeated.

Symphony's eyes journeyed from his tight grasp on her wrist up to his narrowed orbs. "First of all Calvin, let me go. And second, I am a *real bitch* to tell you the truth. There is no point in continuing to lie to you when it's a waste of my damn time and clearly your energy." She disdainfully glanced at his limpness.

"You bitch!" Calvin snapped, extending his arm with a backhand strike to her pretty bronzed face. His diamond-encrusted pinky ring imprinted into her reddened flesh. She clutched her cheek to reduce the sting, tasting a hint of blood on her tongue. Symphony's beautiful grey eyes were fiery red, matching her face.

Calvin and Symphony leered, motionless, both of them stunned at what just happened. Symphony had never been hit by a man a day in her life and definitely never in her face. She was a fighter. Always ready to go to blows when jealous girls taunted her and her cousin Syncere. Never opposed to whooping a bitch's ass. But she'd never fought a man - until today.

"You filthy mutherfucka!" Symphony snapped, the vibrator still clutched in her hand, turning the pleasure tool into a weapon of mass destruction. Banging him upside his head, punching, kicking, scratching - she was beating the shit out of this poor man.

"Fuck. Ouch. Shit. Stop Symphony. Damn." He scurried across the room trying to gather his clothes and shoes from the floor. "Your ass is crazy."

"Crazy? Nigga I will show you crazy." Symphony speedily darted across the bedroom while Calvin was struggling with his pants. She grabbed the bat from her closet. "If you ever put your muthafucking hands on me again, I swear to God I will kill you." She swung, barely missing his shoulder. "Get the fuck out Calvin or I will call the police."

"Symphony, dollface, let's talk about this -" He moved a little closer but backed away to avoid the swinging bat.

"You don't have shit to say to me. Once the police sees this fucked *dollface* -" She paused, shifting her jaw as her face continued to swell. "- your precious dealership will be shut down." Symphony grabbed her phone. "Try me Calvin."

"Symphony, I'm sorry." He pleaded.

"Get out!" She screamed, the tears she'd restrained during her rage now released across her burning cheek. Symphony stood in a defensive stance until she heard the front door close. She ran out of her bedroom, down the steps, bat and phone still in hand. Hurriedly locking the front door as she peeked out of the vertical window to ensure he was gone. She leered until his Audi truck sped out of the driveway.

Symphony caught a glimpse of her face in the mirror hanging above her grandmother's antique console table in the foyer. Her normally glistening amber skin was partially unidentifiable. Face flushed, cheek inflamed, lips swollen, ear puffy - she collapsed to the floor sobbing. Shocked, dumbfounded, unable to digest that Calvin actually hit her. But her bruised and battered face didn't lie. His one strike left significant damage.

Symphony's phone vibrated, frightening her out of her daze. *If this dude is calling me.* It wasn't Calvin, it was her cousin Syncere. *Shit! She's probably on her way.* Symphony pondered, recalling that she and her cousin were going to have breakfast that Sunday morning before they visited their grandmother at the assisted living home.

"Prima. Hey. Um, are you on your way?" Symphony questioned, trying to quell the quiver in her voice.

"Hey Prima. Yeah. We are around the corner. I didn't want to just come in." Syncere paused. "Pri, are you ok? Have you been crying?"

"No. No, I'm not crying. What do you mean *we* are on the way? Is King with you?" Symphony rushed up the steps to her bedroom to see what she could do about her face before her cousin arrived. If Symphony *and* King sees her like this, Calvin was as good as dead.

"Yes. King is dropping me off. We're pulling in the driveway now." Syncere hung up the phone, sliding her almost six month pregnant frame out of the passenger side of the Escalade before her husband King could open the door.

"Princess, slow down. Baby, be careful." King demanded. "Let me walk you up the steps and then I'll come back and grab the bags."

"Symphony never cries, King." Syncere waddled to the front door frantically searching her purse for the key to the house she grew up in. "Something's wrong. The only time she cries is when her mother calls or she tries to reach out to her father."

King nodded in understanding, bracing himself for whatever was going on inside the house. He was concerned about Symphony but was more concerned about his pregnant wife who'd already had a couple scares during this pregnancy.

King placed his hand over Syncere's, halting her entry into the house. "Princess, baby, whatever it is, you need to try to remain calm and stress free. Do you understand me?"

She nodded.

"Syncere! I'm serious. Our baby boy and baby girl need to cook a little longer and I need you to be ok. Bet?" King said.

"Bet. I promise, babe." Syncere opened the door just as Symphony was walking down the steps. She'd tossed on a jogging set and draped her curly tresses to the left side of her face, failing to conceal the redness against her bronzed amber skin.

"Prima!"

"Symphony!"

"What the hell happened to your face?" Syncere and King shouted in unison.

"It's nothing. I'm fine. Just a little accident." Symphony cupped her cheek as she quickly walked past her cousin and cousin-in-law.

"Who did that to your face? That don't look like a mutherfucking accident to me. It looks like somebody hit you in your damn face, Symphony." Syncere closed the distance between them, examining the damage.

"Ouch! Shit, Syncere. That hurts." Symphony moved into the kitchen, still vainly trying to mask the bruises.

King went to grab the coffee and food from the truck to allow Symphony and Syncere some time to talk. He returned after a few minutes, joining the ladies in the kitchen and placed the food on the table. King backed away from the stare down still happening between the cousins and leaned against the arched doorway waiting and listening for whose ass he was about to kick.

"Prima! Answer me. Who did this?" Syncere shouted.

Noticing his wife's discomfort, King removed her coat, laying one hand on Syncere's back and the other on her bulging belly, encouraging her to take a seat at the kitchen table.

"Syncere! I don't want to talk about it so just leave it alone." Symphony paused, tears welling in the corners of her cloudy eyes as she sat with her cousin. "I am not trying to argue with you. It's not good for my peas in the pod."

Symphony's phone vibrated against the table displaying Calvin's name. She declined the call. He called right back. Before she could decline again, Syncere snatched the phone accepting the call.

"Did your trifling old ass hit my cousin?" Syncere shouted. "I don't give a fuck what she did or said, you had no right to hit her in her damn face, you bastard. That's a bitch ass move-"

King seized the phone from his wife's death grip as Calvin was still pleading his case. "Dawg, dawg, just shut up man. You really don't have shit to say if you're responsible for what I see on my cousin's face. But hear me when I say this - watch your mutherfucking back." He ended the call and calmly handed his wife the phone.

Symphony and Syncere recognized the dangerously placid look on King's face.

"King, please don't do anything stupid. His old ass is not worth it." Symphony stared at King, begging him with her eyes.

Symphony and King had established a brother-sister relationship over the time that her cousin dated and married him. No longer calling him Lion King since he despised the nickname, she now called him *Primo* - male cousin in Spanish, to match the nickname for Syncere.

"Primo, please. Promise me you won't do anything to him. Shit, he could probably file assault charges on me." She giggled, until the facial sting was too much to bear.

"I'm cool Symphony. I promise." King closed in on his wife. "Are y'all good? I need to head out. Princess, you ok, baby?" He kneeled down beside Syncere, kissing her forehead, nose, then lips.

"King. Promise me." Syncere locked eyes with her handsome husband.

"Baby, I promise. You trust me?" He questioned.

"Always. I'll be fine. Go ahead and check on the house. I love you." Syncere smiled.

"I love you more." King countered. "Call me if y'all need anything."

The cousins returned to their stare down while they waited for King to leave. Hearing the front door close, Symphony exhaled, walking to the freezer to get some ice for her face.

"I can't believe that bastard hit me."

"Symphony what happened? Has he done this before?" Syncere inquired.

"No. He's never even raised his voice at me before. I think I hurt his little feelings." Symphony rolled her eyes, cringing once she placed the ice pack against her face.

"Prima, what did you say? I can only imagine with your smart ass mouth." Syncere chuckled, spreading the grape jelly over her English muffin.

"We were fucking - well he was fucking. I was laying there thinking about my grocery list when he asked me if *daddy did it for me.* I was tired of lying so I told him no and got my vibrator so I could finish what he didn't even start." Symphony nonchalantly shrugged.

"Prima!" Syncere almost choked on her tea. "You pulled out *Purple Rain* while the man was still in your bed?"

"Yep!" She matter-of-factly responded. "He's lucky I didn't call Jameson while his limp ass was laying there."

"Symphony! You're awful. I mean that is still no reason for him to hit you, but damn Prima. You have to massage his ego or maybe his limp lil' dick to get what you need." The cousins boisterously laughed.

"Stop making me laugh, Syncere. This shit hurts." Symphony paused. "Nobody has ever hit me before, Pri. This is crazy."

"Tell me about it." Syncere mused, understanding all too

well the sting of a slap across the face as she briefly recalled the way it felt during her traumatic rape almost eleven years ago.

"I'm sorry Prima. I wasn't trying to be insensitive. I didn't mean to bring up that memory for you." Symphony repented.

"I know Pri. No worries. I'm just concerned about you." Syncere took a deep breath, reaching towards her cousin's cheek. "What are you going to tell G-ma about this? You never know - this might be the motivation she needs to get up out of that wheelchair and beat his ass." The cousins chuckled.

2

"Symphony Monique James! Who did this to your face? Tell me right now." Symphony's grandmother practically hopped out of her wheelchair.

"G-ma. I had an accident at work." She lied.

Symphony wouldn't dare disclose to her grandmother that a man hit her and she definitely wouldn't tell her that it was Calvin Amos. G-ma knew Calvin's family from around the neighborhood since he went to school with Symphony and Syncere's mothers. Back in the day, Calvin was a big time drug dealer. It was rumored that his car dealership was funded at the expense of many addicts in Haven, Syncere's mother being one of them so G-ma was not a fan of Calvin Amos.

"G-ma, I fell at work. I was rushing to get to a patient and didn't see that the floor was wet." Symphony continued to lie and her grandmother knew it.

"I don't know who you think you're foolin' girly girl, but

I've been around long enough to recognize when a man has put his hands on you." G-ma asserted. "Before you keep on lying, just tell me one thing."

"Yes ma'am." Symphony murmured, ferociously blinking back the flood in her slate eyes.

"Did you whoop his ass?" G-ma questioned knowing her granddaughter was a fighter.

"Yes ma'am." Symphony chuckled.

"Good. I won't ask any more questions then. But you have to take care of yourself, Symphony. You need to stop running behind these young lil boys and old ass men and find yourself somebody who will love you and take care of your heart." G-ma paused. "Me and your grandfather did our best to love you girls unconditionally. To be a role model for what a loving relationship looks like. But it's almost like you are afraid to be loved for the fear of being hurt."

Symphony nodded, as the flood gate of tears freed.

"But look at your face baby girl. You're already hurt, Symphony. Someone who loves you wouldn't harm you like this. They would protect you." G-ma caressed her swollen cheek. Symphony rested her face against her grandmother's soothing touch, weeping.

Syncere silently observed as tears streamed down her glowingly pregnant face. She desired love, marriage, and babies for her cousin. Although Symphony claimed those weren't the desires of her heart, her cousin knew better, recalling their childhood conversations. They'd made plans to live next door to each other while raising their families - two boys for Symphony and a boy and a girl for Syncere. The white picket fence dream had become a reality for Syncere, while Symphony attempted to avoid it at all cost.

The James women continued to talk, the cousins digesting words of wisdom from their grandmother. Before they got ready to leave, Symphony and Syncere made sure G-ma had dinner, a shower, and was comfortably positioned in bed so she could watch a countless number of her favorite Tyler Perry shows.

"I love you so much G-ma." Symphony kissed against her forehead. "I promise I'll be ok. I just need some time to think."

"I love you too, my baby girl." G-ma returned the kiss. "But I know what *time to think* means. You're about to hibernate and I won't be hearing from you for a few days." G-ma was all too familiar with Symphony's need to isolate from the world to get on track; she reluctantly gave her the space to do so.

"Maybe just a day or two." Symphony stiffly grinned.

———————————

IT WAS after seven o'clock when they left G-ma's. Symphony still needed to drop-off Syncere before she could head home and take a hot bath. She was driving her pristine Audi in silence, while Syncere napped in the passenger seat. G-ma's words and the image of Calvin's hand against the side of her delicate flesh played in her mind. Symphony reached for her face as if the swelling and pain were a dream. Calvin hit her so hard, her ear was still throbbing even several hours later. *That bastard.* She mused. The deafening ring of her phone through the car speaker disrupted Symphony's daze.

"It's Calvin." Syncere stated the obvious as she jolted from her slumber. "Prima, answer it. I want to hear what that fool gotta say."

"No. Fuck him." Symphony directed her anger towards the dashboard screen. "He can't say shit to me. Got my damn face looking like I was in a heavyweight fight."

"Symphony! Answer the phone." Syncere shouted. The phone rang for a third time. Since Symphony appeared frozen, Syncere hit the answer button on the dashboard screen to her cousin's dismay.

Silence.

"Hello. Hello. Symphony?" Calvin's hoarse, gruffy timbre resonated through the car.

"Calvin, I swear to God I'm calling the police if you call me again." Symphony paused, aggressively gripping the steering wheel.

"Didn't I tell your ass not to call her?" Syncere yelled, angrily pointing towards the screen as if Calvin was present.

"Syncere, I don't mean any disrespect but I'm not talking to you. This is between me and Symphony." Calvin dismissed. "Your big ass husband was probably the one that sent those mutherfuckers up to my dealership."

Those mutherfuckers. The cousins' flawlessly arched brows furrowed as they stared at each other. Symphony turned into Syncere's driveway confused by Calvin's claim.

"What the hell are you talking about?" The cousins chimed in unison.

"Two big ass twin looking mutherfuckers came to my goddamn dealership threatening me." Calvin was screaming through the phone, sounding like he was ready to cry.

"Calvin, I already beat your ass so why would I need to send somebody to do it again?" Symphony declared. "Goodbye Calvin. Call me again and I *will* have King and his entire construction crew on your ass." She disconnected the call before he could respond.

King saw the car lights in the driveway, assuming it was Syncere and Symphony. As Syncere struggled to climb out of the tiny coupe, King walked out of the door to retrieve his pregnant wife.

"Syncere, why do I keep having to tell you to slow down?" King was trying not to yell as he aided her exit from the car.

"King! What did you do?" Symphony and Syncere shouted.

His wrinkled forehead indicated confusion. "What do you mean what did I do?" King paused. "I ain't done shit. I've been chilling, watching the game, waiting for you, Princess."

"Calvin just called me talking about some twin looking dudes threatening him at his -" Symphony hesitated, as the three of them simultaneously connected the dots.

"King, did you say something to Tyus?" Symphony questioned.

Tyus Okoro was one of King's best friends and the deliciously delightful fine specimen that Symphony craved but was unsuccessfully trying to avoid. She and Tyus met over a year ago when Symphony and her cousin were invited to Brighton Falls for the weekend to celebrate Tyus and his twin brother Titan's 35th birthday. Symphony and Tyus had an immediate connection. He had her feeling things that she'd never experienced. Tyus explored her body in ways that she could only imagine in her dreams. Shit, the *Purple Rain*, didn't make her scream and come and scream and come again like Tyus Okoro.

"Aw shit! I met up with Tyus at Melvin's after I went to the construction site to check on the new house. I may have told him that old man river was fucking with you. And Titan was with him too."

"Ooh. Melvin's. Babe, did you bring me some chicken?" Syncere interrupted, caressing her swollen belly.

"Really Prima? You're thinking about chicken right now." Symphony giggled. "Get your pregnant butt in the house." She turned her attention back to King. "Did you tell him Calvin hit me?"

"Yeah. I did." King paused. "I told him I was going to roll-up on old dude tomorrow but it sounds like he beat me to it."

Symphony was confused. She hadn't seen Tyus in weeks. Why would he risk his livelihood for her? Calvin could've called the police or retrieved one of the many guns he kept in his office at the dealership. She was visibly quivering due to the cool breeze of autumn leaving and winter approaching and the thought of something happening to Tyus because of her messed up situationship.

"Prima, you can't worry about that now. Just call Tyus tomorrow. But for now, go home and get some rest." Syncere embraced her cousin a second longer than usual. "I love you, Pri."

"I love you too, Pri." Symphony blinked back her tears. "I'll text you when I make it home."

King escorted Symphony to the driver's side, opening the door for her.

"Symphony, I apologize for sharing your business. But Tyus cares about you so it doesn't surprise anybody that he would go after old dude like that." King paused while Symphony slid into the seat. "But if Calvin bothers you again, I ain't promising you shit. I will put his ass to sleep. When you're upset, my Princess is upset and I just can't have that."

"I know King. Take care of her. She's just like G-ma, worrying about everybody but herself. She needs to keep those babies in the oven for a few more months." Symphony laughed.

Symphony aimlessly journeyed the twenty minute drive to her house in Haven Point. She lived in the house her grandparents bought almost fifty years ago. She'd done some renovations since her grandmother insisted on gifting her the house but maintained much of the vintage charm. Symphony didn't really want to be alone tonight. She considered calling her young tender plaything Jameson but he would be coming for thigh-aching, good ass sex, but she desired more tonight. Symphony wanted to be held, in addition to the thigh-aching good sex. She made a left onto Loyola Street squinting her eyes to make sure she was seeing clearly. A graphite colored Infiniti QX80 was parked in front of her house. *Oh, shit. Ty. God, you really play too much.* She mused.

Symphony took a deep breath, preparing her mind and body to face Tyus. She couldn't understand what it was about him that made her feel different. He literally gave her butterflies and goosebumps at the same damn time. The brash, out-spoken, bold, fighting Symphony quickly evaporated in his presence. She was almost timid, coy, and bashful around him. Tyus brought out the softer, more gentle side of Symphony - and she hated it. *The quickest way to get your heart broken*, she thought.

Symphony pulled into the carport and exited her car, meandering to the side door of the brick house. She heard the sound of his car door closing as she fumbled with her keys - on purpose. The carport lights automatically illuminated by motion as Symphony unlocked the screen before disarming the deadbolt.

"Symphony." He whispered, careful not to startle her although he knew she saw him approaching. Tyus stood at the entrance of the carport with his hands stuffed in his sweatpants pockets.

"Tyus. Hey. What are you doing here?" She uttered, now extremely self-conscious about the condition of her face under the fluorescent lights, she swiped her curly shoulder-length tresses to cover her reddened cheeks.

"Are you okay?" He questioned, still maintaining his position.

"I'm fine but that doesn't answer my question. What are you doing here Ty?" Her voice was still minimal, but shaky. She was nervous. "King told you I was on my way home, didn't he?"

"I haven't talked to King since we left Melvin's earlier. I came to check on you, Symphony." He began to close the distance between them. "Are you going to invite me in or make me stand out in the cold?" Tyus' sexy grin commissioned tremors through her treasure.

Symphony unlocked the door without a word, simply leaving it ajar. Tyus entered the side door, removing his mocha retro Jordan's, leaving them on the shoe rack in the mudroom. He was familiar with the house and the no shoes rule since he'd spent a few nights there.

Since returning from Brighton a year ago, he and Symphony shared many random nights of pure painstakingly gratifying pleasure. Symphony had been avoiding him for the past several weeks so it had been a good minute since they were together. Tyus craved her - desiring to taste her succulent nectar one more time. Taking his focus from her perfectly plump ass, he followed her into the kitchen.

"Do you want something to drink?" She inquired, grabbing a bottle of room temperature water for herself.

"Nah, I'm good." Tyus leaned against the doorframe with his arms folded and socked feet crossed at the ankles, while Symphony leaned against the counter next to the refrigerator across the room. She was trying not to make eye contact. But she couldn't resist.

Tyus was scrumptious. His lean, yet muscular 6'4" frame was complemented by light brown-sugary smooth skin. Wide eyes, a darker shade of brown that sparkled with a hint of green. He was Will Smith in *iRobot* and *Bad Boys II - not one -* kinda fine. But Symphony couldn't choose between his snowy white impeccable smile or the glorious dimples that were so deep, Symphony would willingly fall into his sunken place.

Tyus stood in her kitchen looking tasty enough to devour

in a chocolate brown Polo hooded jacket and matching sweatpants that miraculously concealed the abundance of his beautiful dick.

As he decreased the gap separating them, Symphony vainly tried to increase the space because she was certain he would smell the heated juices of her saturated treasure. She felt so damn stupid standing there with a throbbing headache, swollen face, and pulsating treasure to match. She wanted to fuck Tyus right on her kitchen island... again.

The feeling was mutual. Tyus could smell her sugary sweet nectar from across the room and he was mesmerized. The combination of lavender and mango infiltrated his airways, requiring him to quell his growing manhood.

"You didn't answer my question, Symphony. Are you ok, Sweetpea?" Tyus continued to shorten the distance until he was standing directly in front of her.

She was gripping the bottle of water so tight, it was certain to explode. He fingered a loose tendril of curly auburn brown hair that fell across her eyes before nudging the hair behind her ear fully, exposing the damage done by Calvin.

"I really should've beat the shit out of that mutherfucker." Tyus mumbled, gritting his teeth in frustration.

"Why did you go over there, Ty? It was already taken care of." Syncere blurted at a whisper, still not making eye contact.

"I could see that lil Mayweather. You beat the shit out of that old ass man." He chortled. "Why the fuck did he put his hands on you in the first place, Symphony?" Tyus probed.

"Why do you care, Ty?" Symphony's misty almond-shaped grey orbs finally connected with his.

"So I see you're on your bullshit again, asking me a question like that." He didn't break his gaze. "But if you need an answer, I care because no man should be putting his hands on any woman."

"So I'm just any woman now?" She questioned, fully aware that she was pissing him off.

Tyus decreased the already nominal space dividing them.

"Sweetpea, why do you continue to play games?" He was so close the warmth of his breath soothed her aching twinge.

"I rolled up on that nigga because he had no business putting his hands on *you*, Symphony. That shit is not ok with me."

He reached around her to open the freezer door, never disjoining their gaze and grabbed the ice pack. Tyus wrapped it in a paper towel gently placing it against her face. She cringed with her eyes clutched tight as he kissed her temple.

"You should get some rest, beautiful."

Symphony opened her eyes, intensely staring at Tyus. She was lightheaded, flinching, not from the pain but the fiery heat generating in the depths of her dripping puss. She unzipped Tyus' hoodie revealing the gleaming white Polo t-shirt caressing his muscly chest before thumbing the waistband of his sweatpants and boxers.

Symphony crept one hand then two into his boxers capturing his expanding shaft. Tyus continued to soothe her cheek with the ice pack while never breaking his gaze. She fondled and stroked as he fruitlessly attempted to calm his desire. Tyus bit the corner of his lip. His swollen dick was

22

instructing him to hoist her onto the countertop and immediately take possession of her puss, while his heart and her bruised face reminded him that she was with another man - an abusive mutherfucker, less than 24 hours ago. This was not the time for their normal fuck-fest rendezvous. He craved the way her pussy suctioned his girth, but Tyus wanted her in more ways than just sex.

"Sweetpea. Symphony. You should stop." Tyus used his free hand to disengage her grip from his dick.

"Ty, I need this tonight." Symphony whimpered against his face, trying to regain possession of his countless curved inches. *I need you tonight.* She mused but gave her words no voice.

"Symphony, baby, you need some rest tonight. I'll stay if you want me to, but that's not what we should be doing right now. Let me take care of these bruises." He motioned towards her face as she recoiled.

Symphony's attitude went from zero to one hundred real quick.

"I don't need a damn babysitter, Tyus." She yelled, removing herself from his embrace. "I'm a nurse. I can take care of my own bruises. We both know what you came here for, so why don't you just let us both get what we need?"

If the depth of his furrowed brow was any indication of his anger level, Tyus was beyond pissed.

"Is that really it, Symphony? You truly believe that's all I came here for?"

Tyus dropped the ice pack on the counter, now trying to find as much distance from her as possible. "Is that all you think I want from you, Symphony? Clearly all you want from me is a good fuck."

Symphony angrily stomped across the kitchen through the archway into the living room standing at the vast window. She and Tyus have had a few disagreements over the past year about the state of their relationship. He didn't understand why they continued to play this game of cat and mouse. One minute Symphony was calling requesting his presence, then the next she was ghosting him.

Tyus did not meet the criteria for her situationships. He had a six year son so a child and baby mama were an automatic no for Symphony. But she couldn't stay away from Tyus.

"I'm not having this conversation, Tyus. A good fuck is what we've always been." She howled.

"Wow!" He breathily mouthed. "That's all we've been, huh? So it didn't mean shit when we had a picnic in the park or drove to Nic's winery for the day or me taking care of you when you had the flu. All of that was just a good fuck, huh?."

Symphony didn't respond. Tyus was dumbfounded that she had the balls to say that shit to him. He was offering exactly what Symphony said she wanted - to be cuddled and caressed. Something more than just sex. But her mouth was malfunctioning. Saying all the wrong shit. Literally word vomit.

"You should probably just go, Tyus." She continued in her stupidity.

"Symphony, are you kidding me right now? I came here to check on you - to make sure you were ok. And because I won't fuck you, you're asking me to leave."

Symphony interrupted. "Please Tyus. Just leave." She demanded. Trembling in tears, she faced the window to avoid his adoring gaze.

"So that's the type of man you want, huh? The kind that would ignore the bruises on your face and just fuck. Instead of trying to take care of you. Protect you." Tyus shook his head in disbelief.

"I don't need your protection, Tyus." She turned for a brief second glaring at him.

"Wow. I guess I know where I stand with you then." He paused, wanting a response but received none.

"Symphony?" He uttered.

Nothing - she remained hushed.

Tyus stared at her shapely frame standing at the window. He could tell she was crying so he slowly walked behind her placing his hand on her shoulder. She jolted.

"You either want to fuck me or you don't Tyus. Since you don't, please leave my house." Symphony aggressively wiped the tears from her face, flinching in pain.

Tyus was bewildered and pissed, yet desperately trying to find a reason to stay. He momentarily paused, as he was about to approach her again but refused to stick around where he was not wanted.

"Man, fuck this." He roared. "Keep some ice on your damn face and take your ass to bed. I'm out." Tyus exited the same way he came in. She heard the door slam then the tires screeched as he bolted down her street.

"Fuck!" Symphony's howl echoed through the freshly painted room.

3

Symphony awakened to the sun disrespectfully beaming through the blinds, interrupting her slumber. It was Monday morning and she was supposed to be at work in an hour. She reached for her cellphone on the nightstand, clutching her face when the twinge of pain shot through her ear. *Shit!* She opened the camera on her phone, praying that the condition of her face had improved after a night of ice packs, warm compresses, and Tylenol. No change.

Symphony had no intention of going to work like this. She grimaced through the pain, tossing two Tylenol in her mouth and taking a sip of water before dialing her friend and co-worker Ledia.

"Hey girl hey." Ledia squealed. "Yes, I want coffee if you're stopping."

"Hey Dia. I'm actually not feeling the best so I'm going to

take the day off." Symphony's morning voice was a bit more raspy than usual.

"Oh my God girl, you sound awful. Do you need anything?" Ledia probed.

"No. I'm good. I'm going to take some medicine and rest. I emailed Mr. O'Neil but can you cover for me? I don't believe I have anything urgent pending."

"Of course, girl. I got you." Ledia confirmed. "Hey, have you talked to Calvin?"

Symphony shuddered at the mention of his name. Why was she asking about Calvin? Dia knew that Symphony was seeing Calvin occasionally but that was the extent of her knowledge. Haven Point was not that big so everybody knew everybody.

"Um, no, I haven't. Why? What's up?" Symphony nervously inquired.

"Girl, somebody beat his ass yesterday." Dia giggled. "Me and my uncle saw him last night picking up some food at Melvin's. He was trying to be incognito with sunglasses on at 8 o'clock at night."

"Wh - what did he say happened?" Symphony stuttered.

"He said somebody tried to rob him when he was leaving the dealership. When he took off those sunglasses, I was like *damn*. His eye was big as hell." Dia cackled.

"Did he know who it was?" Symphony was now sitting on the edge of her bed, praying that Calvin didn't pinpoint Tyus and Titan as the culprits. Tyus said they didn't touch Calvin yesterday so the bruises Dia saw had to be from Symphony beating on him.

"He said some young teenage dudes. He fought them off

until he could reach the gun in his car, but of course, they ran after that."

"Oh, I see." Symphony exhaled a sigh of relief. "Yeah, I'm not really messing with Calvin anymore so I don't know what he has going on."

"I hear you girl. Well let me get off this phone and act like I'm working. I'll check on you later. Let me know if you need anything." Dia offered and Symphony thanked her.

Symphony laid comatose for most of the day. Before she knew it, day turned to night and she hadn't moved from her position on the bed other than to use the bathroom. Since she didn't get an opportunity to partake in a hot bath last night, Symphony padded across her carpeted bedroom into the ensuite bathroom. The master suite was one of her favorite places in the house since the renovations.

The porcelain hexagon-shaped tile floor was cool to her French manicured toes. The white clawfoot tub with a crystal chandelier hanging above was the centerpiece of the room. Symphony purposely avoided the massive mirror framed by large bulb lights. She was not interested in the optics of her face under the luminous glare. Filling the tub until it was steaming, she added lavender bubble bath, eucalyptus oil, and lit a candle. The glass of Malbec was already poured and positioned on the tub caddy. Her bath time ritual was a whole mood.

Symphony undressed, revealing her heavenly naked body. Standing at 5 feet 8 inches of golden amber thickness with rotund breast highlighted by rose gold nipple piercings. An intricately designed superwoman tattoo circled her taut waist from her navel to the small of her back. Symphony's curvy hips and athletic thighs were attributed to genetics and years of competitive volleyball. The scar on her right knee from a torn meniscus was the only flaw on her satiny smooth skin.

Symphony carefully stepped into the tub, submerging every voluptuous inch into the steaming shimmering water. She rested her head against the plush bath pillow exhaling, still reeling from the drama of the past 36 hours. Calvin hadn't called or text anymore, but Symphony took pictures of the cuts and bruises just in case he tried to start some shit. Syncere was blowing up her phone of course, but she was not in the mood to be fixed. Symphony was usually the cousin dropping Iyanla-isms and trying to fix Syncere's life, but now the tables have turned. Tyus hadn't called either, but that was no surprise.

TYUS WAS STILL PISSED...AND hurt. When he left Symphony's house he cursed the entire twenty minute drive home. He lived about five minutes from King in the Bridgeport Hills neighborhood. Tyus needed to talk to somebody about this shit between him and Symphony. But who? It was after 10 o'clock and he didn't want to disturb King's pregnant wife. And his brother Titan was likely with his girl Laiya. The roar of his phone through the speakers was like the answer to an unspoken prayer. It was his twin brother.

"What up bro?" Tyus answered.

"Ain't shit happening. Where you at?" Titan questioned.

"On my way home. I just left Symphony's house." Tyus swallowed hard.

"Oh shit. How is she doing, bro?" Titan probed.

"Bro, man her face is fucked up. The whole left side is red and swollen. I think that mutherfucker even busted her lip." Tyus angrily stated.

"I told you we should've beat his ass. That nigga threatening a gun. Shit, I got a gun too mutherfucker." Titan was just as pissed as his twin brother. "I'm surprised you ain't still at her crib. Was she cool staying by herself tonight?"

"Once again Symphony was on her bullshit." Tyus sighed, as he pulled into his garage. "Man, I was trying to put an icepack on her face and her ass started rubbing my dick. She wanted to fuck right then and there."

"Okay? I don't see the problem." Titan chuckled.

"Dude, I was not about to fuck that girl when half of her damn face was swollen and in pain. I went there to check on her. Be there for her - take care of whatever she needs. But she clearly wasn't feeling that." Tyus sounded defeated and his brother noticed.

"Look bro, that girl has had you on a roller coaster since our trip to Brighton a year ago. She clearly only wants to fuck while you want more. If she ain't feeling that dawg, then bounce." Titan paused. "You ain't got no shortage of women trying to get at you."

"Yeah, but I want *that* woman, bro." Tyus confidently proclaimed.

"Oh, say less. Then you gotta put in work, bro. Be relentless in your pursuit until she gives you her heart. But be careful. It seems like Symphony got some fucked up issues she needs to handle. She may never be ready for what you want to offer. Are you good with that?" Titan inquired, protective of his little brother by only fourteen minutes.

"I hear you bro." Tyus responded, but didn't answer the question. "I'm at home dawg. I'll holler at you."

Tyus walked into his two-story condo with Symphony still on the brain. He padded across the dark living room into his first floor master bedroom. Not bothering to turn on the light, he stripped from his clothes and hopped in bed. He was done thinking about her pretty ass for now.

———————

"HEY GOOGLE, play Mary J. Blige radio." Symphony instructed. She was in the mood to wallow in her distress and Mary J. provided the perfect melody for her misery. "I'm Not Gon Cry" circulated through the steamy bathroom. Perfect. The only problem? Symphony was definitely going to cry. She wasn't necessarily distressed about Calvin hitting her. She was heartbroken that she'd put herself into the situation in the first place. Symphony had wasted much of life's precious time on inconsequential men in meaningless situationships. Engrossed with all the things she wasn't willing to tolerate, instead of focusing on what she desired and needed to bring consistent joy into her life beyond salacious, searing, thigh-aching sex.

Symphony wailed, her tears co-mingling with the lavender bubbles as the continuous sounds of Mary J. Blige's most heart wrenching hits piped through the Bluetooth speaker. Tyus' beautifully bearded face played like a scene from her favorite romance movie. The mere thought of his smile, those dimples, his velvet lips pressed against her forehead impassioned her pulsating private folds. The manner at which he caressed her puffy face. Reverent. Genuine.

Symphony squirmed, sensation trailing through the apex of her thighs. Her nipples were hot and firm, chestnut areolas swollen. Symphony was never the type of woman who was afraid to offer herself pleasure. Since her *Purple Rain* was tucked away in the nightstand, Symphony cupped a handful of warm water over her face, sliding her hands down her neck, then chest until her fingertips rested against her throbbing clit. Softly, gently fondling as she visualized *him.*

Tyus' body was overly chiseled, but he sculpted to perfection in Symphony's eyes. The mold of his sexy physique was imprinted in her mental rolodex. She reminisced about the first time they had sex by the pool at the lake house in Brighton. The way Tyus cuddled, embraced, and caressed her body, gazing into her eyes, whispering repeatedly, *"Sweetpea, you're so fucking sexy."* Symphony was never one for making love. She fucked. But with Tyus, that man salaciously breached every nook and cranny of her body. Leaving no stone unturned. Symphony moaned, drowning out the R&B sounds, as she dipped a finger into her sodden treasure, slowly gliding up to her plump pearl.

"Mmmmhh." The heated water offered additional lubrication. "Shit!" She sighed, repeatedly following the pleasing path.

Tears stained her face as she satisfied herself. Pressing her head against the bath pillow, Symphony was reaching her climax. She swung one leg across the clawfoot tub, small puddles pooling on the floor. One finger then two, drifted in and out and in and out of her plump puss until -

"Ah, shit! Ty!" Symphony screamed his name, desperately desiring his presence. She panted, unhurriedly opening her eyes, but he was just an illusion. Labored breathing, her tears began to cease, body somewhat satisfied as she fell asleep in the tub dreaming of him.

Symphony shivered from the cool bath water and the blaring ring from her phone. *Damn. How long was I asleep?* She mused. Taking a glimpse at the phone, it was Jameson. He'd text her a few times but Symphony didn't respond. She knew exactly what he wanted and typically sex with Jameson would be a welcomed request, but not today.

Jameson Davenport was 26 years of yumminess, seven years younger than Symphony. A thickset, 6 foot, fine ass, coffee brown specimen. Jameson had muscle and mass in all the right places - and was nasty ass fuck. That lil young boy had no limit to what he was willing to do in or outside the bedroom. Shit, he had Symphony rethinking her whole life at times. She completely understood why the one chick threw a brick through the windshield of his black Land Rover. That boy would have you climbing the walls for mercy yet begging him for more.

But Jameson Davenport was a spoiled selfish brat. The youngest of the sexy ass Davenport brothers. Syncere's boss, Justin, was the oldest, then Jeremiah and then Jameson. Fraternal twin sisters, Jeremi and Jaxon, followed. Jameson got everything he wanted, when he wanted it, and refused to take no for an answer.

"What's up J?" Symphony uttered as she wrapped her shivering body in the plush red robe.

"What's up, Symph? You good, baby. I've been texting you. You ghosting me?" Jameson's bass-filled tenor always made her smile.

"Nah J. I was just having a rough day. Was kinda laying low today." She tapped the speaker phone while she sat on the bench at the foot of her king size bed.

"Let me come through. You know I'll take care of you. I'll do that thing you like. I can taste that sweet ass pussy now." He gruffly chuckled.

Whew shit! Jameson told no lies. He would definitely take care of Symphony. And that thing she liked, involved her ass in the air, doggy style, with his substantially thick tongue twisting and turning in ways and places she couldn't even describe. Shit, Symphony cooked that nigga a whole breakfast with freshly squeezed orange juice and homemade blueberry muffins the last time he did that shit.

"Not tonight Jameson." Symphony couldn't understand the words that were coming out of her own damn mouth.

"What? Something must be really going on, Symph. You've never turned me down before." He paused, waiting for a response but nothing. "You sure you're good?"

"Yes, I'm fine, J. I will call you in a few days. I just need to take care of some shit, ok?" As good as Jameson felt against her body, she yearned for more and he wasn't it.

"Alright, beautiful. I'll check on you later." They disconnected the line. For a second, Symphony thought about calling him back. *Remember inconsequential people, Symphony. You're not wasting anymore time.* She mused.

Deciding she didn't want to talk to anybody, Symphony silenced her phone before trekking downstairs to the kitchen. She didn't have an appetite for food but she had to eat something to soak up the bottles of wine she was prepared to drink. Symphony warmed some grilled chicken tenders, popped a bag of popcorn, and grabbed the candy jar filled with snack size Snickers. She placed everything on a tray including two bottles of Black Girl Magic Rose'. Symphony footed up the steps, entered her dusky bedroom, placing the tray on the bed. She closed the door as if she would be disturbed in the empty house. The only light in the room was the TV playing reruns of *A Different World* on Amazon Prime and occasional brightness from her phone when G-ma, Syncere, Aminah, and Ledia repeatedly called or texted. She never responded.

SYMPHONY WAS ISOLATED in her bedroom for two days, only coming out to retrieve more bottles of wine. When the wine was depleted, she escalated to vodka. It was now Tuesday night and Symphony finally checked her text messages to ensure nothing was urgent.

Prima: Symphony I'm worried. We haven't talked since Sunday. Just type anything to let me know that you're ok. How's your face? I love you Pri.

Prima: BTW - I told G-ma I talked to you so you gotta call me now. We don't lie to G-ma remember.

Symphony chuckled because Syncere was right, they never lied to G-ma. Even when they tried, she'd always know it was a lie. Sensing her cousin's anxiety about being dishonest with their grandmother, she texted Syncere. Symphony promised King that she would try to minimize her cousin's stress. And she was determined to honor her word.

Prima: Syncere, I'm ok. I love you too. Don't call me, I'll call you when I'm ready. Tell my babies TT Prima said hi.

Symphony giggled, missing the opportunity to lay on Syncere's stomach to talk to the babies. She shook her head once she saw the three dots indicating that Syncere was typing a response, but they quickly disappeared. Symphony continued to peruse her messages and noticed a text from an unknown phone number but known area code. *Illinois.*

The text simply said, **Call Malynda**. Symphony dropped the phone.

"Fuck! As if things couldn't get worse." She poured another shot of vodka.

4

"Hi. Is Joel Pederson available." Symphony questioned.

"I'm Mr. Pederson. Who's asking?" The tall, hand-some, bearded white man with curly sandy brown hair responded as he walked to the front of the upscale boutique, Tina's Customs. He looked like a movie star.

"Um, my name is Symphony. Symphony James." She paused, inhaling with her eyes closed, then deeply exhaling to gain the courage to continue. "I think I'm your daughter."

"Joel, who is this, honey?" A woman resembling Jackie Kennedy appeared from behind a blue lace curtain. They were the picture perfect couple. "Hello, I'm Tina Pederson. Are you here to be fitted for a dress, dear?" She asked Symphony.

"No, I'm - "

"She's lost and needs directions, sweetie." He spoke to his wife. "I'll walk her out and point her to the highway." Mr. Pederson placed one firm hand on Symphony's shoulder, practically pushing her out of the door.

"Mr. Pederson. Um, Joel. I think you are my father. I really need to talk to you." Symphony uttered, unsuccessfully suppressing the tears bubbling in her beautiful grey orbs, the almond shape mirroring the man in front of her.

"Look young lady. You tell Lyndi that we had an agreement. I've sent checks to her mother every month for the past 18 years. I did what I said I would do if she would just keep her damn mouth shut." He paused, turning to look into the store. "She sent you here, didn't she? What do you need? Money? Are you knocked up? Is that it, you need money for an abortion?" He angrily bombarded her with questions.

"What?" Symphony shouted. "You filthy bastard. No, I'm not pregnant and I damn sure don't need your funky ass money. I came here thinking that after 18 years, you would want to meet your daughter. Maybe you would want to know that I'm graduating from high school at the top of my class and going to college on a volleyball scholarship. I guess I hoped, prayed that you would be different from my mother." Symphony sobbed, balling her fist because she was ready to fight - her father. "I thought maybe if you saw me, really looked at me. You would -" She halted, searching for her inhaler. The rapid rise and fall of Symphony's chest threatened an asthma attack.

"I would what?" Joel Pederson cynically questioned.

Symphony sucked in one puff. "That you - you would want me. As your daughter." She whimpered.

"I'm sorry, but it was a mistake. I can't. I don't." He bluntly declared as he walked away.

Symphony gasped, breathing still labored, just like the day she met her father for the first and last time. She awakened from the unrelenting dream she periodically endured since she was eighteen years old. *It was a mistake.* She mused, reaching towards the nightstand for her inhaler. Lately Symphony's asthma had been giving her trouble, typically flaring when she was under a great amount of stress. The text message from Malynda was enough to cause a full blown medical emergency if she'd allow it to go that far.

It was Wednesday morning. The third day of her isolation. She'd exhausted the wine and vodka. There was Modelo in the refrigerator reserved for when she entertained her *situationships* but she was not that desperate for the gratifying numbness the alcohol offered. Symphony showered because she hadn't bathed since Monday night and her smell was becoming personally offensive. She hadn't done laundry so her favorite robe was dirty. Falling right back into the bed, she was naked with the same *Different World* episodes playing on repeat in the background. *Get your ass up Symphony.* She tried to offer motivation but failed.

Symphony checked her phone to see how many missed calls she had from her cousin Syncere. None. She scrolled through the other text messages from Jameson, Dia, and even her boss Mr. O'Neil asked if she was feeling better. *Tyus still hasn't called. Why would he? You fucked up big time Symphony.* She kept scrolling and abruptly paused when she read the text message again - *Call Malynda.*

Symphony tossed her phone across the king size bed, slightly hoping it would hit the floor and shatter so she could sufficiently ignore the message. She laid her naked frame in the middle of the bed staring at the ceiling. Symphony hadn't been isolated for three days in a very long time. Maybe a day or two, but never this long since high school - since meeting Mr. Pederson. Her normal routine of journaling her feelings, listening to music, meditation, and a few bottles of wine were not working to dismiss her from the distress. The slam of a car door outside roused her from the daydream. The old house was beautiful but the walls were paper thin. She could hear everything. Keys rattled at the storm door then the front door. *Syncere.*

Her cousin was the only person who had keys to enter every door of the house. Symphony was expecting Syncere to show up at some point since she hadn't called or text. She threw on a loose house dress and headed down the steps. Not wanting her pregnant cousin to walk up the steep steps or see the countless empty bottles of wine and vodka spread throughout her bedroom.

"Well thank you for not making my fat ass wobble up the steps. But I would've tried." Syncere giggled.

"Hi Prima." Symphony minimally smiled, happy to see her cousin but still in a funk.

"I brought your favorite soup and sandwich from Sliced & Diced." Syncere walked into the kitchen pulling out plates and utensils as Symphony aimlessly trekked behind her.

"I told you I would call you when I was ready, Syncere." Symphony slid into the kitchen chair, dropping her hungover head onto the table.

"Bitch it's been three days. Your ass is ready." Syncere leered at her cousin, daring her to argue. "I'm sure you're out of wine and vodka by now anyway. But if you were desperate enough to drink that beer - I'm having your ass committed." Syncere fixed the plates and grabbed two bottles of water from the pantry before placing the food in front of Symphony.

"Eat." She demanded.

Symphony stared at the sandwich, determining if she even wanted the fight with her cousin about eating. She decided against it.

"How was your doctor's appointment?" Symphony spoke at a whisper, nibbling on the veggie panini.

"It was good. Your peas are growing, well at least little King is." Syncere chuckled. "He's a bit greedy. He gained weight but his sister didn't."

"I guess he's like his daddy already, huh?" Symphony smiled, and it felt good.

The cousins enjoyed lunch, avoiding any conversation about Calvin, Tyus, or Symphony's isolation and drinking over the past several days. Syncere was just happy to lay eyes on her cousin. Symphony's face was healing, now she had to work on her broken spirit. They finished eating lunch in silence.

"Malynda text me." Symphony blurted, breaking the silence as she hugged her knees against her chest.

Malynda James, Symphony's mother, a timeless beauty with mocha skin matching her father Mylon and smokey grey eyes mirroring her mother Neolla. She was stunning, capturing the attention of every man in Haven Point back in the day. Malynda was genius-level smart, graduating magna cum laude from high school with scholarships from state schools to ivy league universities. *I'm going to be a doctor and an actress.* Malynda often boasted to her friends. She was well on her way attending NYU until the day she met Joel Pederson, a talented instrumentalist, off Broadway actor, and wanna be talent agent. They met when Malynda was nineteen. After a chaotic love affair, the conceited beauty found herself alone and pregnant. Joel Pederson's promises of stardom coupled with his manipulation, a wife, a son, and a baby on the way, drove Malynda psychotic. Clinically.

"What do you mean Malynda texted you? You mean that someone from the mental care facility called you about Malynda?" Syncere nervously inquired.

"No, Prima. I mean Malynda texted me from a 618 area code that was not the facility." Symphony unlocked her phone and navigated to the message before sliding the phone across the kitchen table. Syncere held the phone longer than required to read such a short message.

"Did you text back?" Syncere was visibly shaking, understanding the toll her Aunt Malynda's presence would have on her cousin.

"No." Symphony rocked in the chair.

"Are you going to? Do you want me to?" Syncere offered.

Symphony hunched her shoulders, still rocking. "No. I don't know." She paused. "I'm curious about what's going on with her but I'm... scared. If she's on her bullshit again, I may really hurt her this time."

The cousins glared at each other for what felt like a lifetime. Reminiscing about the last time Malynda showed up in Haven Point. A few years ago she somehow found out that G-ma had another stroke. She blew into town with her Oscar-worthy dramatics, pretending to be a caring doting daughter. She'd been missing in action for almost three years since their grandfather's funeral, where she clowned and had to be physically carried out of the church. This was Malynda's mode of operation; go missing for several years then reappear as if they were all a big happy family. When she popped up at the hospital while G-ma was sick, Symphony and Syncere begged her to leave because she was upsetting their grandmother.

"*Bitch that is my mother!*" *Malynda shouted at her own daughter.*

"*I'm not a little girl anymore, bitch. I swear to God I will drag your crazy ass all through this hospital if you don't leave G-ma alone.*" *Symphony rebutted to her mother. Syncere tried to be the peacemaker until the blue alarm above G-ma's hospital room door sounded.* **Code blue. Code blue. Room 1320** *echoed through the intercom. G-ma's heart rate dropped dangerously low as the nurses rushed in to aid her. Symphony snapped. Fighting her mother in the hospital waiting room.*

They hadn't seen Malynda since then.

Symphony's silent tears were now a boisterous wail infiltrating the paper thin walls. The thunderous sob and vehement pain were palpable.

"I can't Prima. I can't do this with her anymore. She's hurt me enough. I just can't." Symphony screamed as Syncere exited her chair as quickly as her bulging belly allowed, consoling her cousin cheek to cheek. Co-mingling tears from their matching grey eyes dampened the kitchen table. They embraced each other until Symphony's tears ceased.

"I have an idea. Let's order Chinese food for dinner, copasquat on the couch, and watch *School Daze* like we used to when our crazy ass mothers would piss us off." Syncere smiled, thumbing away Symphony's leftover tears. "Before you say no... I'm begging. Please Prima!" Syncere pouted.

"Ugh ok. Only because you're my favorite cousin." Symphony teased, her smile threatened to reach her eyes.

"Bitch I'm your only cousin and I love you so much." Syncere uttered, hugging her prima tighter.

———————

THE COUSINS ORDERED TOO much food and snuggled on each end of the couch reciting every word from *School Daze*. Symphony and Syncere even jumped up to join the classic battle of the Jigaboos versus the Gamma Rays in flawless choreography and singing.

"Ok, Pri. Don't shake those babies out. You will not have King beating my ass." Symphony guffawed. There was a glimmer of light in her eyes as the cousins boisterously laughed. Syncere's phone chimed, disturbing their party.

Tyus: Hey Syn. How are you and my god babies?

Syncere was about to reply when the three dots alerted to another incoming message.

Tyus: Have you talked to Symphony? Is she ok?

Syncere's face brightened as she stared at Symphony. "Prima." She sang. "Somebody is asking about you?"

"Tell my Primo I'm fine and he can have his wife back at any time." Symphony started clearing the Chinese food boxes from the table.

"It's not your Primo who's asking." Syncere cackled. "Let's

play a guessing game. He's a tall caramel tower of fine, a million dollar smile, and prefers to call you his *sweetpea*." She giggled.

"Tyus?" Symphony loudly questioned. "He texted you? Let me see." She snatched the phone from her cousin quietly reading the words, failing miserably to mask her smile.

"Symphony, call him." Syncere gently kicked against her cousin's leg to gain her attention. "Have you even talked to him since the Calvin fiasco?"

"Yeah - and I fucked it all the way up." She whispered, plopping down on the couch. Symphony was prepared to get cursed out once she told Syncere the story.

"Do I even want to ask what you did or said or both?" Syncere inhaled the last eggroll.

"Probably not." Symphony sarcastically chuckled. "To make a long ass story short - he was parked in front of the house when I got home Sunday night. He said he came to check on me. Caressing my face, getting me an ice pack - just being all nice. I wanted him - so I basically grabbed his dick and told him let's just fuck since that's what we both want. He got pissed and left-" She shrugged.

"Symphony! I cannot with you." Syncere clamored, before deeply exhaling. "I'm going to tell you like you told me when I almost ended things with King before they started. Maybe it's time to let that situationship bullshit go. Tyus may have started off that way but he clearly wants more. Do you really think he was ready to whoop on Calvin for nothing - just because y'all fucked? Um, no ma'am. Trust and believe ain't no shortage of va-jay-jay for Tyus Okoro." Syncere paused, trying to glean a reaction from her cousin.

"King said Tyus was fuming when he heard what happened. He confronted Calvin because he cares about you, dummy." Symphony mindlessly stared and listened. "Just like my noncommitment shit was bullshit. So are your *no kids, no baby mama* situationship rules." Syncere scooted off the couch, preparing to stand so she could go to the restroom. Symphony helped her cousin maneuver with that belly.

"Ok Syncere since you have so much to say, would you have dated and fallen in love with King if he had a little baby King and a crazy ex running around?" Symphony probed.

"To have my King? Hell yeah! Without question." Syncere matter-of-factly declared with her hands rested on her stomach. "That man is everything I never knew I needed. So if I had a bonus child and an ex to manage...I would for King Elias Cartwright."

"Wow! Now that's love." Symphony uttered.

"Prima, I understand you're scared and feel the need to protect yourself. Trust me - you know I've been in that place. But every man is not like Joel Pederson. They don't all cheat on their wives, neglect their children, and drive their side chicks crazy. And I'll say it again, every woman in Haven wants a piece of the twin tower so fuck it up if you want to." Syncere started to waddle then paused.

"And who said his son's mother is crazy anyway? You're just making up shit. I've never met her but they seem to co-parent just fine." Syncere walked away, heading towards the bathroom where she responded to Tyus' text. *She's better, just stupid as fuck. You have to be a little patient with her.*

Tyus: I'm a patient man sis, but I ain't Job.

. . .

46

THE COUSINS WATCHED *House Party* movies until Syncere fell asleep around 11 pm. Symphony called King letting him know that his wife was asleep so she should stay all night. For a moment, King, the protector, was about to drive the twenty minutes to get his princess but he acquiesced. After getting her cousin settled in their grandparents' old bedroom, Symphony stared at her phone, desperately wanting to talk to Tyus but what could she say.

Sweetpea: Hey. Can we talk?

After working out, Tyus had been in his office all evening preparing for a business trip to Atlanta the next day. He'd recently started his own accounting and financial fraud investigations firm so he often put in late nights. He did a double take when he saw his nickname for Symphony pop up on his phone. He could only see the name, not the message so he was hesitant. Tyus figured Syncere told Symphony that he'd checked on her. *I hope she ain't on her bullshit.* He mused, knowing all too well that Symphony could get an attitude over small shit.

She's probably asking why I contacted her cousin and not her. He pondered. "Because you always on some dumb shit." Tyus responded to his inner thought. He unlocked his phone and navigated to the message. *Can we talk?* He mouthed. As much as he wanted to hop in his truck and speed to Loyola Street, he decided to chill. Although Tyus hadn't completely disclosed his feelings for Symphony, he knew damn well that she understood his intentions were more than just sex. So yeah, he felt like she had a lot of talking to do.

Ty: Hey. Yeah we can talk. I'm listening.

Symphony honestly wasn't expecting him to respond.

She knew all of the things she should say like *I'm sorry.* But her pride and the brick wall around her heart prevented her from saying anything. Symphony fell asleep clutching the phone, while Tyus checked his messages again for a response. Nothing.

"Man, I'm done." Tyus whispered, closing his suitcase and retiring to bed.

5

Symphony finally broke free from her isolation after the impromptu slumber party with her cousin. Once her face healed, she returned to her regular schedule - work, G-ma, Syncere, but with one modification - no men. She hadn't responded to Jameson's text messages and after initiating communication with Tyus - she never responded to him either. Symphony hadn't heard anything else from Malynda but she didn't expect her mother to remain silent. If she didn't know anything else, she knew Malynda liked to make a scene so Symphony was bracing herself for the dramatics.

The week seemed to breeze by since Symphony was buried in work and planning for Syncere's baby shower on Saturday. It was Friday evening and Symphony was resting since she had a busy day tomorrow. The *Brown Bean Coffee Shop* would be transformed for the *Two Peas in a Pod* themed party. Symphony admitted that she went a bit overboard but spared no expense for her cousin.

After work Symphony picked up a bottle of 19 Criminals red wine and a chicken pizza from *Pi Pizzeria.* She took a bath and draped in her robe, ready to enjoy a quiet evening at home until her doorbell rang. Symphony checked the security camera app on her phone. It was Jameson. *Shit!*

Casually footing across the room into the foyer, she checked her reflection in the mirror and secured her robe before opening the door.

"What are you doing here Jameson?" Symphony unlocked the screen door then crossed her arms in frustration.

"Well hello beautiful. It's been too long. I came to make sure you were in the land of the living." Jameson didn't wait for an invitation to enter. "I came bearing gifts. The lady's favorite wine and dessert." He held up a blue gift bag.

Symphony's mouth watered, hoping his mother, Ms. Ella, made her famous apple cobbler.

"Thank you J." She seized the bag from his hands, verifying the contents, and walked into the kitchen smiling. He swiftly followed. "I was trying to have some me time, but I guess I didn't make that clear the last time we talked."

"Your 'me time' was last week. I missed you, girl." Jameson sexily smiled, undressing her with his devilish eyes.

"I'm sure you had enough to keep you busy." Symphony blushed. Jameson was so damn cute and she couldn't deny it. His jovial and spontaneous personality was contagious. She couldn't be angry or irritated in his presence because he simply wouldn't allow it.

"But I didn't have you, beautiful. You know I need my Symphony fix. You got me feigning, baby." He sang in a horrible rendition of the Jodeci classic.

Symphony giggled as he tickled her waist.

"J! Stop." She swatted his hand away, still chuckling. "Is this wine all for me or do you want to taste it?"

"I want to taste something but it ain't wine." He salaciously smirked.

Jameson grabbed the belt of her robe, pulling Symphony into his brawny frame. He kissed against her neck, trailing a finger down the center of her chest, loosening the robe, slightly exposing her lightly dampened breast. Symphony hadn't had the delicate yet firm touch of a man since Calvin - and since that shit didn't count in her mind, she really hadn't had any release - other than self-imposed. *Remember no inconsequential situationships, Symphony.* She reminded herself, uselessly attempting to retreat, but her treasure was throbbing - shit, aching to be set free. *I'll start over tomorrow. I need this shit.* She mused, graciously following her boy toy's lead.

Jameson continued to trail his hot thick tongue down her neck to her breast, gently licking and tugging each nipple ring. The pain and pleasure delightfully intermingled. Symphony didn't have a chance to react when he removed the wine from her hand then hoisted her onto the counter, guiding his tongue back up her chest to capture her lips. Jameson delivered unyielding, sloppy kisses and Symphony didn't oppose. His tongue twisted and twirled in the most lascivious dance inside her mouth. He had the cutest puppy dog ears that she loved to tug. Symphony drew him in by the ears, urging him to get closer. Jameson unbelted the robe, leaving her naked frame completely exposed.

"Open." Jameson commanded. She obeyed, spreading her shea butter covered thighs wide. Jameson reclaimed the folds of her neck before driving one finger then two into her water-logged puss.

"Ah, shit! J!" She moaned, unconsciously grinding against his fingers. He slithered in and out, up and down before detaching his nectar-coated fingers leaving her private lips dripping wet. Jameson licked her juices from his fingertips like a damn lollipop.

"Damn beautiful. You taste so fucking sweet." He delighted in the last drop. "You want this tongue, this dick or both?"

Fuck! So many great choices. *How's a girl to choose?* Symphony thought to herself. But she knew she needed to make a wise decision. A night with Jameson's tongue *and* dick would have her delirious and passed out until noon tomorrow. Since that wasn't an option, Symphony opted for his tongue only. And she knew Jameson wouldn't debate.

"I'll take the tongue please and thank you." She squealed.

"As you wish, beautiful." Jameson's thick sexy ass strolled to the kitchen table, pulling a chair to the edge of the counter where Symphony's puss was still on display. He clearly was about to be swimming in her ocean for a while. Sitting in the chair, he positioned her thick thighs across his shoulders before kissing against her flushed skin. Jameson planted soft gentle kisses against her pulsating clit and down the layers of her swollen labia, locking his arms around the mass of her thighs before flattening his hefty tongue to lick the entire surface of her pussy.

"Fuck! Jameson!" She screamed, clutching the edge of the countertop, head pressed against the cabinet with nowhere to run.

"Mmmm." He moaned. "Pussy so good I could stay here all night." Jameson grunted before diving back in. Sliding two fingers back into her depth, he licked and stroked and stroked and licked with unabated pursuit. Jameson had thoroughly examined every curve of Symphony's body so he knew exactly what to do for her to explode. But he teased, slowing his pace to a crawl, tongue-kissing every fold of her jewel at a merciless pace. He flicked the tip of his tongue against her clit as his fingers gently escaped the suction of her folds. A gasp escaped her mouth.

"Look at me, Symphony." He demanded. Symphony was barely coherent, almost unable to follow directions. Panting, narrow-eyed, she glanced down just in time to see him lick her creamy goodness from his fingers with her juices glistening against his smooth skin. He plunged back into her sodden hole tongue first - slurping, sucking, nibbling, withdrawing her surplus. She was empty, bankrupt, completely spent.

"Oh my goodness. Ah, shit! J!" Symphony screamed, grabbing his ears for leverage as she rode his face. He secured her legs, his tongue and lips rapidly kneading her clit.

"Shit. Shit. Shit." Symphony sang.

She ready. Jameson mused with a smile as he made his

final attack acquainting his fingers with her walls one more time.

"Aaahh! J-J-J!" Symphony screamed, pushing his head away. But he was unmovable, clutching her thighs until her convulsions ceased. Kissing up her stomach, across each nipple, up her neck, then capturing the full of her mouth with his treasure-flavored kisses. He lingered there for a minute, trailing his fingers up and down her thighs until she was stable.

"I'll let your tasty ass get back to your *me time.*" Jameson kissed against her forehead before aiding her from the counter. "Can I use your bathroom?"

"Of course." She whimpered, still out of breath and a little wobbly. Symphony ambled across the kitchen into the living room, collapsing onto the couch. Several minutes later, Jameson exited the bathroom and kneeled beside her.

"You good, baby?" He cupped her chin, planting one last kiss against her lips.

"Yep. All good." She breathily laughed.

"You know where to find me if you need me." Jameson stood, peering down at her. "Symph, don't fall asleep girl. Come walk me to the door."

Symphony jolted. She'd fallen asleep that damn quick. Taking a deep breath to get herself together, she rose, belting her robe as she walked Jameson to the door. He extended a final goodnight and she secured the door before returning to the couch with every intention of eating her pizza. But she peacefully slumbered instead.

TYUS SPENT the week in Atlanta for business and had just landed back in Haven. Still no word from Symphony. He didn't understand the purpose of her messaging him as if she wanted to talk but then go ghost - again. Symphony was playing games as usual and he was not in the mood. When Tyus said he was done, he meant that shit.

Looking deliciously sexy in all black everything - suit, shirt, tie, shoes, he exited the airport heading to Mosaic Bar and Grill to meet Titan and Lennox for drinks. After a week of business meetings all day and corporate dinners at night, he was ready to unwind with his boys. King couldn't join the crew since his baby shower was tomorrow and Syncere was not having it.

"What's up, Tyus? How was the ATL bro?" Titan pulled his brother into a hug. "Your ass walking in here like double O seven and shit."

"Whatever bro. I came straight from the airport so I didn't have time to change clothes." Tyus loosened his tie while the trio of fine black men gained the attention of every woman in the bar.

"We got you a Macallan coming, dawg." Lennox chimed. "How have you been, man? I haven't seen you in a minute."

"Dawg, my schedule is crazy. Business is good so I'm not complaining." Tyus paused, as he noticed a familiar set of eyes staring at him. "Give me a second. I'll be right back."

Tyus sauntered across the restaurant towards the bar in the opposite corner, nodding greetings to the ladies who wished he was coming their way. He halted his pursuit at his target.

"Natalie McNeese. It's been a long time. Or excuse me Natalie McNeese Wright." Tyus sexily smiled, resting his hand against the bar beside her.

"Tyus Okoro. Oh my goodness. It has been way too long." Natalie stood on her 4 inch red bottoms, pulling him into an embrace. The scent of bergamot and citrus intoxicated her as she inhaled.

"What are you doing in Haven? You left sunny California for 40 degrees and rain?" Tyus inquired.

Natalie McNeese was Tyus' high school sweetheart and his first - everything. She was still beautiful but had been crazy as hell. Natalie and Tyus had a whirlwind dramatic ass relationship to be so young. He thought she was the love of his life, but he was terribly mistaken. They parted ways when he moved to Atlanta to attend Morehouse College and she got accepted into the University of Southern California.

"My parents moved back last year to take care of my grandfather. Unfortunately, he passed away a couple weeks ago so I've been here helping them settle his estate." She explained.

"I'm sorry to hear that. You have my condolences." Tyus remained standing as she returned to her seat.

"Thank you. Take a seat Tyus. We should catch up." She nibbled at her bottom lip, eyeing him from head to toe.

"And by the way, it's just Natalie McNeese again. He wasn't *Mister Right* after all." She paused, sipping her fruity-looking drink as she continued to examine Tyus' muscular frame.

Tyus smirked, recognizing the familiar flirtatious behavior. "Oh I see. Well, I'm sorry to hear that as well." He paused, observing her matured physique. She still had those deep ass dimples that used to drive him wild. "I'm actually here with my brother and a friend. So I should get back."

"Titan's here?" She peered around the bar. "I should go say hello."

"Nah. I would advise against that." Tyus chuckled, aware of his brother's disdain for Natalie.

"Have breakfast with me tomorrow." Natalie blurted as Tyus began to walk away. "It's just breakfast with a friend. We are still friends right, Tyus? We have too much history not to be."

"Um, I promised my son I would take him to breakfast so I'll have to pass." Tyus attempted to exit again when she grabbed his arm.

"Oh wow. You have a son. Is there a wife too?" She inquired but Tyus had a feeling she wouldn't give a damn if there was.

"No. No wife."

"Lunch then?" She eagerly offered.

Tyus thought of a million reasons why he should say no given the history with this woman. "Ok. An early lunch." He sighed, already regretting his decision. "I have to go to my boy King's baby shower tomorrow at 3. We can meet at *Sliced and Diced* since the shower is down the street at the *Brown Bean*."

"Perfect! It's a date." Natalie practically squealed as she typed her number into his phone.

Tyus returned to the bar with his friends trying to avoid

the snickers and sneers. "Just shut the fuck up. I don't want to hear it." He chortled.

"Yo! Is that Natalie McNeese from high school?" Titan bantered. "Your first fuck and first heart break, Natalie? What is she doing here? And without her millionaire Dr. Wright."

"Her grandfather died." Tyus took a sip of his whiskey. "And she's no longer Mrs. Wright."

"Aww shit! Leave that shit alone, Tyus. She was never *Mrs. Right* for you. I have never wanted to hit a woman in my life but I was ready to fuck her up when she pulled that bullshit."

"Man that's been over fifteen years ago. If I'm over it, you should be too." Tyus leered at his brother.

"Aye. Y'all see me sitting here right?" Lennox snapped. "What the hell are y'all talking about? What did she do?"

"She's a liar and a bitch. And I can hold a grudge longer than a mutherfucker." Titan quipped and the men all heartily guffawed.

"It's a long ass story, Len, that I don't want to get into. I want to finish my drink, maybe get another one before I go home to crash." Tyus' tone and expression were laced with seriousness. His brother and friend quickly changed the subject.

———————

THE NEXT MORNING, Tyus was elated to see his six year old son Tyus Anthony Ramos Okoro, Jr. (TJ). He picked up TJ around 9 am for breakfast at his son's favorite place, IHOP. Tyus and TJ's mother, Gia, didn't need the courtroom to dictate his financial commitment or visitation. He took very good care of his son and Gia couldn't complain. As long as he wasn't traveling, Tyus had TJ every other Thursday through Monday. He would pick up TJ from school on Thursday and take him to school on Monday morning where his mother would resume her duties that evening. On the off weeks, he'd usually take TJ to dinner one or two nights a week.

"Hey Dad, can I spend the night with Grammy and PopPop tonight?" TJ asked as he stuffed Mickey Mouse shaped pancakes in his little mouth.

"I thought we were hanging out this weekend, lil man. And stop stuffing your mouth before you choke." He reached up to wipe TJ's face. "You are a sticky mess." They laughed.

"Well, PopPop bought me a new Lego and Grammy said we can make cheeseburgers and fries." TJ grinned, revealing nothing but the cutest gums.

"So you're ditching me for Legos and cheeseburgers. I see how you do me." Tyus guffawed, admiring his namesake who mirrored everything about him except his eyes. "Yes, you can spend the night. But don't call me at 10 o'clock to pick you up once the Lego is done and burgers are gone, you understand?"

"Yes Sir." TJ saluted with a smile.

Tyus dropped off TJ at his parents' house as promised. Typically he would want his son all to himself during the weekend, but Tyus didn't mind tonight since TJ was spending the week with him while his mother was on a girls' trip with her sisters.

After spending a few minutes with his family, Tyus returned home and got dressed to meet Natalie before the baby shower. He arrived at *Sliced and Diced* at 2 pm as planned. It was now 2:15 and Natalie wasn't there. She'd text that she was en route. That was fifteen minutes ago. Tyus glanced at his watch for the third time. It was 2:40 and Natalie still hadn't arrived. A few minutes later she rushed in profusely apologizing for her delay. But Tyus had a feeling this shit was intentional.

"Natalie, you're late. I told you I had somewhere to be at three." Tyus was irritated.

"Tyus, I'm sorry. Mother had me running around this morning. She told me to tell you hello by the way." Natalie talked non-stop.

"Natalie. Stop." Tyus stood to leave, but she thought he was pulling out a chair for her to be seated. "I have to go."

"Let me go with you." She nudged his chin, encouraging him to look at her. "Tyus, I just want to spend some time with you. You know, catch up. Talk about old times. I'm sorry I was late. I'll make it up to you. Please, let me go with you."

Tyus reluctantly acquiesced as an image of Symphony popped in his head. He had been prepared to completely ignore her during the baby shower, but he still felt disturbed about bringing Natalie. *But Symphony had her chance. She hasn't called in over a week.* He mused, opening the restaurant door for him and Natalie to exit and head one block to the coffee shop. A decision he prayed he wouldn't regret.

THE COFFEE SHOP where King proclaimed he first fell in love with Syncere, *The Brown Bean,* had truly been transformed. Every surface was draped with green, yellow, and white polka-dots - tablecloths, napkins, and chair bows. If it stood still, Symphony had it decorated to coordinate with the *Two Peas in a Pod* theme. The candy bar and dessert tables were even adorned with images of two little green peas kissing. Symphony busied herself as the caterers delivered the food to the kitchen. Elegant finger food foods, sandwiches, and delectable salads prepared by King's personal chef, and Melvin's fried chicken - a special request from the mommy to be. Guests began to arrive at exactly 3 o'clock greeted with the signature alcoholic or non-alcoholic coffee inspired cocktail named, 'Syncerely My King.'

Symphony's friend Ledia picked up G-ma who was beautiful in her green, white, and yellow sweater to match the decor. Symphony hurriedly greeted her grandmother then ensured everything was ready before Syncere arrived. King texted that they were five minutes away. The shower wasn't a surprise, but Syncere gave her cousin and sorority sister Aminah creative freedom on the theme. Her only requirement was the fried chicken.

Syncere and King strolled into *The Brown Bean* hand in hand glowing with anticipation. Their eyes collectively brightened as they observed every meticulously thoughtful detail. Syncere's eyes watered searching the room for her cousin, knowing that she was the primary brainchild behind this spectacular event.

"Do you like it, Prima?" Symphony squealed with Aminah following closely behind.

"I absolutely love it!" Syncere embraced her cousin with tear dampened cheeks. "It's amazing. I'm speechless. Seriously, everything is so beautiful. Thank you, Pri. And you too Minah."

"You ladies outdid yourself. For real. It's wonderful. Thank you." King chimed, massaging the small of his wife's back.

"Syncere, you look beautiful, baby girl." G-ma interrupted. Syncere was gorgeous in a canary yellow long sleeve maxi dress, her freshly braided hair in a high bun with her signature gold hoop earrings. Since her feet were swollen, she opted for metallic gold Gucci sneakers.

Symphony positioned the guests of honor at the head table before returning to her hostess duties. Sauntering through the room in a fitted high waist army green skirt, ivory long sleeve bodysuit, and peep toe camouflage green boots, Symphony was feeling herself. Her curly golden brown afro was partially pulled into a ponytail with loose tresses hanging against her shoulders. She mingled, laughing with various guests until she felt a shift in her spirit. Her body quivered as contractions slithered through her spine. It was *him*. She could smell the bergamot mixed with his natural aroma. Symphony's body could sense Tyus in the atmosphere before ever laying eyes on him. She wanted to turn around to observe the frame that held the sexy scent but her juices were already beginning to saturate her thong.

"What's up King? Hey Syn. You look amazing. This is an

old friend of mine, Natalie McNeese." Symphony heard his bass-filled timbre echo in the background.

Natalie? What the fuck? She internally screeched, hesitantly shifting her stance to examine the situation. *Hmm. She's pretty. But who the hell is she?* Symphony pondered.

Tyus stood with King, Titan, Lennox, and Nicolas as he searched the room for *her.* He didn't want to, but his traitorous ass heart and manhood couldn't help themselves. His eyes landed on Symphony. *Damn she is gorgeous.* Tyus surveyed her from the curly brown mane to those pretty ass toes and he was mesmerized. Symphony turned in his direction and they held an adoring gaze for a moment too long before she darted into the kitchen. Tyus saw everything he needed to see. She was beautiful, stunningly sexy, and he wanted her - now.

"Um, fellas, excuse me for a minute." Tyus interrupted, departing from his crew before they could say a word.

"Where is he going in a hurry?" Lennox questioned.

"Man, you know where he's going." Nic stated as he, King, and Titan chimed almost in unison, "Symphony."

Why the fuck can't I just stay away. Tyus debated as he continued his pursuit towards the kitchen, navigating through the crowd as he quickly greeted family and friends. Natalie was getting reacquainted with some old schoolmates from the neighborhood, giving Tyus the perfect opportunity to get away.

"Hey everyone. Can I have your attention please? We are going to begin serving the food in about five minutes. Please grab a drink from the bar and take a seat. Thank you." Aminah announced.

"Uh oh. I guess you will be rushing off next, Nic." Lennox bantered.

"Why do you say that?" Nic questioned, sipping on his cognac-spiked coffee.

The fellas sang in union again, "Aminah." Nic unsuccessfully attempted to act unphased but he'd been smitten with Aminah since King and Syncere's wedding at his family's winery in Brighton Falls.

"What's up with y'all, bro? She seems cool with that pretty ass smile." Lennox chimed.

"That's a great question, dawg. Aminah is um -" Nic struggled.

"Complex?" King offered. "If she's anything like her sorority sisters, complex is the only word to describe her." They laughed. Nic nodded in agreement, keeping his focus on Aminah.

While Aminah played hostess, fruitlessly trying to avoid the penetrating stare of Nic's anthracite eyes, Symphony escaped to the kitchen pretending to get the food organized. The caterers had things under control and were ready to begin serving the guests. To delay her stay in the kitchen, she aimlessly began rearranging the charcuterie board as if the gouda and pepper jack cheeses were out of place. Tyus made his way through the crowd with minimal attention when he approached the double doors leading to the kitchen.

"Symphony." Tyus whispered. He had a way of saying her name that always gave her this butterfly-goosebump combination.

Symphony continued to diligently arrange the assorted

crackers. "Yes, what can I do for you?" She stated without looking up, knowing damn well it was him.

"Symphony, look at me." Tyus demanded, stepping into the kitchen. "How are you?"

She inhaled deeply, blinking back the mistiness against her cloudy grey eyes. Symphony cleared her throat. "Hi Tyus. I'm ok. How are you?" She uttered.

"I'm ok. It's good to see you." He began to close the distance, leaning against the stainless steel prep table next to her. "Let me see your face."

"Tyus, my face is fine. No need to worry anymore. The bruises are gone. Everything is healed." Symphony declared.

"But are you, Sweetpea? Healed, that is?" Tyus depleted the miniscule gap examining her face. He was happy to see that the visible bruises were gone. But he was concerned about the condition of her heart.

"Why do you care, Ty?" She glared into his honey brown eyes.

"I've answered that question already so please don't ask me again." He held her glare to reinforce his earnestness. The caterers cleared the kitchen to set up the food in the other room. "Can you answer me please?" He requested.

"She's pretty." Symphony blurted, trying to redirect the conversation. "Your friend. Y'all look good together. I'm happy for you, Ty." She paused, distancing herself from him so he couldn't smell the stench of lies.

"Man, why do I keep fucking with this woman?" He snapped, not intending for his internal frustration to be made public as he rubbed a hand down his face, exhaling.

"This woman?" Her attitude was rapidly budding. "So I'm just-"

Tyus quickly condensed the space she created as he denied her potential rant, placing his finger against her lips. "Just stop. Please, just stop." He sighed.

"Symphony, I don't know what else to do. I told myself that I was going to come here today to celebrate King and Syncere - and ignore you. Until I saw you. I keep telling myself to leave you alone - I'm not the type of dude she wants. Convincing myself that I'm done with you. After last week I should be pissed. I *am* pissed. Really shouldn't have shit to say to you, but I can't - " Tyus paused, dropping his finger from her mouth as he hung his head in frustration.

"You can't what, Ty?" Symphony whispered, so close her inhale was indistinguishable from his exhale.

"I - I can't let you go. I just can't stay away." Tyus and Symphony held their glare for what seemed like hours but only seconds ticked away. He cupped her chin, gliding his massive hand up her cheeks, kissing the places that previously held swollen bruises.

Tyus landed a kiss against her ear and whispered, "Whenever you're ready to talk, I'm still ready to listen." He kissed against her forehead before exiting the kitchen. Symphony audibly exhaled, relinquishing the breath she'd been holding.

6

Symphony was silent as she drove G-ma home after the baby shower. All she could think about was Tyus. *I can't let you go.* She replayed his words on rewind in her pretty little head. The words did more than just produce the normal butterfly-goosebump combination. His admission caused Symphony to visibly quiver from her freshly arched brows to her flawlessly manicured toes. She was breathless, immovable, awestricken - and turned the fuck on.

The intensity in his beautiful eyes and sincerity of his tone terrified Symphony because she felt every ounce of his adoration. *But will he be able to put me first? Make me number one. Will he really choose me?* She mused, interrupted by her grandmother's gaze.

"You ok, girly girl?" G-ma inquired, already knowing the answer.

"Yeah, I'm okay, G-ma. Just tired I guess." Symphony lied again.

"I don't like this lying version of my Symphony. Since when can't you tell your G-ma the truth?" She paused. "You know you can say anything to me."

"I know. I just -" Symphony huffed. "I don't like this version of Symphony either G-ma."

"Can I offer you something, baby girl? And I just want you to listen." G-ma questioned. Symphony nodded. "Stop running from that man Symphony."

"What? Running from what man?" She played dumb.

"I thought I asked you to just listen." G-ma's stern glare hushed Symphony immediately. "Now, like I said. You need to stop running from Tyus. Stevie Wonder and Ray Charles put together can see that you all have something going on beyond just sex."

"G-ma!" Symphony shouted, blushing with embarrassment.

"Girl please. Don't play coy with me. Let me finish." G-ma rolled her eyes. "I saw the way he looked at you today. And I saw you too. You weren't expecting him to walk in there with a woman on his arm. But that's what happens when you keep a good man waiting. There's a line of women praying you'll make a mistake. But he came to you. I saw him rushing into that kitchen looking for you. So that tells me all I need to know."

"Am I allowed to talk now?" Symphony questioned, causing G-ma to chuckle and nod her approval. "What does that tell you, G-ma?"

"That he cares for you, Symphony. You can't see that because you're too busy fooling with Calvin's old ass and Ella's boy James or Jamie. Whatever his name is."

Jameson. She silently corrected because she wouldn't dare do it aloud. Symphony's eyes bulged and slightly vomited in her mouth at her grandmother's knowledge of her situation-ships. She remained voiceless, pleading the fifth, not admitting to anything.

"You don't have to admit it because I already know. And I know that Calvin is the bastard who hit you." Symphony aggressively pressed the brake, slightly jerking her and G-ma towards the dashboard as they leered at each other. "Baby girl, the streets have been talking long before you and they will keep talking especially when you put your business out in the streets."

Symphony pulled into the half circle driveway in front of G-ma's building waiting for the aide to get the wheelchair. "Tyus said he can't let me go. But he has a family already." She whispered.

"He has a *son* already." G-ma clarified. "Has he even given you any reason to believe that he and his son's mother are a couple?" G-ma didn't give Symphony time to answer.

"No. I'm sure he hasn't. You are just making up stories in your head baby girl so you can find any excuse not to fall in love with this man. But it may be too late, Symphony." G-ma caressed the top of her hand. "Your mother's story is *not* your story. She made her choices and lives her life. Wherever she is." Symphony remained silent, deciding not to tell her grandmother about the text from Malynda.

"You have to make your choices, live your life girly girl." G-ma caressed her granddaughter's cheek. "Tyus said he can't let you go. But is that what you want? Do you want him to let go?"

Symphony hesitated, envisioning the moments she and Tyus spent together over the past year. It had been more than just sex, albeit amazing sex, but they had a connection. Laughing, talking, sharing their dreams. She missed the way he cuddled, caressed, and stroked her hair as he inhaled her flavorful aroma. And Symphony craved, shit she was hungry for more.

"No ma'am. I don't want him to let me go." A single tear fell from her misty eyes. "I think I need him." She cried.

"Then go get him, baby girl." G-ma matter-of-factly stated with a smile. Symphony kissed her grandmother and helped the aide get her settled. She walked back to her car when her phone buzzed. *Syncere.*

"Hey Prima." Symphony answered.

"Hey Pri. I just wanted to thank you again. Me and King had so much fun." Syncere sniffed.

"Prima, are you crying again? Girl stop." Symphony giggled. "I know you would do the same for me."

"Yeah, I would. If marriage and babies are what you wanted. But you said you don't, so I guess I'll keep throwing bomb ass birthday parties." Syncere chuckled and cried. Her hormones were a mess.

"Yeah, that is what I said, huh?" Symphony sighed as she slid into the driver's seat.

"Go see him, Symphony." Syncere whined. "Y'all need to talk. You have one perspective, he has another, but no one is trying to figure out what the two of you could even be together." Syncere paused. "Well, I take that back. Tyus has tried, but when your ass kicks a man out of your house because he wouldn't fuck you - what is the man supposed to think?"

Symphony didn't want to hear it but she knew her cousin was right. She needed to talk to Tyus and explain what was really going on with her. Symphony was feisty and would speak her mind on just about anything, but when it came to Tyus, her feelings stayed trapped in an unattainable vault.

"What if he is still with that chick?" Symphony rolled her eyes as if Syncere could see. "Who was she anyway?"

"I know for a fact he is at home and that chick, I think her name is Natalie, is not with him." Syncere slightly squealed, but Symphony was hushed. "King's never met her but Titan said they dated in high school and he can't stand her. Titan called her a fake ass Whitley Gilbert." Syncere guffawed. Even Symphony had to laugh at that. "She lives in LA though so I don't think you need to worry."

"Hmm. So she just pops up. I'm sure that's not a coincidence." Symphony proclaimed.

"Girl, just go see that man. If she's there then you know where you stand with him." Syncere paused. "Or better yet, you say you're a boss bitch, call his bluff. Knock on the door and see which one of y'all he wants to stay."

Syncere waited for a response but Symphony was silent. "Pri? Heffa, are you getting on the highway? That's the fastest way to get to Tyus' house."

"Shut up Syncere. I know how to get to his house." The GPS sounded in the background, *you will arrive at 105 Barrington Drive in eleven minutes.* "And for the record, I *am* a boss bitch."

"Yeeesss bitch!" Syncere shouted, recognizing Tyus' address. "Call me tomorrow when you get from under that man. Love you boo."

SYMPHONY'S HANDS began to tremble against the leather-wrapped steering wheel as she turned onto Barrington Drive. The full moon illuminated the serene tree-lined street with single family and two story homes. She crept slightly past the front of his house as if she was casing the place, pausing in front of the driveway. There were no cars out front and Tyus always parked his truck to the right in the two car garage and his motorcycle occupied the other side. So the chances of him being home alone were high. She contemplated if she should park on the street or in the driveway or if she should call or just knock on the door. *What if that Natalie chick rode with him and she's in there getting that good dick?*

Symphony was in her head - bad. She turned into the driveway but just kept her foot firmly planted on the brake. Sitting with the car running, staring at the black and bronze address plaque outlining the numbers 105 with her eyes over and over. *What the fuck are you doing Symphony?* She mused, turning the music volume down as if it would help in her decision making ability.

Inhaling deeply to calm her nervousness, she scrolled through the contacts on her phone to get to Tyus' phone number. *I'll just call him.* Five minutes later with the phone still positioned in the palm of her hand, she was motionless yet trembling. *Oh my God Symphony. What is happening?* Syncere was the one who experienced panic attacks - not Symphony. But that's exactly what she believed was happening. She didn't feel short of breath like she would with her asthma. No chest pains or lightheadedness, she just couldn't stop shaking. Symphony dropped the phone in her lap, clasping her sweaty hands together to quell her anxiety.

"Ok Symphony. Get it together. Get it together." She whispered. "What are you going to say? Maybe I should practice." Her quivering voice whimpered repeatedly, "Ty, I'm sorry. It's me not you. I don't know what is wrong with me." She shook her head, nervously tapping against the steering wheel. "No, no. That's stupid. You need to just tell him the truth." She paused, repeating again. "Ty, I'm sorry." Symphony was having a bit of a breakdown.

Tyus got home after the baby shower, declining his brother's offer to go to Melvin's. Natalie was somehow under the impression that they would grab a drink after the shower but she was sadly mistaken. He walked her to her car and respectfully declined her offer for dinner first, then a movie, and then she put all of her cards on the table basically offering her pussy on a platter. She continuously insisted, forcing him to sternly reject. *"Natalie, it was great seeing you but this will not happen. We can be friends but that's really all I can offer. I hope you understand."* She didn't understand but Tyus didn't care. He made sure she was safely in her car when he departed and headed home.

Tyus replayed his encounter with Symphony, somewhat regretting that he was so forthcoming with his emotions, but he couldn't continue to play this game with her. She either wanted him or she didn't. *It's not that hard.* He pondered as he walked into his living room taking a seat in the recliner after pouring a glass of Macallan 15. Tyus clicked the remote to turn on the 70 inch flat screen TV. Lebron and the Lakers were playing tonight so he was elated to just chill. Taking a sip of the aged scotch, he saw headlights from a car turning into his driveway. He was praying it wasn't Natalie because he didn't want to hurt her feelings. Tyus footed across the room to peep through the espresso wooden blinds. The moon glistened against the familiar shiny black Audi Coupe. *Symphony.*

Tyus slightly smiled as he stood there watching her. He couldn't determine if she was on the phone or what the hell she was doing, but she was just sitting. At least 10 minutes ticked by and she still hadn't exited the car. His smile diminished into concern. Tyus contemplated calling her, but he didn't want to scare her off. He had to make a decision and fast - go retrieve her from the car right now, or risk Symphony driving away without a word - which she would do. She'd clearly come to his house for a reason and Tyus was desperate to find out why.

He grabbed a sweatshirt since it was a bit chilly outside. Pleasantly crowding the grey sweatpants with his toned thighs, he stepped into Nike slides and exited the front door as discreetly as possible. Symphony was in a deep daze, not even realizing that he crossed in front of her car. With one hand in his pocket, Tyus gently tapped the window with his knuckles trying not to startle her. She jolted, finally acknowledging his presence. Gazing at him with a counterfeit smile, her glossy grey eyes melted his heart. She'd been crying. But why? He reached for the door handle but it was locked. He tapped on the window again.

"Symphony. Are you ok?" Tyus bent down to get closer so that she could hear him through the window.

Instead of exiting the car, she partially rolled down the window. Her foot still rested on the brake. But she was hushed, silent.

"Symphony. Sweetpea, are you ok? Can you please come inside?" He pleaded. "Why are you just sitting here?"

"I was practicing, Tyus. Trying to figure out what I would say to you. But it's all wrong. It sounds crazy - I sound crazy." She mumbled as the tremble of her hands intensified. "I should probably just go. I shouldn't have come." She quickly released the brake, causing the car to move forward before she aggressively stomped against the brake stopping the motion. Symphony's breathing remained labored.

"Symphony, put the car in park please. Don't leave. Please. Just stay." Tyus knocked against the window again as she parked the car, still lifeless peering out of the windshield. "You don't have to say a word. Just come inside." He bent further to capture her eyes through the cracked window. Her hands trembled and the blank stare across her angelic face terrified him. He'd never seen Symphony like this - vulnerable, sensitive, fragile. Tyus was concerned and definitely wouldn't allow her to leave.

"Baby, please." He begged, tone laced with trepidation.

The sound of him calling her baby was like an automated Stepford wife-like command. Symphony swiftly rolled up the window and killed the ignition. She grabbed her purse before exiting the car, standing, waiting for the next instruction. Tyus wrapped her in his arms, ushering her into the house. Symphony stood in the foyer as if she was a stranger in his home. It had been a minute since she'd visited so she wanted to get reacquainted with his domicile.

Symphony observed the vaulted ceilings with the industrial looking fan spinning although it was cold outside. The tan oversized sectional was positioned in the middle of the room facing the massive television. Every gaming system known to man sat on floating shelves framing the television. She could see straight through to the modern grey and brown eat-in kitchen. He'd been drinking as she observed the opened bottle of whiskey on the island.

"Do you want to come in or are you going to stand there?" Tyus questioned, untangling her clenched fingers to guide her to the couch.

"I forgot to take my shoes off." She whispered, still robotic as she sat on the edge of the lounger.

"Let me help you." Tyus offered. He sat next to her and lifted her leg to rest on top of his exposing her milky thighs. The touch of his hand against the back of her knee re-ignited the butterfly- goosebump thing. Tyus sexily smirked, noticing the hairs on her arms standing at attention. He slid his hand down her smooth legs slowly unzipping her boots as he stared at her. With narrowed eyes, he gazed trying to discern the pain and sadness that resided within her smokey orbs.

Symphony cleared her throat, the Louis Vuitton cross-body still clutched under her arm.

"Hey. What's going on? Tell me what happened." Tyus stroked a finger down the curve of her face. "I'm worried about you, Sweetpea."

"I'm fine Ty. Can I have some water?" Her voice nervously

cracked. He obliged, not ready to dispute her *I'm fine* response.

Tyus returned with a bottle of Voss water and a glass. He poured the water, resistant to place the glass in her shaky hands. His gaze was relentless. Although he understood that he needed to tread lightly, Tyus wasn't about to let her off the hook. This fragile uncertain version of Symphony was new to him.

"Are you ready to tell me what you're doing here?" He paused. "I'm happy you came but I must admit I'm shocked."

Symphony sipped her water trying not to make eye contact with Tyus. She had no clue what she was about to say to this man but she had to say something and fast. Silence fell over the room for what seemed like hours but only a few minutes depleted.

"I don't want to go crazy like my mother." Symphony blurted in a whisper as her grey irises flooded. This was going to be a grueling conversation for her, but she desperately needed to release the pain and confusion she'd been feeling long before the text from Malynda.

"My mother has spent most of my life in and out of mental institutions because of my father. He was married with children when she got pregnant with me. He promised her that she was number one and that they would be a family. But when his wife found out about the affair, he had to choose and he chose his pregnant wife and young son."

The torrent tears that were being held captive escaped her cloudy eyes. She'd cried about her mother *and her father* many times before but these tears were different. This cry was in the arms of a man that she adored more than she cared to admit.

"Symphony. Baby, it's ok. I got you. Just let it out. It's ok." Tyus caressed the nape of her neck as she wailed against his chest. She lifted from him, almost hyperventilating trying to finish what she started.

"My mother was obsessed with him - calling, going to his house, his job. She was completely insane over that man." Symphony aggressively wiped the tears from her puffy face. "Malynda, my mother, always blamed me for his decision. Hated me because we were not his number one priority." She huffed trying to catch her breath. Tyus continued to caress her hand in an attempt to calm her nerves.

"So I've never been the type of chick to be in a relationship, Ty. I figured if I avoided men that came with any type of baggage like an ex-wife or... kids, they would never have to choose between me and their family. My father didn't choose me, so why would anybody else?"

Tyus released a deep breath hearing her admission. Now it was starting to make sense. He recalled instances when Symphony would go ghost because he had to adjust their plans or his schedule didn't align with her expectations due to his responsibilities for TJ. Nobody was ever going to disrupt the relationship between him and his son, but Tyus knew that whatever woman entered his life, she would be his number one priority in addition to his son.

"So you think because I have TJ, I don't have room for you in my life?" Tyus nudged her drooped chin, forcing her to look at him. "Hmm? Am I right?"

"Ty, you have TJ and Gia. They are your priority." She muttered.

"I know my priorities, Symphony. I don't need you to remind me or try to use them as an excuse for why you don't want to be with me." Tyus exclaimed.

"I never said I didn't want to be with you, Ty. I - I just don't know if I'm built to be the woman you need me to be." She paused, lips quivering. "Or the woman you and your son deserve."

That statement shattered Symphony's already broken heart. She wanted Tyus desperately, but she didn't want him to have to deal with her trauma and damage when he had other priorities.

"I'm gonna go, Ty. I shouldn't have come. I need to go." Symphony stood, scrambling to grab her boots as he clutched her wrist pulling her into him.

"Symphony, please don't run away from me. Baby, I'm a grown man. I know what I want and what I need." Tyus cupped her chin, canceling any available space left that separated them.

"Look at me, Symphony." She obeyed as he continued. "I want you, Sweetpea. I've always wanted you. I can't change what's happened to you in the past. And I can't change the circumstances that gave me TJ. But Symphony, I know if we tried to do this - to be together, I would choose you. Every time."

"I don't know if I am ready. How do you know you're ready, Ty? What if you decide there's no room for me... in your heart?" She worthlessly attempted to disconnect but his unshakeable clasp made it impossible.

Tyus pressed his forehead against her temple. "Sweetpea, I have room in my heart because my heart has been waiting for you, baby. It's always been you, Symphony." He kissed against her left cheek, then the right, then gently captured her pouty lips. They glared at each other, blushing and caressing. She smiled.

"And your ass was trying to leave when we had all this good shit to say to each other." He teased, attempting to lighten the mood. They chortled through his healing smile and her cleansing tears.

"You didn't know I was this fucked up did you? All that good ass sex had you disoriented." Symphony grinned as Tyus boisterously guffawed.

"You damn right. A nigga been craving that pretty pussy." Tyus bit the side of his lip as he wiped the stream of tears from her face. He tenderly, gently seized her plump glossy lips as he whispered, "Baby, I've missed you. I need to taste you- feel you." He halted his pursuit. "But you have to promise me you'll stop running from me, Sweetpea. Promise me you'll try. That's all I'm asking is that you'll make an effort."

"I promise. For you I will try." Symphony paused, resting her lips against his. "I promise." They stayed enmeshed, breathing each other in, replenishing the oxygen they'd been deprived.

"Ty?" Symphony broke the silence.

"Yes, baby?"

"Can you fuck me now?" She sexily grinned.

Symphony's savagely beating heart was pounding furiously against her chest. She pulled him closer to prevent the impending heart attack she was certain was approaching if he didn't occupy the folds of her sodden treasure expeditiously.

Tyus parted her lips with his heated thick tongue, grazing the structure of her gorgeous face with his fingertips. He reluctantly relinquished her lips as the length of her neck was calling for him to be there. He kissed and nibbled against the folds of her citrus scented neck. Still playing in her crevices, Tyus unzipped the fitted skirt, disrobing her while unhooking the snaps on the body suit. They simultaneously and hurriedly lifted the shirt over her head as he released her ponytail caressing his finger through her curly tresses. Symphony was standing there exposed and sexy as hell. The saturated dark green thong and matching bra on display.

"You are so fucking sexy Symphony. Damn girl!" Tyus yelped.

He traced his hands down her center removing the wettish thong. Tyus kissed from her nape to her chest, halting to unhook the satiny bra revealing her buxom swollen breasts. He was obsessed with her nipple rings, kissing, biting, and tugging against the warm shiny metal with his teeth as he fondled her clit with his fingertips. She squirmed, feeling gratifyingly tickled. Symphony continued to stand on display while Tyus sat on the couch in front of her. He played with her navel, kissing and licking every detail of her waist tattoo.

Tyus glared directly at Symphony, dangerous but sexy as he reached one monstrous hand between her thighs, firmly nudging her athletic curvy legs open wide, then wider. He stealthily slid off the couch, still surveying her as he positioned his body between her legs, his mouth coming in direct alignment with her pretty pussy. Symphony rested her hands against the top of his head. Endeavoring to keep her balance, she quivered in anticipation.

Tyus teased her, blowing his fiery salacious breath against her dripping treasure. The hot and cold sensations caused her to moan, tossing her head back watching the ceiling. Journeying up the length of her thighs with soft kisses, he returned his attention to her private lips. Gently kissing the crown of her swollen jewel, he slowly kneaded and fondled, daring her to flounder.

"Aahhh. Ty, please." She pleaded.

Tyus caressed her plump rotund ass with both hands as his imposing snake-like tongue slowly glided into her jewel circling in slow motion against her pulsating drenched walls. He twisted, turned, tousled, deliciously puncturing her puss with the tip of his flaming hot long ass tongue.

"Shit Ty. What the fuck is that? Don't stop. Please bae. Please." She begged. That damn tongue of his was like an anaconda. Slithering in and out of her hole at a steady pace, mercilessly manipulating her clit. The candied juices dripped from his face. Humming, he joyously delighted in her creamy goodness. He nibbled at her swollen folds before Tyus drove his blazing tongue back into her ocean, this time accompanied by one finger then a second finger. The salacious trio weakened her knees. She fought to stay upright. Tyus was relentless, never coming up for air. He licked and sucked and nibbled on repeat. Symphony's athletic thigh power was stripped away with every lick, twist and turn. Her body was limp.

Tyus firmly secured her holding on to all of that bodacious ass.

"No, no, Sweetpea. Hold that position baby. I promise you are about to come." He teased.

Tyus adjusted his head, tossing it back further between his shoulder blades, wearing her inner thighs as earmuffs. He clenched his arms tighter around her thighs and ass, encouraging, welcoming her to take a seat on his face. Tyus' fingers and tongue intensely competed for the title probing deeper and deeper and deeper.

"Fuck! Ty! Shit, baby. I'm cumming." She paused, fighting to breathe for a minute. "Ah!" Her howl echoed. His tongue fiercely made love to her jewel. He growled like an animal famished and eager to devour its prey.

"I'm-still-cu-cumming, Ty." Symphony screamed, her knees buckled as she became unraveled, collapsing. Tyus captured her limp frame, pulling her down to straddle him seated on the plush carpet. She found refuge in the folds of his neck. Labored breathing, panting, squirming... and still cumming.

"What-the fuck-was-that? That-shit? Shit-Ty. Shit. I-Can't-You." Her words were disjointed and somewhat incomprehensible. *A bitch is speaking in tongues.*

"I'm not even going to try to make sense of that." Tyus chuckled as he trailed fingertips down her spine. Covering her neck with aromatic treasure scented kisses.

"Symphony, look at me." She obliged. "Baby, do I need to

get a condom? Have you been with anybody since our last time?" He inquisitively probed already knowing the answer.

Symphony delayed her response, kissing the juices from his face, not wanting to ruin the moment. Tyus raised an eyebrow seeking an answer.

"Um, Calvin... when that shit happened with him. We used a condom but I understand your concern." She uttered, a bit embarrassed.

"Nobody else?" He probed, very aware that old man river wasn't the only person she was dealing with.

"I haven't been with Jameson, Ty. Not like that. I haven't had sex with him in several months. Well before the last time with you." Symphony truthfully declared.

It had been three months since the last time Symphony and Tyus had sex. She'd only been with Calvin one time since then and participated in Jameson's gift of oral sex.

"Have you... been with anybody?" She inquired.

"No. I haven't." Tyus definitively declared. Symphony felt like shit.

"I'm sorry Ty -" He hushed her with a kiss against her lips that quickly escalated into a treasure-flavored invasion of the mouth that delighted all of her senses.

"Sweetpea, I told you it's always been you." He whispered.

Symphony navigated her tongue around the surface of his neck, nibbling at his Adam's apple before journeying to his chest. She gently grazed her teeth across his nipples. He flinched. She giggled, sneaking her hand into his sweatpants releasing the monster. Symphony caressed and stroked his dick from the base to the tip - salaciously endearing his shaft.

Shit, she couldn't deny it, Tyus had a pretty penis. Buttery caramel brown with a light ombre effect at the head. That damn head - it curved slightly to the right, perfectly positioned to hit every nook and cranny of her puss.

Symphony slowly rose to a squat, hoisted above him. All her portly smooth pussy was on display. Tyus pulled his pants down past his knees releasing more of the ombre beast. She licked her lips, trying to decide if she wanted to taste it or ride it. Symphony possessively clutched his dick sliding it against the dampened folds of her private lips. She had to take this shit slow. It had been 90 days since the amplitude of his girth and immeasurable inches entered her throne. Symphony carefully guided him into her treasure. *Fuck!* She mused, eyes rolling backwards as her jewel walls stretched to meet his demand. The pleasure was perfect and the pain was magnificently merciless but welcomed at the same damn time.

"Ty." She moaned.

"Symphony." He grunted.

"Baby, you feel so fucking good." They crooned in unison.

"Damn, Sweetpea. I missed your fine ass. How can you be so damn wet and tight?" Tyus grunted through his teeth.

Symphony was trying to provide an explanation but Tyus captured her inexplicable words and moans with his mouth, reclaiming authority of her lips. Incessantly thrusting, pounding, thrashing, Symphony's motions grew more intense, feverish. Tyus gripped her juicy ass, his upstroke challenging her downstroke. The basketball game clock ticked in the background with the Lakers down by one with 13 seconds to go and Lebron taking the final shot. Symphony urged Tyus deeper, harder, faster. He watched her ride the shit out of him. Tyus and the game were on countdown - reaching a climatic finish. *Five, four, three, two, one...*

"Fuck, Sweetpea! Symphony! Shit! Baby don't stop. Don't stop!" Tyus' bellow echoed through the vaulted ceiling. He tightly palmed her ass leaking all of his gooey goodies inside her jewel as Lebron made the game winning shot.

"Aah! Shit! Damn girl." He grumbled.

Symphony rode the gas out of his tank but not before he unleashed the magic of that damn curved dick. Tyus was insatiable. Instantly hardening to ensure she was completely satisfied.

Symphony gleefully hissed his name, "Tyus!"

He gripped her neck, pleasingly choking as his girth became heavier and her fulfilment grew stronger, "TYUS." She howled.

A thunderous downpour of bliss escaped her body. Symphony reached the pinnacle, gladdening in a breathtaking, long overdue climax. She was fully prepared to dispose of *Purple Rain* if this was the lustful relations that Tyus was planning to consistently deliver.

"Bae, I missed you too." Symphony whimpered, body lightly quaking with aftershock. His dick sang to her like a lullaby because her ass was fast asleep.

7

Tyus perched on the charcoal grey chaise in his bedroom gazing at Symphony as she slept. The hum of the sweetest snore was like music to his ears. It was a little after 6 am and he'd been observing her for at least an hour. The curve of her angelic face, satiny smooth light brown sugar skin and pouty plump lips that he wanted to devour all over again. Tyus wanted to kiss her just to see those gorgeous grey eyes open for a quick second. Eyes that held so much heartache, disappointment, and wrath. He had so many questions. There were a multitude of missing details but Tyus didn't want to press.

While Symphony wore a rigid ruthless exterior, her interior was still a brokenhearted little girl seeking love and acceptance. Unfortunately, the two people who were granted the job to provide unconditional adoration were the ones responsible for the demise of her ability to truly love and trust.

Symphony roused from her slumber reaching for Tyus but he was gone. She jolted, quickly rising from the comforts of the weighted blanket to search the room for him. Tyus sat on the chaise in the dark corner of the room eyeing her like an ambush predator, sitting patiently awaiting his prey before stealthily launching a surprise attack. He sexily grinned in the shadows, watching as her angst from his absence shifted to delight once she caught a glimpse of his enticing frame. Symphony's nipples hardened with every rise and fall of her chest at the sight of him.

"Was I snoring?" Symphony whispered. "Sorry if I woke you." She repositioned, shivering from his entrancing stare and chill of the room pulling the plush white blanket over her naked shoulders.

Her sweet, serene voice pleasantly disrupted his musing.

"Nah, you're good. I don't require much sleep. I didn't want to wake you with my early grand rising." He softly chuckled.

Symphony smiled, patting the empty side of the bed, encouraging him to join her. Tyus lifted an eyebrow pointing a finger to his chest and mouthed, *"You want me?"*

She nodded, biting the side of her lip. Tyus momentarily remained motionless, then aimlessly sauntered across the room ready to capture his prey. He entered from the foot of the bed with a snake-like slither lifting the covers to expose her goosebump covered flesh. Tyus leisurely kissed, licked, and nibbled from her white painted toes to her pursy lips inhaling the delectable morning aroma.

"Good morning, beautiful." Tyus kissed the tip of her

chilled nose. "Is it too cold for you? I can adjust the heat or turn off the fan."

"No. I'm good." She shuddered. "You are heating up things just fine."

Tyus took that as approval to proceed. He passionately glared at her, enthused that he was finally able to view those enchanting argentine eyes again. He seized the arc of her face, caressing her cheeks with the pad of his thumb studying her. He hovered over Symphony, still gazing as he caressed down her left arm then the right. Tyus pinned Symphony's arms on each side of a head of curls scattered across the pillow. With a firm, yet gentle grip, his gaze remained deep, penetrating, daunting. A slightly dangerous smile formed at the corners of his sexy lips. Symphony's breathing was strained and laden. She didn't know if screaming for help was appropriate or just surrender to the seductive battering he was about to administer.

"You are so damn pretty, Symphony." Tyus paused, combing his fingers through her hair. "Your hair." He caressed. "Your eyes." He brushed his lips against her eyelids. "Your nose." He pecked. "And my personal favorite, your lips." Tyus planted tender kisses before parting her lustrous lips, their tongues intertwined in the most divine dance.

Tyus' dick ached for Symphony and her pussy was pounding for him. He was ready to pounce, but he yearned to relish in her beauty, allure, and sexiness.

"Can I take my time, Sweetpea?" *Can I make love to you?* That was the real question but he didn't want to scare her.

Symphony couldn't catch her breath. She was hyperventilating. *I might need my damn inhaler.* She mused, but the cure wasn't Albuterol, it was Tyus. She craved him. His touch was imperative to her overall well-being.

"Yes, Ty. Please." Symphony breathlessly begged.

Tyus slowly entered her. Teasing her dampened folds with the ombre tip of his dick. He labored there for a moment, glaring into her eyes. Suddenly, Symphony was spellbound. Overcome with a familiar, yet undefined emotion. She only experienced this sentiment with Tyus. *Was it love?* She silently questioned before gasping as Tyus filled her. Occupying all of the available space in her treasure. Inch by salacious inch, knocking against every juicy drenched wall. He stroked slowly, steadily, deliberately driving her insane.

Symphony was disoriented, overwhelmed, her body melted into the ecstasy of his chiseled frame. The weight of his body and his dick were deliciously heavy. The pleasure outweighed the satisfying suffering as her river parted, succumbing to the demand of his substantial girth. Tyus was making love to Symphony - and she felt every inch and ounce of his adoration. Overwhelmed by *him* and her emotions, she shed a single tear.

"Ty!" She moaned.

"BAE!" She screamed.

The mind blowing climax caused a flood of torrent tears staining the stark white pillow. Tyus cradled her, diminishing the possibility for separation. He continued to pleasantly pound into her convulsing flesh until he reached his pinnacle. They slumbered, Tyus never withdrawing from her jewel.

SYMPHONY AWAKENED around noon with a blissful ache between her thighs. She was drunk, tipsy off of Tyus. Smiling as she reached for him, the bed was empty again. Symphony reluctantly exited the comforts of the plush king size mattress. *Damn I need to get one of these weighted blankets.* She pondered, footing her naked frame into the bathroom. Symphony was desperate to find Tyus, so she cleaned the pertinent parts of her body instead of showering before throwing on one of his t-shirts. A delectable scent from the kitchen circled the air. Symphony padded down the hallway into the great room eyeing a shirtless Tyus in the kitchen. She bit her lip, still desiring this man even after a feverish night and morning of fucking...or lovemaking... or both. Symphony didn't know how to categorize what was happening with Tyus.

"Hey sleeping beauty." Tyus' resounding timbre broke her daze. "You hungry?"

"Starving." She giggled as she closed the distance between them. He clutched her waist, resting his lips against her forehead before patting her ass.

"Have a seat. I made brunch." Tyus continued preparing their plates before popping a bottle of champagne to mix with the orange juice already in the glasses.

"Whatever it is smells wonderful." Symphony perched at the kitchen table, grabbing a grape out of the fruit bowl on the table.

"Well, I snagged a plate of chicken from the baby shower yesterday and made some waffles and eggs to go with it." He proudly smiled. "Is that cool for you?"

"Most definitely. Thank you for brunch, Ty." Symphony blushed.

Tyus placed the plates on the table as he sat down beside her. He led them in prayer before digging into the delicious meal. Symphony was famished. She devoured her food in record time.

"You really were starving, huh?" Tyus chortled. "I guess a night and morning with a nigga like me can do that you."

"Oh you're really feeling yourself, Mr. Okoro." She chuckled, gently tossing a grape at him.

"I think you're feeling me too, Ms. James." He sexily grinned, wiping his mouth with the napkin.

"Whatever." Symphony coyly laughed. They sat in comfortable silence for a few moments reminiscing about their night.

"Can I ask you a personal question?" Tyus blurted.

"Um, sure." She sipped her mimosa.

"When's the last time you talked to your mother or father?" He gazed, trying to determine if she was ready to disclose any details.

"I, um, haven't seen or talked to Joel since I was 18 years old." She paused, refusing to give him any other title outside of his name. "My mother, well it's been a few years but I recently got a text message from an unknown number asking me to call her."

"Did you call?"

"Nope."

"Are you going to?" He probed. "Or better yet, do you want to?"

Symphony deeply exhaled. She secretly wished that one day her mother would just be normal. That Malynda would not bring drama and anguish into her life. But Symphony was smart enough to understand, when someone shows you who they are, believe them. And Malynda had shown her ass on multiple occasions.

"My mother causes me a lot of anxiety. She can produce a wrath in me that's frightening. It's like I snap and just lose it." She paused, blinking away the mist building in her eyes.

"Sweetpea, I didn't mean to dredge up these memories." Tyus reached for her, encouraging her to sit on his lap. She obliged, laying her head against his shoulder.

"I hit her once." Symphony blurted. "She kept saying the meanest things. *You're a mistake. I should've had an abortion. He loved me until I decided to keep you.*" A tear fell against Tyus' chest and his heart plummeted. "I slapped her, then she slapped me back, and I snapped. I kept pounding and punching and hitting - for every mean thing she'd said and done to me my whole life."

Symphony wept, unable to comprehend why it was so easy to share her deepest trauma with Tyus. He rubbed his fingertips up and down her spine, silently offering his support. Inspiring her to find respite in the comfort of his arms. Tyus detected worry and trepidation in her saddened eyes. He was pissed about her painful past, wishing he could make it disappear while knowing the best thing he could do was protect her heart.

"It's ok baby. Look at me." He nudged her chin. "I -" Tyus

paused, clearing his throat as *I love you* danced on the tip of his tongue unspoken. "I'm here for whatever you need. Whatever you decide, I won't let anybody hurt you."

Symphony and Tyus sat noiseless as he continued to caress her as she calmed. The vibration from his phone shuddered them both. A picture of the cutest snaggletooth little boy with his grandparents brought sunshine to Tyus' eyes. Symphony's stomach quivered a little, softened by his reaction to his son while uneasy about what she'd committed to. *For you, I'll try.* Symphony recalled her promise to Tyus. She attempted to remove herself from his stronghold, but his clutch was steadfast.

"What's up lil man?" Tyus beamed, as the most adorable giggle blared on speaker phone.

"How'd you know it was me, Dad." TJ was tickled. "It could've been Grammy or PopPop because I don't have a phone."

"Yeah but I knew you would be calling soon. What have you been up to today?" He questioned, with Symphony still on his lap.

"Nothing much. Grammy cooked pancakes and PopPop let me have coffee...oops." Tyus could only imagine the look on his son's face after his slip of the tongue.

"PopPop let you have coffee, huh. Now I have to deal with you climbing the walls all day." Tyus shook his head laughing.

"What are you doing, Dad? What time are you picking me up?" TJ probed.

"I'm having lunch with a friend right now and I'll be there to have dinner with you, Grammy, and PopPop around five o'clock. Then you're coming home to finish your reading and go to bed for school tomorrow."

"Is your friend a girl or a boy?" TJ giggled, causing Symphony to even chuckle a little. She covered her mouth trying to be discreet.

"Why are you so nosey lil man?" Tyus guffawed.

"You won't answer so that means it's a girl." He squealed in laughter. "Is she pretty?"

Symphony snuck away from his grasp busying herself in the kitchen anticipating Tyus' response to his namesake.

"Yeah lil man. She's very pretty." Tyus winked at Symphony.

"Ok Dad. I'm about to go to the store with PopPop. See you later." TJ hurried and just like that he hung up.

Tyus chuckled. "The joys of a six year old." He mumbled, walking into the kitchen to help Symphony with the dishes.

"He sounds adorable." Symphony wore a miniature smile. "And he loves his Grammy and PopPop." She laughed. "Me and TJ have something in common."

Tyus could sense something was off. She was jittery, nervous.

"Yeah he does." Tyus placed his hand atop hers, halting any movement. "What's wrong, Sweetpea?"

"Nothing. What do you mean?" She asked.

"You've washed the same plate at least three times." He dried her hands with the towel. "Something is wrong? Don't shut down... talk to me."

Symphony glared at him, her demonous mind told her to exit immediately, you're *not a priority for him*, while her restorative heart recalled his comforting words, *I'm here for whatever you need.*

"I, um, I guess I was hoping to hang out a little longer. But...I should probably go." She began to amble away before Tyus captured her wrist, pulling her into him.

"Symphony, you're more than welcome to stay and join us for dinner." He paused. "But I honestly didn't think you were ready for that."

Symphony stared misty eyed, her mood shifted instantaneously. "I'm not." She firmly declared, stomping away like a jealous juvenile.

"Symphony, wait." Tyus called after her as she disappeared into his bedroom. He didn't follow.

Several minutes later Symphony appeared in the living room fully dressed as Tyus sat on the couch paying no attention to the football game.

"Ty, I'm about to head out." Symphony whispered, embarrassed by her behavior. She knew she'd fucked up - again.

"I'll walk you out." Tyus was visibly irritated. He rose from the couch motioning for her to walk towards the door. He yanked the hoodie from the closet by the front door. His face was stone cold, no smile, no smirk - not even a frown. He was externally emotionless, while internally enraged and annoyed. Tyus thought he'd cracked her steely impenetrable barriers, but now he felt like they were back at square one.

They walked to her car in awkward silence. The sun beamed but there was still a chill in the air for more reasons than one. Symphony clicked the key fob to unlock the car as Tyus opened her door. She hesitated.

"Ty-"

"Symphony." He interrupted, connecting with her eyes for the first time since she had her little tantrum. "If we're going to have a problem every time I interact with my son, then we need to just let it go now. TJ is not negotiable. I already told you, I know my priorities, and I want you to be one of them, Symphony." He exhaled, rubbing a hand down his face. "But I'm not going to beg you or force you to be a part of my life. A life that will *always* include my son as long as I have breath in my body."

"Ty, I-"

"Enjoy the rest of your day, Symphony." Tyus pressed his lips against her forehead, deeply inhaling her scent as if it would be the last time. "And you're not a mistake. Not to me." He whispered as his lips grazed her ear. He walked away towards the house, closing the door behind him.

Symphony stood at her open car door, lifeless, although her heart fiercely pounded, she felt comatose, unconscious. Her heart rate elevated, chest rapidly rising and falling. She was hyperventilating. Symphony slumped into the car frantically searching her purse for the inhaler. She took one puff then two, breathing deeply through her nose, exhaling out of her mouth, repeatedly. A minute expired as she gained enough composure to pull out of his driveway. She eyed the view of his house as it drifted further and further away, finally disappearing from her rear view.

Symphony cried silent tears. "Call Prima." She instructed the auto dial in her car.

"Hey Prima!" Syncere shrieked. "You're finally able to walk with your nasty ass."

97

"Syncere." Symphony wailed.

"Pri, what's wrong?" Syncere's tone quickly shifted from excitement to concern.

Symphony inaudibly bawled. "I fucked up, Prima. Again."

8

It had been almost two weeks and Tyus hadn't responded to Symphony's endless outreach. No response to her text messages. He didn't even attempt to let the phone ring and then go to voicemail - nope he was consciously declining her calls straight to voicemail. Tyus contemplated blocking her number for about a half a second. He was still hurt and annoyed, but he privately held out hope that Symphony would get her shit together.

Meanwhile, Natalie was doing exactly what G-ma said...taking advantage of the situation when another woman fucked up. She'd delayed her return to LA, claiming her parents still needed help, but her real reason was Tyus. Natalie was relentless in her pursuit - bringing him lunch to his office, buying groceries to cook him dinner, she'd even joined him on a few runs through the neighborhood. She was doing the most but her efforts were in vain. Tyus still had Symphony constantly on the brain.

"Tyus, mother and daddy would love for you to join us for dinner this Sunday." Natalie had been chatting non-stop since they'd arrived at Melvin's for lunch. Earlier, Tyus was just about to leave Nate's Barbershop when Natalie called to see if he could join her for lunch. He was already planning on picking up food so he agreed to meet her. Tyus crossed the street and walked the half-block to Vivre Salon where Natalie was getting her nails done. It was an unseasonably warm day for November so the streets were crowded with people taking advantage of the sunshine. Natalie grabbed Tyus' arm as they meandered down Main Street to walk the two blocks to Melvin's. Tyus' stomach dropped a bit when he saw Syncere and another agent from Davenport Realty coming out of *The Brown Bean* just as he and Natalie were about to cross their paths. *Shit!*

Tyus saw the steam brewing behind Syncere's familiar grey eyes. She was pissed on her cousin's behalf.

"What's up Syn?" Tyus disjoined his arm from Natalie.

"Hello Tyus." Syncere dryly responded, only acknowledging him.

"Hi Syncere. You are almost ready to pop." Natalie giggled, interrupting the stare down.

"Hello. Naomi, right?" Syncere rolled her eyes. *Petty Princess strikes again.*

"It's Natalie."

"I'm sorry, what?" Syncere didn't attempt to conceal her irritation.

"My name is Natalie. You said Naomi." Natalie corrected.

"Oh, got it. You all have a nice day. Good day Mr. Okoro."

Syncere rolled her eyes. Tyus knew some bullshit was coming after that 30 second encounter.

"Tyus? Are you listening to me? Will you join me, mother, and daddy for dinner Sunday." Natalie repeated.

Noticing his eyes were focused elsewhere, she followed Tyus' line of sight. Symphony and Ledia walked into Melvin's dressed in their hospital scrubs laughing and talking. He couldn't take his eyes off of her. She was beautiful, even in the pale yellow scrubs with black girl magic pins all over the top. Symphony had her hair braided in cornrows, similar to how she wore it when they first met. Tyus still didn't discontinue his gaze although Natalie was frantically waving her hands trying to gain his attention.

Symphony was in her own world as she and Ledia found an available seat during the lunch rush. Suddenly, she felt that familiar shift in the atmosphere. She experienced him penetrating through her body like a cold breeze even before she saw him. Tyus was the only man that ever made her puss throb in anticipation of connecting with his eyes. She turned on the heels of her tie-dye graphic Crocs searching the room for him.

Symphony's breathing was labored as they connected. She had to be seated but maintained a watchful eye on him. Symphony didn't know if he would ignore her like he'd been doing. She stared, blushing, hoping, praying that she would see a glimpse of her Ty - not the pissed off version who's been disregarding her. Tyus' eyes brightened with a miniature sexy smirk at the corner of his mouth until he saw a familiar face step into focus behind Symphony.

"Hello dollface. It's been a while." Calvin's gruff voice

rudely interrupted her eye sex with Tyus. Calvin reached to touch Symphony's arm and she instinctively yanked away rising from her seat.

"Don't touch me." Symphony muttered, attempting to remain calm.

"I was just saying hello, Symphony." Calvin moved in closer. "Can't we get past our personal issues?" He whispered, attempting to be discreet.

"Get past our issues? You must be crazy as hell." Symphony's voice elevated, causing a bit of a scene.

"Excuse me." Tyus said to Natalie. Wiping his mouth, he stood to his full imposing height prowling towards his Sweetpea. Tyus crept across the muddy brown laminate floor like Denzel Washington. His amble was slow and sexy, yet purposeful. Symphony eyed Tyus approaching and she knew this shit was about to go left real fast.

"Do we have a problem here?" Tyus was dangerously positioned in that familiar ambush predatory stance. One hand in his pocket and the other combing through the fine hairs of his goatee. This would not fare well for Calvin.

"Are you her bodyguard now, man?" Calvin nervously chuckled, appraising the muscly frame that was 20 years his junior and at least 4 inches taller and 40 pounds heavier.

"I can be." Tyus stood, straight face, hands now crossed at his crotch.

Damn, I wanna fuck him right now. Symphony mused as she admired her deliciously fetching protector. She glanced at Ledia whose mouth was gaped open, enamored by Tyus' sexiness like she wanted to fuck him too.

"You clearly can't hear too well, old man. My instructions

were simple - run the other fucking way if you ever crossed paths with Symphony James. If you even thought about her, immediately change your mind. If a scent reminds you of her sweet ass pussy, find something else to smell. Is that not what I said? Was I unclear?" His fiery eyes narrowed.

"Look young blood. I don't want no trouble. I was just saying hello." Calvin backed away.

"So we're clearly having a communication issue because hello shouldn't even leave your tongue when it's directed to Symphony James." Tyus closed the distance between him and Calvin.

"Ty, just leave it alone. Please." Symphony rested her hand on the bulge of his arm peeking through the burgundy sweater.

He glared at her, digesting the silvery sparkle of her eyes that he craved.

"No worries, Sweetpea. Mr. Amos was just leaving anyway because he didn't want any trouble. He wouldn't want the pictures of your face showing up at the police department. Stories of the abusive car dealership owner spreading across town wouldn't be good for business. Or, maybe I should investigate how Amos Audi was financed. Everybody knows those financial records are fiction. Shit, best sellers." Tyus leered at Calvin daring him to say another word.

"Go ahead and enjoy your lunch, Sweetpea." He pulled the chair out for Symphony, still eyeing Calvin as he began to exit Melvin's.

"Thank you, Ty. But you didn't have to-" Tyus interrupted before she could piss him off with her words.

"Just leave it at *thank you,* Symphony. I know I didn't have to, I wanted to." He glared, desperately wanting to kiss those pouty glossed lips.

"Tyus, honey, what is going on?" Natalie wrapped her arm around his waist.

He didn't respond, maintaining his attention towards Symphony.

"Are you sure you're okay?" He probed.

The sparkle in Symphony's eyes was replaced by fiery flames aiming for Natalie's head. *Honey!* She leered at Tyus before dropping her head.

"I'm fine." She snarkily responded. Tyus was tempted to snatch her up and literally shake some sense into her sexy ass physique. But he acquiesced.

"It's nice to see you again, Sympathy." Natalie deviously smirked. But she had no clue the type of bitch she was dealing with.

"Girl, don't act like you don't know my damn name." Symphony spoke to Natalie but kept her eyes on him. "Tyus, you betta get your girl, *honey."* Symphony rolled her eyes.

"You ladies enjoy your lunch." Tyus backed away, eyeing Symphony as he departed. Symphony's cell phone rang, disrupting the stare down between her and Tyus. She dryly answered.

"Hey Prima."

"Pri, I tried to call you because I saw Tyus about 30 minutes ago. I think he was going to Melvin's and that chick was with him. Were you still going to Melvin's for lunch? I was trying to catch you before you ran into him." Syncere warned.

Symphony watched as Tyus and Natalie left the restaurant.

"Too late." She whimpered.

───────────────

Natalie talked non-stop as they walked back to her car from Melvin's. Tyus heard nothing. All he could hear was Symphony's voice, smelled the coconut hibiscus aroma. He shuddered from the thought of her light touch, but the wrath in her eyes was infuriating and heartbreaking. Yeah he was still pissed, but he needed to make it clear that he was not fucking with Natalie.

"Tyus?" Natalie huffed. "Can we just go to your place?" She rubbed his face, standing on her tippy toes trying to kiss him.

"Natalie, I have work." His brow furrowed.

"You're the boss, right? So you call the shots." Natalie caressed his chest steadily journeying her fingers to his crotch before he firmly clutched her hand.

"Natalie, why are you still in Haven?" Tyus questioned, moving her other hand from his face.

"What do you mean? I'm helping mother and daddy." She nervously responded.

"You keep saying that but it's been almost a month. Your grandfather's estate was that complicated?" Tyus was skeptical.

"Tyus, you remember how important granddad was. So yes, it's complicated."

"I remember he owned a butcher shop that's been closed for years." Tyus rebutted. "Why are you really here, Natalie?"

"Tyus, I just figured since you're single and I'm single we could try again. Rekindle what we once had. We were so in love." Natalie reached for him again only to be denied.

"I was so in love. You lied." Tyus was placid, standing with his hands stuffed in his pockets.

"Tyus, that was so long ago. We were kids talking about marriage. It was too much too soon."

"You're right... it was too much and we were young. I know that now but you could've told me that to my face instead of pretending like you were going to attend Spelman while I was at Morehouse. I drove to your house that morning ecstatic about our road trip to Atlanta. Only to be greeted by your parents telling me you were on a plane headed to California. *Natalie is going to USC, a real school.* Your snooty ass mother said that shit to me. They took so much pleasure in giving me that letter since they didn't think I was good enough for their perfect little girl." Tyus chortled.

"I still remember that bullshit ass letter...*Tyus, I'm sorry but I literally met **mister right** during my visit to USC. Michael Wright and he's going to be a doctor.* And you got what you wanted, Natalie, so why are you here?" Tyus questioned again.

"Michael left me." She blurted. "He's been cheating for years and he says he's in love with that woman. They're going to be a family. He didn't choose me, Tyus." Natalie leaned against her car covering her face with both hands weeping.

"Natalie, I'm sorry to hear that. I really am. But I'm not the one for you. I never was. You're reacting from a broken heart. Not because you really want to be with me." He lifted her chin to capture her eyes.

"You really love her don't you?" Natalie smiled, delicately wiping tears from her cheeks.

"Who?" Tyus' brow furrowed.

"Symphony." Natalie nastily rolled her eyes.

"Why would you say that?"

"I saw how you looked at her. Today, and at the baby shower. Shit, everybody could see. You used to look at me that way, Tyus. Awestricken, protective, mesmerized. Back then I didn't know what it meant, but now I do. Now... I wish I had a love like that." Natalie sighed, sliding into the passenger seat. "Good luck, Tyus. I really hope she's the one. She'd be crazy not to choose you." She smiled, and just like that Natalie was gone.

SYMPHONY WAS EXCITED to spend the evening with her cousin after running into Calvin and Tyus earlier that day. The cousins were going to Vivre Salon to have a girls' night with their hair stylist and friend Deeny. Since Syncere was seven months pregnant and was having periodic pain in her feet, Symphony and King made the executive decision that she would cease driving. Symphony pulled into the driveway of her cousins' beautiful new home - shit, mini mansion in

Haven Point. She'd swapped her work scrubs for a black jumper and high top wedge sneakers. The unseasonal warmth from earlier disappeared, replaced by a cold November night. King opened the door before Symphony could knock.

"What's up Primo?" Symphony cheerfully greeted King but he didn't look happy.

"What's up Symphony?" King sternly greeted as she entered the foyer.

"Um, you ok King? You look like somebody pissed you off." Symphony carefully questioned. She didn't mess with King when he was angry.

King's eyes narrowed as he observed Syncere when she appeared from their master bedroom. "Somebody did, but that's neither here nor there."

Symphony quickly realized where his frustration was targeted.

"King, I'm not about to argue with you anymore. I'm fine." Syncere's irritation matched her husband.

"Syncere, you're right. We are not about to do this here but this conversation is not over. And so we're crystal clear, I do not approve of this little outing." King was fuming but Symphony was still clueless.

"Um, I am not trying to get in the middle of a domestic dispute -" Symphony stood with her hands up. "- but what's the problem?"

"Tell your cousin about the Braxton Hicks contractions and how bad your feet were hurting and swollen today." King paused, leering at his wife with frustration and concern. "She doesn't need to be going anywhere. Justin and Ms. Ella had to make her leave the office today to get some rest."

"Prima, we don't have to go-"

"I'm fine!" Syncere shouted. "Pri, let's go." She demanded, reaching to open the door as King laid his hand on her shoulder.

"Princess. Please slow down." He kissed against her forehead then her lips. "I'm sorry I yelled, and I love you." King whispered as Syncere returned his sentiment.

Symphony helped her cousin to the car, driving Syncere's SUV since the Audi Coupe was a tight squeeze for the mommy to be.

"Prima, what was that about?" Symphony inquired, as she slid into the driver's seat.

"King is just being dramatic. I have two big ass babies floating around in me. My damn feet are supposed to hurt." Syncere cried. She pretty much cried about everything these days.

"Syncere, don't be out here trying to be strong. You're not superwoman. If your feet hurt, sit your ass down." Symphony stressed and Syncere remained silent.

Ten minutes later, they pulled in front of Vivre Salon. The *closed* sign was illuminated but Deeny was patiently waiting to hang with her friends.

"Hey momma!" Deeny squealed, placing her hand against Syncere's stomach. "I think that belly has grown since the baby shower."

"Girl it has. I'm so ready for these babies to vacate my body." Syncere giggled, then directed her words to her belly.

"Mommy is just kidding. You keep on growing until you're ready."

Syncere reclined in the pedicure chair since it was the most comfortable, sipping on her sparkling grape juice.

"Ok Prima, let's get right to it. What happened with Tyus today?" Syncere probed, now stuffing her face with pizza.

Symphony deeply exhaled, deflating her rosy cheeks. "I know this is girls' night but do we have to talk about me? Why can't we talk about Deeny and Nate?"

"Because ain't shit going on with Deeny and Nate." Deeny matter of factly stated. "I'm living vicariously through y'all." They all guffawed.

Symphony proceeded to get Syncere and Deeny up to speed about the showdown between Calvin and Tyus. Retelling the story pissed her off even more. The image of Natalie cuddled against Tyus set her soul on fire. An hour later, she was still pissed.

"I should've beat that bitch's ass." Symphony blurted.

"Damn Symphony. You are always ready to fight but never ready to talk things through." Deeny chortled. "That girl didn't do anything to you. You handed her Tyus' fine ass on a silver platter when you walked your crazy ass out of his house that day."

"Facts." Syncere nonchalantly nodded, still stuffing her face.

"What else do you want the man to do? He said he can't let you go - that you're a priority. Tyus seems to be giving you everything that you need, and some shit you didn't even know you wanted. And you're just taking, taking, taking. But what are you giving him?" Deeny lifted an eyebrow, taking a big gulp of red wine.

"And you committed to trying, Prima. Made a promise to the man but your ass tried for like one hour and then you reverted back to your bullshit." Syncere chimed.

"So this is pick on Symphony day I see." She pouted.

"Prima, we are not picking on you. We just want you to see what you have right in front of your face before you're sittin' up wondering what you could have been with Tyus, instead of enjoying what you and him can be right now. I know you care about Tyus and I believe he knows it too but the man can only take so much." Syncere paused, slowly gliding out of her seat to go to the restroom.

"Yeah, Symphony. All we're trying to say is get your shit together, girl. Damn." Deeny boisterously laughed. " I'm so sick of y'all finding these fine ass, Mandingo ass men to love y'all and you act a fool." Deeny laughed, hugging Symphony shoulders.

"Ouch! Shit!" Syncere's screams echoed from the back of the salon.

"Syncere, what's wrong?" Deeny leaped from the salon chair.

"Prima! Are you ok?" Symphony ran to her cousin.

Syncere was hunched over bracing herself on the dryer chair with one hand, caressing her belly with the other. She abruptly danced on her tippy toes like she was stepping on hot coals. The pain was excruciating. "Oh my God. I need to sit down."

Symphony and Deeny helped Syncere rest in the dryer

chair. Deeny scrambled to find something to elevate Syncere's feet.

"Shit! My feet, my legs hurt so bad." She breathily panted. "Oh my God. Prima, I can't breathe." Syncere was panicking.

"Prima calm down. Practice your breathing." Symphony blew and counted with her cousin. Syncere's skin was flushed, she felt dizzy and suddenly nauseous.

"Deeny, call 911." Symphony shouted, recognizing that this may be a serious medical emergency, much more than a panic attack.

9

"**W**hat's up bro? Thanks for the invite to the new crib, man. This is dope." Tyus dapped King as he entered the massive two story foyer. Unpacked boxes were scattered across the floor.

"Thanks man. We still have a lot to do before the little princess and king make their grand entrance." King chuckled.

"Damn, dawg. What is it like, in two months?" Tyus paused. "Where is the momma to be anyway? She's probably still pissed at me."

"Man, her strong-headed ass went with Symphony to hang with Deeny at the shop. Against my recommendation." King was still pissed and would tell anybody who would listen. "But I heard about your run in today and yeah, Princess is still pissed." They laughed.

Tyus and King footed across the foyer into the living

room. King grabbed two Coronas from the refrigerator and padded further into the house entering his man cave.

"Man, you would've thought I was in trouble at school. My ass got so nervous when I saw Syncere." Tyus chortled. "And you know Natalie tried to make that shit look like much more than what it was. But that wasn't the end of it. Once we got to Melvin's, Symphony walked in. Then that nigga Calvin drug his old ass in there trying to talk to her."

"Please tell me you finally whooped his ass. Or did Symphony beat his ass...again?" King and Tyus laughed.

"Nah, I didn't but I think he got the message." Tyus paused. "But real talk King... what the fuck am I going to do about Symphony?" Tyus rubbed a hand down his face laced with irritation.

"Oh so we're getting straight to it, huh?" King laughed. "Well fuck the beer, we need something stronger for this conversation." He trekked to the bar grabbing two glasses and poured the Macallan double cask.

"Like her cousin, Symphony is complicated. I'm not sure how much you know about her story, but she's been through some shit with her mom. And it's kinda fucked with her head. If you're willing to be patient then understand that the shit she pulls is not about you - it's how she deals with her pain. If that ain't the life for you then let it go." King shrugged.

Tyus sat back in the chair and deeply exhaled. "It's for me dawg. She's for me." Tyus declared. "I've been trying to help her through the pain- "

"But will you love her past her pain? No matter what the

outcome is for you." King interjected. He was very familiar with what Tyus is going through.

"Yes. Without question." Tyus did not delay. "I - I think I love her, man."

"You think or you know?" King raised an eyebrow, inquiring.

"I'm not going to force Symphony to do anything, but I know I'm in love with that woman." Tyus declared, smiling as he shook his head at the revelation.

"Then tell her. Over and over and over again. Then again some more." King chuckled. "I don't get enough of telling my Princess how much I love her because I know it helps erase some of the bullshit that crowds her head and heart."

Tyus nodded his understanding.

"It's about shock and awe with those James girls." King reclined in his chair. "You gotta do something big to gain and maintain Symphony's attention."

Tyus was silent but was devising a plan.

The men chatted a little longer until the blaring ring of King's phone disrupted their conversation.

"What's up Symphony?"

"King, I need you to stay calm. I'm taking Syncere to the hospital." Symphony tried to take her own advice. She was trembling but fairly calm although King could hear the commotion in the background.

"What! Symphony, what happened? Where is she?" King sprang from his chair, terror in his eyes.

"Her feet were in a lot of pain, but then she got dizzy and nauseous, so I thought it would be best to get her to the hospital. We're in the ambulance?" Symphony's voice quivered.

"Ambulance!" King shouted, scrambling to find his shoes and keys. Tyus held up his car keys signaling to King that he would drive. He didn't know what was going on but he would do whatever necessary to support his friend.

"Symphony, can I talk to her?" Hearing Syncere's cries in the background ripped through his soul.

"King." Syncere grunted in pain. "Babe, it hurts so bad. I should've listened. I'm sorry. King, I can't lose our babies. Oh my God." Syncere cried.

"Princess, it's ok. You and our babies will be fine. I'm on my way, baby. I promise you're going to be fine." King frantically exited the front door as he hopped in Tyus' truck and they sped off to the hospital.

———————————

THE AMBULANCE PULLED up to the emergency room door at St. Gabriel Hospital where Symphony was a nurse. She hopped out of the ambulance along with the EMTs attending to her cousin. Syncere was still having pain in her feet and her blood pressure was elevated. The ER nurse met them at the door transporting Syncere to be seen by a doctor. Symphony tried to leave the room so the nurses could do their jobs but Syncere screamed for her to stay in the room. Symphony obliged.

Tyus and King busted through the emergency room doors fifteen minutes later.

"Syncere Cartwright. My wife. She's pregnant." King loudly blurted at the receptionist, aggressively fisting the desk. "Syncere Cartwright. She was brought here in an ambulance."

"Yes sir, Mr. Cartwright. Let me check with her nurse to determine if you can go back. Please have a seat." King didn't move as the nurse dialed a number and then disconnected. "She's in room 4 but there is already someone back there, sir. There can only be one person in the room at a time, Mr. Cartwright. You'll have to wait sir."

"Lady, take me to my wife!" He shouted. Tyus placed a hand on King's shoulder trying to quell his next move. Just as King was about to climb across the desk to choke that poor lady, Symphony walked through the double doors.

"King. She's crying for you. You need to get back there. She's in so much pain." Symphony was panting, unsuccessfully trying to blink back the ocean of tears in her eyes. King sprinted, disappearing down the hallway.

Symphony's breathing was labored as she aimlessly turned in circles, discombobulated, afraid.

"Symphony." Tyus' soothing voice echoed like a dream. Symphony turned around and locked eyes with him. How did she not see him standing there? She huffed and puffed, trying not to cry. Tyus extended his hand, pulling her body tightly into his frame. Symphony sobbed, releasing the adrenaline and fear crashing through her body.

"I can't lose her. She can't lose the babies. It will destroy her." Symphony paused, capturing his eyes. "Please tell me she's going to be ok, Ty. Please. I - I can't lose her. She's my best friend - my everything."

Tyus ushered Symphony across the waiting area to take a seat. He caressed her, rubbing his fingertips up and down her spine, whispering against her ear, "We should pray." Tyus was often a man of few words but when he spoke they were meaningful.

Symphony clasped her hand in his, resting her head against his chest as he prayed.

"Dear Heavenly Father, thank you for your continued grace and mercy. Loving God, we come to you today asking that you will comfort and heal Syncere in her time of suffering. Shelter her and the two blessings that you have granted her from any hurt, harm, or danger. Cover Syncere and King that they may have confidence in your powerful grace and that they will put all of their trust in you. God, I thank you that Syncere and the babies belong to you and that you are in control of everything that happens from our first breath to our last exhale. In the name of the Father, Son, and Holy Spirit. Amen." Tyus affirmed, as Symphony echoed with tears staining her face. She didn't relinquish from his calming embrace and he didn't desire her absence.

They settled in the waiting room for what felt like hours but only thirty minutes ticked off the clock before King returned to the waiting area.

"King. Is she ok?" Symphony darted across the room before King could say a word.

"Yeah. Her blood pressure is still elevated and she's dehydrated. They're giving her fluids and some medicine to get her pressure down. They want to keep her overnight for observation. The swelling has started to go down and she's not in as much pain." King explained.

"And the babies. Are they good?" Tyus chimed.

"Thankfully yes. Strong heart beats - everything looks good with them." He exhaled a breath, releasing the visible tension.

"I know they are going to put her on bedrest and she will not be happy." Symphony declared.

"And I don't give a damn. If I have to tie her ass to the bed, I will." King shook his head. "Princess is just so damn hard headed." He walked away blinking back the mistiness forming in his eyes.

Symphony was acutely aware of King's desire to release his tears and anguish with his friend so she excused herself and hurriedly returned to Syncere's room.

"Hi Prima." Syncere groggily greeted as Symphony appeared from behind the curtain.

"Hi Prima." Symphony thumbed away a single tear caressing her cousin's face.

"I'm so scared." Syncere silently cried. "King is so upset. I should've listened."

"Stop it, Syncere. King loves you and he's just concerned. You and my little peas in the pod are going to be just fine. Listen to those heart beats. They're strong just like you and me." Symphony and Syncere connected temple to temple as tears flooded their matching grey orbs.

Symphony sat with her cousin until she fell asleep and was transitioned to a hospital room. King entered the room determined to stay with his princess. He could not be persuaded to go home to get some rest. Fully prepared to tear the entire hospital apart if another person told him he couldn't stay with his wife. Symphony peered at Syncere and King with his head cradled in her cousin's hand as she slept. She adored the way King loved and protected her cousin. She could rest knowing Syncere was in good hands.

"King, I'm going to head home. I'll be back in the morning. Well it is morning, so a few hours." She extended her arms for a hug. "I won't call G-ma until she can actually talk to Syncere. Otherwise she'll go crazy if she can't hear her voice."

Symphony planted a kiss against her sleeping cousin's forehead.

"Oh, shit. I rode in the ambulance and my car is at your house. I guess I'll have to order an Uber." She tossed her head back, frustrated, and exhausted.

"I can take you home Symphony." Tyus' thunderous tone sounded from the doorway where he quietly lurked. He was the comfort she didn't know she needed. They locked eyes as Symphony simply nodded, unable to comprehend or articulate anything in that moment.

It was almost one o'clock in the morning and the frigid temperature sent a quiver through Symphony since she'd left her coat at the beauty salon during the haste. The adrenaline that kept her warm hours earlier was no more. Tyus engaged the remote start on his truck as they stood in the hospital corridor waiting for the car to warm. Her teeth chattered when the automatic sliding hospital doors opened releasing a gust of chilled wind. He removed his coat to blanket her, wrapping his corded arms around her shivering frame.

Tyus was in protective mode, observing their surroundings before they walked to the car. She noticed the same fiery look of protection on Tyus' face that she just admired on King. Symphony missed Tyus, so she took this opportunity to digest him. She deeply inhaled, intoxicated by the deep seasoned aroma of Cuban cigars he smoked earlier, the spicy vibrance of whiskey entangled with sweet bergamot. Symphony was beyond drunk in love. She was damn near plastered like a college frat boy. How dare he stand before her so savagely manly hypnotizing her with his entrancing essence. *Fuck!* Symphony mused as she visibly shuddered from the thump in her treasure.

Symphony. Sweetpea. A voice rang in her ears. She thought she was hearing things. "Symphony? You ready?" Tyus lifted her chin. "Where was your head at?"

"Um, huh? Nowhere. Just thinking about Syncere." She kinda lied.

"Syn is going to be fine. Let's get out of here. The car should be warm." Tyus quickly ushered her to the car, securing her seatbelt before jogging around to the driver's seat. Symphony jolted, chattering her teeth again this time with a loud squeal through her clenched pearly whites.

Tyus chuckled. "You are so dramatic. It's not that cold."

"Ty, it is fr-ee-zing." She dramatically shrilled. They warmly guffawed and it was delightful.

"If you say so." Tyus continued chuckling, enjoying a carefree moment with her. "I'll take you home and come back in the morning so you can get your car from Syncere's house."

"Ty, it's fine. I can just get my car tonight."

"Symphony." He turned to her, fiercely gawking. "I would

really prefer to take you home so that you are not driving at two o'clock in the morning. You've had a rough night and you're tired. It's not a problem for me to come back in the morning."

Symphony thought for a second to rebuttal with some *I'm a boss bitch black woman who doesn't need a man to do shit for me* type of statement but instead she acquiesced, allowing Tyus to simply care for her.

"What if I don't want to go home?" She blurted, eyeballing his velvety lips.

"Then tell me what you want, Symphony." He licked his lips, drawing attention to her second favorite part of his anatomy.

Symphony hesitated, exhausting all the logical and illogical options. She was desperately trying not to fuck up this moment as she'd done in the past.

"Ty, I don't want to be alone tonight." She cracked a coy smile.

"Say less, Sweetpea."

LESS THAN THIRTY MINUTES LATER, Tyus pulled into his garage. Symphony dozed off shortly after leaving the hospital. He gently scooped her into his arms and entered the side door of his house. She was still comatose, her head resting on his shoulder. Tyus padded down the hallway into his room settling her on the king size bed. He removed her shoes as she shuffled from the tickling sensation. Tyus snickered, tempted to awake her in a ticklish fit.

He undressed her, finding one of his t-shirts to cover her gorgeous body. Tyus observed Symphony and he was captivated. Entranced by the light hum of her snore and the way she pouted her glossy lips when she slumbered. He desperately missed Symphony and desired to enfold her into an unyielding cuddle. But he decided to abandon his desires and sleep on the couch.

Symphony roused from her sleep around 5 am peering throughout the familiar dark grey and blue room. She lengthened her arm, stretching across the king size mattress but something was missing - Tyus. She perched on the edge of the bed eyeing the chaise in the dark corner of the room where he usually meditated in the early mornings. It was vacant. Symphony was wearing one of his Morehouse t-shirts. Her brow furrowed, no recollection of getting undressed. But more importantly she wondered where Tyus was. She tip-toed across the plush carpeted floor exiting his room, navigating her way down the dusky hallway. The flickering light from the TV slightly illuminated her path.

Tyus was shirtless and sound asleep on the couch. Symphony was unsure if she should cuddle up next to his exquisitely gooey butter skin or curse him for leaving her alone last night. She intently observed him, crafting every ridiculously insane reason why he would sleep on the couch instead of with her. *Maybe he's really done this time. Does he want me anymore? Is there someone else? You really fucked up this time Symphony.*

"Symphony." She quaked at the sound of his raspy

morning tone and the realization that she was caught gaping. "Why are you just standing there staring at me?" He patted the couch cushion requesting her presence near him. "Come and talk to me so I can banish the bullshit that's circulating through that pretty little head of yours."

Symphony pointlessly tried to suppress the blush forming within her cheeks as she ambled to the couch. She hated and appreciated that Tyus knew her so well. She squatted on the couch keeping distance between them.

"Closer." He whispered. She moved slightly.

"Closer." He urged as she left a miniscule gap.

"Just a little more. I promise I won't bite." Tyus playfully grinned. She obliged.

"What's wrong Symphony?" He asked.

Her hands began to tremble, the butterfly-goosebump shit returned and the word vomit was brewing. *Don't fuck this up Symphony.* She encouraged.

"What happened last night, Ty? Why did you sleep out here? I could've slept on the couch." Symphony probed.

"You fell asleep in the car so I put you in my bed. And I wouldn't dare allow you to sleep on the couch." He declared.

"Ok, but you didn't answer my other question. Why didn't you sleep with me last night in your bed?" Symphony rested her shapely hip against the couch cushion crossing her arms.

Tyus repositioned on the couch to ensure that he was intently focused on her eyes.

"Honestly, Symphony, I wouldn't have been capable of keeping my hands off of you. I wanted to comfort and caress you, but I know that's not your only expectation. And I refuse to satisfy you physically, when I am not given the opportunity to penetrate you emotionally....to access your heart."

Symphony gasped, breathless. Every defense she thought she possessed instantly dismantled.

"I'm sorry, Ty. I don't know what's wrong with me. Well I guess I sort of know what's wrong but -" She sighed. "You fill my heart in ways I've only imagined and there's so much I want to express to you but my stupid ass mouth just spits out the dumbest shit. Just self-destructive."

Symphony smacked her palm against her forehead. "I'm literally a Boogie Down Production walking billboard for self-destruction, Ty."

Tyus snickered because this woman was silly as hell, even in her distress. He trailed a finger up her thigh then rested his hand over her heart. It pounded against his palm threatening to pierce her fleshiness.

"Symphony, if you would take a moment to stop and feel instead of always thinking something or someone is going to hurt you - you'd be able to listen to your heart." Tyus kept his hand motionless. "Speak to me from your heart, Sweetpea."

"Tyus, I -" She roughly swallowed to keep the tears she felt peaking minimized. He tapped lightly against her goosebump covered skin encouraging her to continue.

"Ty, I'm sorry. I completely fucked up. I shouldn't have walked out like a damn two year old." Symphony hesitated. "I - I was just -" She paused again and he gently tapped again. Every time Symphony stuttered her words, Tyus drummed his fingers against her quivering flesh.

Misty-eyed, Symphony cried. "Tyus, I want to keep my promise if you'll let me. I want to try. With you? I - I've - *tap,*

tap, tap. I've missed you, Ty." She mightily swiped her tears audibly exhaling through babbling lips.

Tyus smiled that beautiful toothy grin she loved.

"See that wasn't so hard, Sweetpea." He drew her into his frame, caressing her sultry body, inhaling the sweetest mango aroma. "Baby, I missed you too."

10

Two weeks swiftly flew by, sending Symphony and Tyus on a whirlwind romance. Since they rekindled at the hospital, the dashing couple had been inseparable, alternating living spaces throughout the week and the weekends when Tyus didn't have TJ. Symphony was committed to actually trying this relationship thing with Tyus which included his son. She'd video chatted with TJ, discovering he's the cutest sweetest six year old she'd ever seen.

It was Friday night and Tyus had been in Chicago since Tuesday visiting a few construction sites for King since he was hesitant to travel while Syncere was on bedrest - or house arrest as she sarcastically called it. Symphony didn't realize how much she would miss their connection while he was gone but it was a sensation that she craved daily and one second without him was becoming unbearable...and Symphony abhorred the feeling. She'd never relinquished her mind, body, and soul to any man and Tyus had her splendidly consumed. *This man got me cooking and shit.* She mused, preparing her specialty chicken and broccoli alfredo for their dinner date tonight.

Symphony beautifully set the dining room table with candles, wine, and her grandmother's fine china. She pulled her fluffy curly afro into a high ponytail and draped in a hip-hugging long sleeve black dress. Symphony sang and danced to the jazzy melodies of Jill Scott trumpeting from the Google Home in her kitchen. The blare of her phone hindered her joyous reverie. Expecting Tyus to call, Symphony shouted, *"Hey Google, answer call."* The call connected through the speaker and she immediately greeted the caller.

"Hey Bae. Did you just land?" She cooed.

"Bae? Are you preparing to entertain a gentleman caller, daughter?" Malynda's cigarette smoke-filled throaty pitch and prissy bitch tone echoing through the kitchen sent a spark of uneasiness through Symphony's veins.

"What do you want, Malynda? I haven't responded to your twenty thousand text messages so why would I want to talk to you?" She inquired but didn't expect a coherent answer.

"Twenty thousand? I see your dramatics have not deteriorated." Her mother declared.

"Well I learned from the best didn't I? Ms. Malynda James, doctor and actress wanna be." Symphony's voice was laced with indignation as she exhaled, rolling her eyes. She began aggressively chopping the tomato for the salad, banging the knife against the wooden cutting board.

"Don't sass me, daughter." Malynda paused. "You didn't answer my question. Who is Bae? Your gentleman caller." She posed again.

"Will you stop calling me daughter! You are not Thanos and I'm not Gamora. Contrary to your twisted mind, we are not in a Marvel movie." Symphony yelled, rapidly chopping until she pricked her finger with the knife.

"Shit! Ouch!" She hurried over to the faucet applying cold water to the wound. Symphony and Malynda remained hushed as Symphony busseled through the drawer looking for a bandage.

"I have to go, Malynda. But for the record, I don't have a gentleman caller. That's your shit. I have a man."

"Still using such language with your mother I see. Daughter, we really need to talk. I have something I need to talk about-" Symphony canceled her mother's comment before it really started.

"I don't want to hear it. Whatever you have to say... I can't - not today." She audibly expelled a breath, unsuccessfully releasing the seething frustration that only her mother could induce.

"I will text you tomorrow to find a more appropriate time for us to talk." Symphony lied, but that was the only way her mother would acquiesce. She disconnected the call before Malynda could agree.

Fuck the wine. Symphony pondered as she peered at the bottle of red wine on the table. She footed across the kitchen to the freezer to retrieve the bottle of Tito's. *Fuck a shot glass.* Symphony tossed the vodka bottle back, inhaling two massive gulps. She cringed from the sting, then counted and breathed until she calmed.

The pasta was warming in the oven, salad was done, and the bread buttered. She was ready to plunge into the protective consolatory arms of her man. Tyus called from his car to determine if she needed anything before he arrived. Symphony was giddy with anticipation but extremely distressed by the brief yet counterproductive phone call. She'd only chatted with her mother for maybe five minutes but the lasting impact of Malynda's harm was plastered all over Symphony's pretty face. She allowed the soothing effects of the vodka to penetrate attempting to tranquilize before Tyus arrived. The ring from the doorbell produced an immediate smile accompanied by the butterfly-goosebumps mixture.

"Hey Bae." Symphony instantly melted into him. Firmly tossing her arms around his neck, squeezing a little bit tighter than intended, Tyus didn't have the opportunity to cross the threshold.

"Sweetpea. It's cold out here, baby. Let me in." He chuckled, maintaining his hold on her waist with one arm while he closed and secured the door quickly reverting back to their embrace.

"I take it you missed me, huh?" Tyus reluctantly released her but he needed an extended glimpse of the ashen grey orbs he loved.

"I did miss you, Ty." She smiled, but it didn't reach her eyes. And he noticed.

"Symphony." Tyus firmly uttered her name in his distinct way as he cupped her chin examining those eyes. "Baby, what's wrong? And before you even consider it, please don't tell me nothing. I can see the anguish that resides in those beautiful eyes." He laced a finger down the curve of her face.

"Ty, I'm fine. Why do you always think something is wrong with me?" Symphony began sauntering into the living room. Tyus removed his coat and followed behind her. He pulled her into him searching for answers.

"Sweetpea, when are you going to realize that I know you? I know every curve of your face - every glisten in your eyes. The meaning of every smile, scowl, and smirk. When those eyes narrow into thin slits, you're pissed or trying to control the word vomit." Tyus sexily grinned, never ceasing his gaze as he ushered her to the couch. "And those trembling hands -" He clasped her quivering fingers into his, placing them against her chest. "- they are the first indicator that something is bothering you. Talk to me, baby."

Symphony squinted, eyes narrowly thin, proving Tyus' point about the ensuing word vomit. She quelled the initial *I can handle this shit on my own because I'm a boss bitch* though, opting for the truth instead.

"My mother called." Symphony whispered. "She's been texting me a few times a week for the past month and I've never responded. Malynda claims she wants to talk but she never has anything worthwhile to say. It's like her main goal is to piss me off. And she always succeeds." She pouted, leaning her head against his shoulder.

"I'm sorry she upset you, Sweetpea. What can I do?" He massaged his fingers against her neck.

"Not much can be done to change Malynda James." She shrugged.

"No offense, but honestly, I could care less about Ms. James." He shrugged.

"It's ok. You can call my mother a bitch. I have." She chuckled.

"Symphony! I wouldn't go to that extreme. Right now, the only James woman I'm responsible for is you. I'm not going to let anybody hurt you, Symphony, especially your mother. Tell me what you need." Tyus was stern, protective.

"Well first, I need a kiss because I missed you like crazy. Second, I need you to enjoy this amazing dinner I've prepared. And third, I need you to carry me upstairs and ravish every inch of this sexy ass curvy body." Symphony sexily grinned.

"In that order? Or can I rearrange some things?" They chuckled as he slowly captured her lips with genteel, intentional, tender kisses.

Harmonized soft moans provided the most sensual backdrop as the gentle kisses escalated. Tyus licked her smooth pouty lips before parting her mouth with his searing plump tongue. He caressed her earlobes, stroked her cheeks, kneading against her nape, caressing up the back of her head - driving Symphony completely nuts. They were lost in that kiss - disoriented, unhinged and wanton with desire.

Beep. Beep. Beep. The oven timer sounded, not breaking the impassioned rhythm of the tongue-lashing.

"Bae. Dinner is ready." Symphony panted, mumbling through kisses as his lips trailed down her neck. "Aren't you hungry, Ty? Don't you want to eat?" Her inquiry caused a fiery gaze from Tyus.

"Yeah baby. I want to eat." He lustfully smirked, licking

his lips, causing a tidal wave in her treasure. Symphony was dripping...like wet wet. Desperately needing a dry pair of panties because her thong served no purpose. He inhaled the ambrosial bouquet scent fused with the saccharine sweet delicacy simmering from her puss. His heaviness pressed against her frame, forcing her back against the couch.

Tyus' imposing hands stroked up her thighs lifting the dress exposing the sodden wet thong. Her pretty naked puss playing peek-a-boo through the sheer fabric. He beamed at her, elated that she stayed moist and ready for him. She smiled, sliding her bottom lip against her teeth. They were jointly intoxicated by each other's desire.

Tyus wasted no time, removing her dress and his pants almost at the same time. His pretty ombre penis was firmly erect, waving hello because he missed his sweetpea too. The anticipation of his curved girth caused Symphony to pant, quiver, and quake. Her mouth was ready to devour his dick while her body was prepared to enthusiastically welcome him into the depths of her pussy.

"Aahh! Ty!" She moaned, simply from the consolidation of their flushed skin. His seduction was calculated, unhurried, but assured. He was teasing her, sucking, licking, nibbling, and biting everywhere but where she begged him to be.

"Please Ty. Bae please." Symphony pleaded.

"You don't have to beg for this dick, baby. I promise I'm all yours." Tyus whimpered against her private lips. He hovered over there, his breath humid, steamy against her glistening jewel. Tyus' heated lips tongue-kissed her sweltering puss like he was making love to it. Twisting, turning, probing, licking to the continued beeping playing in the background.

"Tyus. Baby. I need to feel you." Symphony moaned, fisting the throw pillow eventually tossing it across the room. She arched her back, head thrown between her shoulder blades gripping the back of the couch because she was plummeting - literally and figuratively. Falling more in love with Tyus with every caress, stroke, fondle, and sweet embrace.

Insatiable, craving his heaviness within her waterlogged walls and him desiring to occupy permanent residency amidst her juicy ocean. Tyus journeyed up the length of her frame taking a pit stop at her stone hard nipples, tugging the rose gold rings before inhaling them one at a time into the cavernous depths of his mouth.

"Ty please!" She yelped. Enfolding his manhood with both hands, carefully guiding that damn curved head into her saturated folds.

"Shit!" They whimpered in unison.

"Sweetpea, damn girl. You feel like heaven...every fucking time." His strokes were slow, deliberate, inhabiting every square inch of her pulsating treasure. Tyus could feel the throbbing against his dick. The weightiness of Tyus' penetration grew deeper, more intense. He felt like she was an extension of him unable to distinguish where she began and he ended.

Symphony welcomed his every stroke, graciously consenting to inch by glorious inch, by curved inch after inch.

"Ty! You feel so fucking good." She moaned. "Ty I -, Ty I -" She cried.

"You what, baby? Tell me, Sweetpea." Tyus didn't cease his merciless pounding. He was ready to fuck the *I love you* right out of her. Dismantling every one of her complicated, crazy layers with every stroke.

"Tell me Symphony." He commanded, slowing his pace to a crawl, teasing.

"Bae." She screamed at the edge of her pinnacle. "I'm coming."

Tyus shifted positions, resting on his knees with her legs draped across his shoulders driving harder, deeper, faster. Her guts were guaranteed to be all fucked up after the gratifying beating he delivered.

Symphony joyously screamed his entire government name, "Tyus Anthony Okoro, Sr." A bitch even added a suffix, the dick was so damn good. She buried her face into his chest, labored breathing, attempting to conceal the single tear that brimmed. Tyus meticulously thrusted into her one more time reaching a magnificently mind blowing climax. He collapsed onto her, still leaking his gooey goodness inside. She marveled in the warmth of the skin to skin connection, cuddling and cooing like a newborn baby.

"Bae." She whispered.

"Sweetpea." Ty rebutted.

"Let's go eat." They chimed in unison, chuckling, basking in a blissful afterglow.

11

Almost two weeks passed since Malynda called and Symphony had been ignoring her, only responding with, *I'm too busy to talk right now.* It was Thanksgiving morning and Symphony spent the night at Tyus' house. Although they had a magnificent date the night before and an even more splendid early morning of love-making, Symphony had an attitude because Tyus had to travel again next week. His business was picking up, requiring him to travel to Atlanta and Chicago a bit more. Her words said *she understood* but her funky mood spoke otherwise.

Tyus was in the shower preparing to spend the morning with his parents and TJ and was going to meet Symphony over King and Syncere's house later in the evening for dinner. Syncere had been on a tirade about not seeing her friends and G-ma since being on bedrest for the past three weeks so it was no question that the holiday dinner would be at the Cartwright's.

Tyus' phone rang and TJ's picture popped up. Symphony figured TJ was probably calling from his mom's phone to see what time his dad was picking him up. Seconds later the phone vibrated against the nightstand. A text message from Gia's phone. *TJ never sends a text.* Symphony pondered, lifting up in the bed to glance at the message before it disappeared.

Gia: Can you bring orange juice for the mimosas?

Why the fuck would Tyus need to bring Gia orange juice? She mused, furrowed brow, and her grey eyes squinted to a fine line.

"Sweetpea, are you sure you want to drive? I can pick you up after brunch and we can go to dinner together." Tyus sauntered out of the bathroom, his glistening caramel skin on full display, fresh haircut and his no shave November beard nicely groomed. Symphony licked her lips at the delicious sight, irritated that her traitorous ass treasure was throbbing for this man that she was supposed to be pissed at.

"Nah, I'm good." She pouted, laying against the dark grey tufted headboard with her arms crossed over her naked flesh. "Um, Gia needs orange juice for you all's mimosas." She spat.

Tyus continued to dry off then stepped into a pair of black Polo boxer briefs. Her pout, stank ass tone, and childish body language were all too familiar.

"Okay?" He calmly responded, pulling a matching black t-shirt over his head. "I heard my phone ring. Did you talk to her?" He aimlessly moved about the room, pissing off Symphony even more.

"No, I didn't talk to her. Why would I answer your phone, especially when your son's mother is calling?" Symphony jolted her naked body out of the bed, snatching her overnight bag from the floor.

"Well how do you know she needs orange juice?" Tyus could care less if Symphony answered his phone or investigated every text and phone call. He had nothing to hide.

"I saw the text, Tyus." She snapped.

"Oh, so we're checking each other's text messages now." He teasingly questioned.

Symphony leered at him but didn't respond, just continued to vigorously pull out clothes from her bag. She'd already showered so she was ready to get dressed. Symphony stomped into the bathroom.

"I didn't realize this was a family affair, Ty. You said you, TJ, and your parents were having brunch. Not Gia!"

"I asked you, begged you, several times if you wanted to come to brunch, Symphony." His reserve remained as he dressed in dark distressed denim jeans, perching on the lounge chair lacing his Timberland boots. "And you said no...several times."

"You conveniently left out the fact that TJ's mother would be spending Thanksgiving with you as well. Like one big happy family I guess." Symphony yelled from the bathroom as she aggressively brushed through her curly mane.

"You are always on some bullshit. Is this about Gia or is this about you? Sounds like you're only regretting your decision not to go because she'll be there." Tyus huffed, pulling the hunter green sweater over his head.

Symphony walked out of the restroom but couldn't prevent her sudden pause, gazing at him in that sweater highlighting the slight green in his eyes and cuddling every inch of his muscular abdomen.

"What the fuck difference does it make if Gia will be at brunch.? You didn't want to go, right?" Tyus declared.

"Tyus that's not the point - "

He held his hand up, halting any further comment.

"Answer the question. Did you want to go when I asked you at least four times in the past week?" He inquired.

Symphony was about to speak every word but an appropriate response.

"Yes or no, Symphony?" He demanded.

"No." She harshly whispered.

"So you don't have shit to be mad about."

Tyus snatched his wallet from the nightstand leaving her perched in the bathroom doorway. He walked into the kitchen checking his refrigerator for orange juice and yanked the new bottle out, slamming it on the counter. Thankfully, it was a cardboard container.

Tyus was pissed, slamming shit and mumbling his frustrations under his breath. Symphony finished dressing in a burgundy cowl neck sweater dress and knee-high heeled suede boots. She sauntered into the living room with her purse and overnight bag. Tyus looked up from his position on the couch. He now had to pause, examining the way that dress hugged her curves. He loved when she pulled her hair into a high curly ponytail exposing her long velvety neck.

"I'm about to leave. I thought you would've been gone by now. Wouldn't want to disappoint the family by being late." She sarcastically bantered, while her hands trembled. "I guess... call me later if you want."

Tyus leered at her, fiery eyes expressing all of the shit he wouldn't dare say aloud.

"Your ass is something else." Tyus mumbled under his breath. "Get your shit and let's go." He grabbed his keys and the orange juice from the kitchen island.

"I'll just see you later Tyus." She retorted.

"Symphony!" He yelled before taking a breath. "Get your stuff. You are going with me because I'm tired of this shit and it's getting settled right fucking now."

He held the front door open, motioning for her to exit. Her feet remained bolted to the shiny hardwood. "Now, Symphony." Tyus demanded and she stubbornly obliged.

They rode in silence. No music, no talking, not even a damn hum. Symphony was almost afraid to swallow too loud. Tyus tightly gripped the steering wheel while he drove through Haven Point to get to Grover Heights. She had no clue where he was going because Gia didn't live in either neighborhood. He pulled his truck up to an old two story brick house very similar to her grandparent's home. Two cars were parked in the driveway and two more under the extra wide carport.

"Tyus, where are we?" Symphony whispered but didn't make eye contact.

Tyus remained hushed, slamming the car door then walked to the passenger side to retrieve her. He grabbed the orange juice from the back seat then signaled for her to start walking.

"Ty - "

"Nah. We'll talk later. Just come on." Tyus continued up the steps and rang the doorbell. They heard the pitter patter of feet running then the locks disengaged before the door opened.

"Dad!" TJ jumped in Tyus' arms, clutching his dad's neck with his eyes clamped tight. When he opened them, he yelled, "Ms. Symphony!" He reached for her, pulling Symphony into a joint hug with his dad. Symphony didn't realize she was holding her breath when those little arms cradled her neck. She smiled.

"Dad, you said Ms. Symphony couldn't come. You wanted to surprise me didn't you?" TJ released the cutest giggle.

Symphony gazed at TJ. She'd seen him several times on video chat but to have an up close and personal visual of him gave her chills. He was a miniature Tyus - face, smile, ears, hands, everything except his eyes.

"Tyus Anthony Ramos Okoro Jr.! Why are you answering the door like you pay some bills?" A voice resounded in the background. A petite yet curvy woman with smooth olive skin and coal black short curly Halle Berry-ish hair appeared. Her eyes were citrine in color matching TJ's.

"Hi Tyus. Happy Thanksgiving. Come in. It's chilly out there." The woman motioned for them to enter while TJ was still hanging on Tyus' neck.

"Happy Thanksgiving Gia." Tyus placed TJ on his feet. "Gia this is-"

"Mommy, this is Ms. Symphony." TJ interrupted. "I told

you she was pretty. Daddy said she wasn't coming but they surprised me." He giggled.

"Well you are the party planner TJ so the more the merrier." Gia smiled and extended her hand to Symphony. "Nice to meet you. Happy Thanksgiving. Everybody is in the kitchen."

Symphony wore a counterfeit smile, glancing at Tyus, she mouthed, "Everybody?"

TJ grabbed his dad and Symphony's hands pulling them into the kitchen. He then shouted, "Happy Thanksgiving. Let's eat." Everyone burst out laughing. TJ was a bit of a character to be six years old.

"Hi son." A man about Tyus' height and a smile that matched his and Titan's pulled him into a hug. The man peered around Tyus, noticing Symphony. "Well hello, pretty lady. You must be Symphony James? I'm Theodore Okoro." He greeted before his wife interrupted.

"Theo move. Let the girl get in here good." While Tyus and Titan were identical twins, their mother was Tyus' true twin. Her smooth caramel skin was the epitome of black don't crack. A chocolate brown chin-length layered bob accentuated her young look. She was beautiful.

"Hello dear. I'm Racine Okoro, Tyus' mother. I've heard a lot about you. You are absolutely gorgeous, dear. I have been dying to meet you." Mrs. Okoro pulled Symphony into a hug.

"Hello Mr. and Mrs. Okoro. It's nice to meet you as well." Symphony cleared her throat before smiling. She was a nervous wreck. Tyus had been talking about her - to his parents, nonetheless. Symphony tried to stay close to Tyus but he truly wasn't fucking with her. He took her coat and ambled down the hallway. There were so many people spread throughout the eat-in kitchen and connecting living room. She glanced around the room trying to guess the association to Tyus, nodding her head recognizing Titan and his girlfriend Laiya. Tyus remained quiet, still visibly frustrated as he vainly attempted to act normal.

"Symphony, these are my parents, Raphael and Marita Ramos. They are our gracious host this year." Gia's raspy voice was laced with an authentic Spanish accent. Symphony smiled, shaking their hands, seeing where Gia inherited her beautifully black curly hair.

"And this -" Gia motioned to a woman who was just as petite and equally pretty, a little thicker than Gia rocking waist-length box braids. "- this is my girlfriend Roselyn."

"Call me Rose." She extended her hand. "It's nice to meet you. TJ can't stop talking about Ms. Symphony." Rose laughed, pulling Gia closer. "I'm glad we get to put a face with a name."

All of the blood drained to Symphony's feet. She kept blinking, trying to register what Gia just said. *Girlfriend?* Symphony was wordless, shocked, dumbfounded. She had so many questions.

"Um, it's nice to meet you Rose. TJ has definitely become my little buddy." She chuckled, feeling Tyus' eyes on her. Symphony glanced at him as he lifted an eyebrow as if to say, *see I told your ass to trust me.*

Everyone sat down to eat brunch. The menu was a deliciously interesting combination of southern soul food - fried chicken, pork chops waffles, grits, cheese eggs, and a touch of Mexican compliments of Gia's father who bragged about cooking the Huevos a la Mexicana coupled with black beans, homemade tortillas, and salsa. Symphony was in heaven. And so was TJ, he laughed and flashed his toothless grin all afternoon, enthusiastic about having his entire family together.

"Ty, can I ask you a question?" Symphony was seated next to him and whispered. He nodded but no verbal response.

"Gia said TJ was the party planner. What did she mean?"

"Two years ago, TJ decided that he wanted to spend one holiday with all of his family. He didn't want to split his day between my family and Gia's. Going to one place for breakfast then another for dinner every holiday. When we asked him what he wanted...this was it - time with all of his family at the same dinner table. He started a new tradition at only four years old." Tyus beamed, glancing at the head of the table where TJ proudly sat. Symphony joined his elation. TJ was a pretty remarkable kid. And Symphony was feeling like shit - again.

It was almost 3 o'clock when everyone began to disperse. Tyus' parents left first to get on the highway headed to southern Missouri to visit some of his mother's family. Titan dapped his brother as he and Laiya left to spend Thanksgiving with her family, indicating they would stop by King and Syncere's later tonight. TJ laughed, ate, and talked himself into a coma so Tyus carried him to the bedroom he had at his grandparent's home. Symphony stood at the kitchen island, observing, admiring how gentle Tyus was with TJ.

"They have a pretty special relationship. I sometimes find

myself staring at them too." Gia voiced from behind Symphony. "He's a good dad. No, correction, a great dad. Under the circumstances, I'm truly blessed." Gia continued to observe the two Tyus' until they disappeared down the hallway into the bedroom.

"Circumstances?" Symphony questioned, peering over her shoulder at Gia. "What do you mean?"

"You don't know the story, huh? You've never asked Tyus how we met?" Gia grinned.

Symphony shook her head. She'd always wanted to inquire about Gia but didn't really desire the gritty details of his past relationship. And he didn't seem keen on disclosing them.

"Over the years, I've learned that Tyus is a don't ask, don't tell kinda man. If you don't ask, he will never tell. I'm sure you were concerned about any baby mama drama. But Tyus and I were never in that kind of relationship to warrant any drama. We barely knew each other." She chuckled through an exhale.

"Um, pardon me. Come again." Symphony almost choked on the mimosa.

"Before Tyus moved back to Haven to start his own company, we both worked at Coca-Cola in Atlanta. I was in sales and he was in finance but we didn't know each other. Almost seven years ago, the company sent a group of promising underrepresented talent to the National Black MBA conference in Chicago. The last night of the conference, Diageo sponsored the bomb ass party and the vodka, rum, and whiskey were freely flowing. His group and my group of work friends were really drunk and hella flirty."

"Tyus and I discovered that we were both from St. Louis, he graduated from Morehouse and me from Clark-Atlanta. One thing led to another and I found myself in Tyus' hotel room." Gia shook her head, glancing at Rose who had clearly heard this story before.

"I left his room before he woke up thinking I would never see him again. About eight weeks later, I found out I was pregnant. Twenty - nine years old, struggling with my sexuality and pregnant with a stranger's baby. I was so drunk that all I remembered about him was - a cute, Will Smith looking brother named Tyus with the funny last name. I was keeping my baby no matter what he wanted but thought he should at least be able to state his position on the matter. And the rest is his history."

Symphony gasped. "So a one night stand? And y'all have never....ya know, done it again?" She probed.

"Nope. Now if I was into men like that, I definitely would've done that shit again. Because I'm certain you are fully aware that Tyus is a hell of a man." Gia coyly cackled. "But it would've been a lie."

"Damn! That's a hell of a story." Symphony's mouth was still gaped.

"Right!" Rose squealed and the ladies boisterously guffawed.

"Sounds like y'all are having too much fun." Tyus entered the kitchen as the ladies hastily quieted. "Symphony, we should go. Gia, can I talk to you for a minute?" He questioned.

Tyus and Gia quickly connected on next week's schedule for TJ.

"I like her for you. She's feisty. Won't take none of your bullshit." Gia laughed.

"I guess feisty is one way to describe Symphony James." He glared at her, fully aware that a serious conversation about the future of their relationship was necessary.

Symphony grabbed her coat and thanked the Ramos', Gia, and Rose for their hospitality.

12

Tyus and Symphony got in his car heading to her house instead of going to King and Syncere's right away. He desperately needed to clear his head; have an honest and transparent conversation with her before they engaged in any more holiday festivities. Symphony was surprised when he turned on her street pulling into the driveway.

"You're not coming to dinner anymore are you?" Symphony blurted, assuming he was too pissed to deal with her today.

"We need to talk." Tyus responded, killing the engine and stepping out to open her door.

This is not good. Shit! Symphony pondered, hesitantly entering her house, hanging their coats before walking into the kitchen. Symphony always found herself pressed against the kitchen counter while Tyus leaned against the archway with his arms crossed anytime they needed to *talk*. The silence that lingered between them was eerie and disconcerting.

"Symphony, you make it extremely fucking hard to love you." Tyus blurted, voice almost at a whisper. The hurt and frustration were palpable. "I don't have a reason to lie to you. Have I ever given you a reason not to trust me? But every damn time I think our relationship is advancing, I get knocked the fuck back. I've never lied to you Symphony and I never will. If I'm not here, you are at my house. When I'm out of town, I'm talking to you every night until you fall asleep and you're the first person I see when I step off the damn plane." He deeply exhaled, shaking his head. "You can answer my phone at any time. Here, take the damn phone because I don't care." He pulled the phone from his pocket, extending it to her. "I don't have shit to hide, Symphony." Tyus looked defeated, ambling to the couch, leaving her in the kitchen. He tossed his head back against the cushion, rubbing a hand down his face.

"I don't want Gia, Symphony. She is TJ's mother, that's it. And as you can see, Gia doesn't want me. There's never been anything between us. We made a mistake but vowed that TJ would never be slighted, never feel like he was a mistake."

"I know, Ty. Gia told me the story." Her shaky voice resounded from the kitchen.

"But you shouldn't have needed to hear it from Gia to believe me." Tyus snapped. "I'm sorry. I didn't mean to yell. Symphony, can you come here please?" He requested.

She crept through the archway from the kitchen like a kid ready to receive their punishment.

"Closer." He directed. She complied, laying her phone on the table as she sat on the edge of the couch.

"Do you want this, Symphony?" He motioned a finger between the two of them. "Do you want *me*?" Tyus questioned, glaring directly into her misty grey eyes.

Symphony blinked, allowing the tears to escape. "Yes, Ty. Yes, I want this and more importantly, I want *you*, bae." Symphony slowly eliminated the distance between them, unfolding his corded arm. "I think I've always wanted you."

Tyus wanted to believe the veracity of her words, but he was cautious yet deeply captivated.

"Are you certain, Sweetpea? Because I don't bullshit commitments. When I'm fucking in, I'm in - 100 percent. Everything that you've shared with me about your mother, your father. All the shit you've trusted me with. But if what I'm feeling...what I believe you're feeling is all a lie, then we just need to part ways right here, right now. That shit will hurt like hell, but I -" Tyus refused to complete his sentence dismissing the wretched thought.

"Ty. Baby. I always seem to be the one saying I'm sorry. Always doing or saying some stupid shit. But I am truly sorry, Ty. It's just... sometimes it's easier to be prepared for the worst so the shit won't hurt as bad." She shrugged.

"Maybe with some other niggas but not with me." Tyus snapped. "If you keep holding yourself hostage to what happened when you were a kid, the mistakes your parents made, you'll never stop fighting, Symphony." Tyus ran his finger down the bridge of her nose. "Baby, I need you to stop fighting. You can take your *boss bitch* crown off sometimes.

Let me protect you. I promised you I would never hurt you and I meant that shit."

Symphony silently cried as Tyus placed his hand over her heart. That simple gesture immediately softened her barriers, allowing her to feel - *him.*

"I want this commitment. I want to be with you, whatever that means, whatever it looks like - as long as I'm with you." Symphony caressed his face, kissing against his cheek, then the corner of his lips uttering, "Please accept my apology. I don't want to be difficult for you to...love." She whimpered. The duo had never exchanged the sentiment verbally, but that was the first time Tyus alluded to loving her.

The gentle kisses rapidly intensified. Their tongues passionately twirling, heat sweltering between their thighs. The buzz of Symphony's phone against the glass top cocktail table disrupted the pending satiation. Jameson's face with the title *Baby Boy* glared on the screen. Both Tyus and Symphony stared between each other and the phone as it continued to vibrate.

"Are you going to handle that or do I need to?" Tyus tilted his head, staring at her because at this point, Symphony belonged to him - and he was fully prepared to provide clarity to any mutherfucker that needed to know.

Symphony nervously answered the phone because she knew Jameson was liable to be parked outside of her house, ready to come in and deliver some holiday cheer. Symphony held Tyus' gaze.

"Hey Jameson. Yeah, um... Happy Thanksgiving to you too. No, that's not a good idea anymore. Hey J - I mean Jameson, listen. I... um - I'm in a relationship now so we can't see each other anymore. Yeah, I'm dead ass serious." She paused, her eyes still locked with Tyus as she listened to Jameson express his disappointment that he couldn't do that thing she liked one more time. He reminded Symphony that she knew where to find him if necessary. "Yeah, I know. Bye Jameson."

Tyus didn't ask any questions about her chat with the boy toy because he really didn't care as long as the situation was handled. He resumed the salacious tongue dance, caressing his fingers through her hair, fondling her slightly exposed thighs.

"Bae, we're going to be late." She whimpered, lip quivering.

Tyus remained hushed. Slowly, meticulously, and deliberately stroking up the length of her thighs, manipulating every inch of her thick bodacious frame. His masculinity was evidenced by the substantial bulge pressing against his zipper.

"Ty, you know how Prima gets when I'm late." Symphony's voice still at a fluttering shiver. Her actions contradict her words as she assisted him with removing her clothes.

She was on the brink of an orgasm simply from his touch. Tyus remained voiceless, his animalistic nature brewing. After the intensity of the conversation, he was voracious, greedy for his Sweetpea - unable to get enough of her savory gem. Tyus continued his carnal pursuit, rendering Symphony late for the holiday dinner.

Symphony and Tyus arrived at her cousin's house at about 6:30 pm - dinner was scheduled for six. Symphony had to take another shower and change clothes after her and Tyus' rendezvous on the couch that continued in the bedroom.

"You know she's pissed right?" King answered the door. "Tread lightly because mommy-to-be is on the prowl."

"See Tyus, I told you." Symphony hit against his abdomen. "It was his fault. I swear I was trying to get away."

"Man, I don't want to hear that shit." King waved his hand and meandered into the great room.

"Symphony Monique James." Syncere shouted. "When I said six, I meant that I wanted to eat at six, not thirty minutes later."

"Hi Prima. Happy Thanksgiving and I love you too, boo. Thank you for inviting us to Cartwright Castle." Symphony teased, kneeling in front of her cousin and kissed her 3-carat wedding ring as if Syncere was the God*mother*. The entire room boisterously laughed.

"Y'all stop playing and come on in here and eat. My daughter is carrying two babies so you know she's hungry." Syncere's mother-in-love, Lorna Cartwright, pronounced.

"I know that's right. I'm hungry too." G-ma chimed in from the kitchen.

"My grandbabies need to be fed. Let's eat." King's father, Elias Cartwright's similar bass-filled voice, rang from the living room.

The twelve person dining table was elegantly set family style. G-ma and Momma Lorna, as Syncere and Symphony lovingly called King's mother, cooked enough food to feed all of Haven Point. Baked and fried chicken, beef roast, macaroni and cheese, green beans, broccoli and rice casserole, sweet potatoes, homemade rolls. G-ma even made her grand-daughters' favorite red velvet cream cheese rum balls - no rum for Syncere though. The table was filled with people stuffing their faces, laughing, talking in fellowship. Even Aminah was in town which meant Nicolas was there too. They thought they were slick, always miraculously showing up in Haven at the same time when she lived in Monroe City and he lived in Brighton Falls.

"What does everybody have going on this weekend? I need to live vicariously through you all since dictator King is holding me hostage." Syncere chortled, teasingly eyeing King.

"You damn right. And I will maintain absolute power over you until Dr. Ingler delivers two healthy babies in about seven weeks and ensures that you are in good health." Syncere leaned into him as King kissed against her forehead.

Random responses to Syncere's question such as resting, black Friday shopping, and working danced across the table.

"Me and Symphony are going away for the weekend." Tyus chimed to Symphony's surprise.

"Wait, what? We are? Ty! Since when? Where?" The multitude of questions flowed from her tongue.

"Since a couple weeks ago when I planned the trip." He nonchalantly responded. "We leave tomorrow afternoon."

"Bae, I can't leave G-ma and Syncere at such short notice." Symphony leaned over whispering in his ear. "And I thought you were traveling for work next week?"

"It's handled, Sweetpea. I promise." Tyus lifted her chin towards him. "You trust me?" She nodded.

"Don't worry about us." Syncere and G-ma harmonized then giggled.

"Prima, we will be fine. G-ma is staying here for the weekend and Aminah and Momma Lorna will be available to help." Syncere assured. "Go and have fun, girl." She winked.

"Why do I feel like I've been set up?" Symphony blushed. "You knew about this didn't you, Pri?"

"I plead the fifth." Syncere mummed her lips tight, motioning as if she was locking and throwing away the key.

The men began to transition into the mancave after dinner while the women gathered at the massive kitchen island to enjoy coffee and dessert. But not before Tyus snatched Symphony into the hallway bathroom.

"You're not upset are you, Sweetpea?" He traced a finger down her cheek.

"No Ty. I'm just concerned about being gone with Syncere in her condition. What if something happens?" Symphony's expression laced with anxiety.

"King will contact us and we'll be on the first plane back if anything happens. I promise." He paused. "Baby, I just want us to get away from Haven for a little while. We've both been working like crazy. But we won't go if you're not going to be able to enjoy yourself."

"No bae. I want to be wherever you are." She kissed his lips. "Where exactly are *we* going to be?" She chuckled and continued kissing, trying to seduce an answer out of him.

"Nah, baby. These lips are sealed." Tyus mumbled against her lips. "While your kisses are so damn delicious, you will have to do more than that to get me to talk."

Symphony trailed her fingertips down his chest, fondling his growing manhood.

"Symphony. Stop playing." Tyus' dick and his tone were firm.

"So what if I bend all of this ass over in these tight jeans? Will that change your mind?" She turned around, positioning her ass directly against his dick, grinding. Tyus smacked against her butt, then caressed to soothe the sting.

"Save that shit for later, baby." He declared as they exited the bathroom.

Syncere was slowly waddling towards her master bedroom near the front of the house. She passed the bathroom eyeing Tyus and Symphony sneaking like two teenagers.

"Get y'all nasty asses out of my bathroom." Syncere giggled. "Prima, come and help me for a second."

Symphony walked with her cousin to the bedroom. Syncere grabbed the two medicine bottles from the nightstand and trekked across the room to the ensuite to get a cup of water.

"You seem to be moving just fine. What did you need my help with?" Symphony inquired, resting on the velvet tufted bench at the foot of the oversized bed.

"I just wanted to steal you away for a few minutes. I feel like we haven't talked in a while." Syncere sat in the mustard yellow reclining chair.

"Pri, we talk almost everyday." Symphony shrugged in confusion.

"I know but we're usually talking about G-ma or the babies. You know I'm nosey. Has Malynda called anymore?

Are you going to see her? How are things going with Tyus? Have you met TJ yet? Or his mother?"

"Damn, Mary J. Blige. What's the 411?" Symphony blurted as the cousins cackled.

"So y'all just gone leave me with G-ma and Momma Lorna, huh?" Aminah snuck into the bedroom. "What y'all talking about?"

"Nah, we was leaving you with Nic so y'all can hurry up and fuck. Gone get that shit over with." Symphony blurted into laughter.

"Ugh, heffa! I hate yo' nasty ass." Aminah chuckled. "It's not like that. Nic is cool, but y'all know I'm not ready for that."

"Leave her alone, Prima. Minah, we'll discuss you and Nic when you're ready. Hurry up and answer my questions, Symphony. Y'all know King will be sniffing me out in a minute." Syncere stressed. "Ok, where was I? Malynda - Tyus - TJ - TJ momma... go." The ladies giggled.

"Malynda will be quick. She hasn't called anymore because I told her that I will contact her after the holiday. TJ and I are definitely video chat buddies but I actually met him today. As well as his mother Gia. And Gia's *girlfriend*." Symphony paused, waiting for the *bitch what, you're kidding me* comments.

"Wait. Bitch what? Did you say girlfriend? As in female?" Syncere sat up on the lounger to ensure she was hearing correctly.

"You're fucking kidding, right? Tyus' baby momma got a girlfriend?" Aminah chimed.

"Yep. Her name is Rose. They've been together for almost three years."

"Well damn. Ok then Gia. Get yours sis." Syncere chuckled.

"It's a crazy dynamic but it actually seems to work. I haven't probed Tyus for too much information yet, but you know a bitch got hella questions." They cackled. "But seeing him with TJ today was - wow. It truly warmed my heart." Symphony blushed, recalling how enamored Tyus was with TJ.

"I like this look on you, sis." Aminah smiled. "Tyus got you glowing and shit."

"Right?" Syncere chimed. "You're just so tranquil and carefree with him. I haven't heard you say that you were about to beat a bitch's ass in a few weeks." They guffawed.

"Yeah, Ty definitely calms me. Something happens to me when he simply says my name or calls me baby. I turn all *Coming to America*, whatever you like, barking like a dog, submissive wife and shit." She reenacted the classic movie scene.

"Wife?" Aminah shrieked. "Do we hear wedding bells - the future Mrs. Symphony Okoro?" She questioned as Syncere quietly squealed, rapidly clapping her hands together, grinning in agreement.

"No ma'am!" Symphony shouted. "The subject has not and will not come up."

"Ok so maybe marriage is a bit much right now, but is love a subject that you're willing to broach?" Syncere probed. "Do you love Tyus, Prima?"

Symphony was momentarily hushed, considering her

cousin's words. Her heart didn't want to comprehend a second without Tyus. She craved him when he was gone and fancied every moment they spent together. Symphony shared her innermost secrets, desires, and dreams with him - conversations that were typically reserved for Syncere's ears only.

"It's like the cosmos convened and decided to finally get their shit together and be on my team for a change." Symphony chuckled. "Tyus unselfishly offers a level of adoration, passion, and devotion that I've never experienced from a man. Even if they wanted to, I wouldn't allow it. He's not intimidated by my crazy boss bitch attitude either."

"So he's not one of your situationships?" Aminah probed.

"No." Symphony quickly retorted. "Ty is...a relationship. A commitment. I trust and believe him when he says he won't hurt me - or let anybody hurt me." She smiled.

Tyus was truly the human manifestation of unspoken wishes that Symphony was too afraid and stubborn to give a voice. Symphony's dewy eyes landed on her cousin's mirrored slate orbs. She was in such a daze, she didn't realize Syncere was standing before her.

"In the words of my wonderful therapist, the good Dr. Jacky - *my dear, that is love.*" Syncere cupped her cousin's chin, kissing against her forehead. "I'm so happy for you, Prima."

The three sorority sisters and best friends hugged. Each of them fully understands their plight of enduring personal traumas while seeking redemption, healing, and love. Syncere found her couple of forevers. Now it was Symphony and Aminah's chance.

"Princess? Is everything ok?" King's baritone whispered as he lightly tapped on the bedroom door. The ladies chuckled since King found his princess just as Syncere said he would. *That's the shit I'm talking about.* Aminah mouthed, admiring the way King protected Syncere.

"Yeah, babe. Everything is great. We're on our way out." Syncere blushed.

The ladies rejoined the rest of the family in the living room. A vicious game of tunk ensued between the grandparents and great grandparent-to-be, ending with G-ma talking a lot of smack to Mr. Elias.

"Don't let this wheelchair fool you, Eli." She cackled loudly, shuffling the cards preparing for another win.

Syncere stuffed herself with non-rum rum balls until she fell asleep on King's lap. Aminah and Nic found themselves on the enclosed patio with a bottle of Toussaint Winery's finest port. Symphony observed them, recognizing the giddy blushing smile plastered across Aminah's face. *I wish they would just do the good deed already.* Symphony mused as she sauntered behind Tyus who was talking to his brother Titan, enfolding her arms around his waist.

"You ready, Sweetpea?" He kissed her forehead.

"Yeah. I clearly need to pack for a trip tomorrow to an unknown place." She teased.

Tyus and Symphony said their goodbyes and drove to her house so that she could pack. She tried every trick in the book to get him to disclose the secret vacation location. The only hint he gave her was to pack light. Tyus layed on her bed giving a thumbs up or thumbs down rating of the jumpsuits, dresses, and sexy lingerie she randomly tossed into her suitcase.

After an hour of fussing and ranting about the pressures of packing for an undisclosed location, Symphony was tired and sleepy. She crawled into the bed where Tyus was already dozing. Laying against his bare chest exhaling deeply, enthusiastic about the slumber in her near future.

"So what was that shit you were talking in the bathroom earlier?" Tyus awakened, pulling Symphony to straddle him. She smiled, welcoming his offer to put her to bed properly.

13

The airport was bustling with holiday travelers. Tyus and Symphony arrived two hours early for their 12:40 pm flight. She'd given up on trying to guess the location since he remained tight-lipped. Tyus took great pleasure in being the cause of Symphony's budding attitude. He laughed every time she pouted when he asked her a question or snatched away when he tried to carry her bag. Tyus was going to milk this until he had no choice but to tell her where they were going. He flashed the electronic tickets on his phone, only requiring her to show her passport to the TSA attendant. She was irritated, while Tyus continued to delay. Stopping at the restroom, grabbing coffee, and even belaboring in the bookstore knowing damn well he wasn't about to read a book. He clutched her waist, tickling and nibling at her neck to make her laugh. She fruitlessly ventured to hold the scowl she'd been wearing but Tyus' command over her was powerful.

"Stop Ty. I'm still mad at you." Symphony whined.

"Well stop being mad. We're here now, Sweetpea." He signaled his head towards their departing gate. Symphony stared at the gate 18 monitor as it slowly flipped through the departing flights. She impatiently waited for their flight time to appear, nibbling at her burnt orange manicured nails. She mouthed, *flight 1203 departing St. Louis to Cabo San Lucas.*

"Mexico!" Symphony's shout echoed through the terminal. "Bae! Are we really going to Mexico?" She beamed, jumping into his embrace.

"Yes, Sweetpea, we're going to Mexico. You still pissed at me now?" He kissed her cheek as they sat at the gate waiting to board.

The gate attendant announced for first class passengers to line up and Tyus grabbed her bag. With a furrowed brow, Symphony stared at him trying to figure out where he was going.

"You coming or you're staying?" He inquired.

"Oh shit! First class too?" She questioned. "Oh you trying to get all of my treats this weekend, huh?" Symphony giggled as the attendant scanned their tickets and they meandered down the bridgeway.

"That's the plan." Tyus winked.

After a long night of lovemaking, Tyus and Symphony slept the entire flight. Waking up momentarily during the no plane change layover in Dallas and long enough to get a couple free first class drinks. Almost six hours later, they landed in Cabo San Lucas, Mexico.

Tyus admired Symphony's excitement as she gazed out of the car window heading to their resort. Her eyes almost bulged out of their sockets when the SUV pulled up to the Breathless Resort & Spa. The resort was stunning. Symphony audibly gasped when they entered the airy hotel lobby with ivory marble floors, stone lined walls, a floor to ceiling waterfall creating a calming atmosphere. Tyus checked into their room while Symphony happily accepted the fruity cocktail from a young man dressed in the resort uniform.

"Bienvenida a Cabo la bella dama. Welcome to Cabo, pretty lady. I am Miguel and I will be your personal butler this weekend."

"Gracias Miguel." Symphony smiled.

"Bienvenido a Cabo senor. Welcome to Cabo, sir." Miguel greeted Tyus when he appeared behind Symphony.

"Gracias." Tyus handed Miguel the room keys as instructed by the desk attendant. They walked hands clasped as the butler gave them a brief tour of the resort before showing them to their suite.

"Ty, this is too much. It's so beautiful." Symphony beamed. "Thank you bae." She snuggled against his solid chest, holding on to him for dear life. Symphony was overwhelmed, enamored with the way Tyus cared for her.

"You're welcome, Sweetpea. But we're just getting started." He kissed into her curly tresses.

Approaching the massive wooden door with gold letters reading Suite 13, Miguel instructed the couple on how to use the coded entry feature while he used the room key, opening the entryway to a beautifully breezy king suite. They were welcomed by the most breathtaking view. The colossal stark white room with bamboo wooden accents appeared to extend for miles into the water. Symphony extended her hand as if she could touch it.

The sliding collapsible floor to ceiling door opened the room to the private balcony and pool. Tyus and Miguel stepped aside in choreographed unison to allow Symphony to bask in the magnificence of the glorious site. Symphony swung around to gaze at Tyus. He methodically surveyed her misty grey eyes. Their stares were more passionate and salacious than intended. The butler cleared his throat to pull them from their daze before exiting to retrieve the luggage.

"Ty. Bae. I - I don't know what to say." She brushed away the single tear escaping her eye. "I'm speechless and I always have some shit to say." They chuckled as he pulled her into his firm frame. "It's gorgeous, bae. Absolutely stunning."

Tyus cuddled behind her and she positioned her neck to one side to allow him easy access for kisses. "Symphony, why are you crying, baby?" Tyus caressed her face.

"I'm just happy. That's all. I've been on trips before but this just feels different...special." She cracked a miniature smile, unexpectedly overwhelmed with emotions. Symphony didn't quite understand who she was becoming. Always crying and shit. This man had her completely unequivocally intensely entranced.

The sweet pecks to the neck quickly amplified to an impassioned tear-filled tongue lashing. The knock on the door disrupted Tyus' ability to probe further. It was Miguel with their bags.

"Senor Okoro, your dinner reservation is scheduled for 8'oclock. Does that still meet your needs, senor?" Miguel questioned.

"Yes, thank you." Tyus nodded as the butler exited. He turned to Symphony with a blushing grin. "Baby, let's get freshened up. I'm ready to show you your first surprise."

"Um, Ty. I think I'm standing in all of the surprises I need this weekend." She chuckled.

TYUS STOOD on the private patio meditating to the sound of the ocean waves while waiting for Symphony to finish getting dressed. He was handsomely enticing in white linen pants and shirt that complimented his brawny chest and powerful thighs. Tyus looked like a tall drink of honey and Symphony was ready to get a little sticky. She stood in the bathroom doorway consumed, absorbing every inch of him. *Damn!* She mused, enthusiastic about their dinner date but momentarily saddened that she wasn't in this big ass bed being instantly filled with the heaviness of his dick.

"Hey." She coyly uttered.

Tyus slowly turned with one hand in his pocket. He gasped. She was exquisite.

"I don't remember approving or denying that dress, baby." Tyus sexily grinned as he eased one thumb up in the air giving his consent.

Symphony looked like a Greek goddess in a Kelly green halter dress that was completely backless. The top provided only enough material to cover her glorious breasts. The ruched fabric at the midriff snatched her taut waist before freely flowing just above the sparkle on her strappy sandals. Symphony's curvy thighs played peek-a-boo through a deep front split. She completed the look by gathering her thick tresses into a high bun adorned with gold jewels. She was simply beautiful.

"Sweetpea, you are...wow...baby, damn." Tyus blushed, shaking his head because he was literally speechless. He was fully aware of her beauty but there was something about the way the green of her dress reflected against those damn argentine eyes.

"Symphony, babe, you are breathtaking. Seriously, you look beautiful." Tyus sauntered towards her planting a sweet kiss against her temple, cradling the small of her back.

"Shall we?" He extended his arm and she happily obliged.

"Let's." She smiled.

Their suite was in the private section of the hotel so a luminated golf cart transported them to the main lobby of the resort. When Symphony and Tyus exited the cart, she felt like Julia Roberts in *Pretty Woman*, reveling in the stares, oohs, and ahhs of passersby as she and her handsome suitor confidently strolled to their destination. Symphony's brow furrowed, confused as they continued to walk past the row of resort restaurants. *Where are we going?* She pondered but wouldn't dare ask. Tyus took way too much pleasure in surprising her so she went with the flow this time.

Their butler Miguel ushered them to the edge of the sandy beach. The radiant light of luminaries brightened the walkway, leading the hand-holding couple to a cabana beautifully decorated with white sheer drapes, candles, and red roses. One white couch facing the ocean surrounded the maple dining table. A bouquet of flowers and a silver bucket chilling the champagne acted as the centerpiece. Symphony admired the floral scent, patiently anticipating the taste of the expensive-looking champagne but she honestly wouldn't know the difference. Miguel motioned to the couch encouraging them to be seated before he spoke with another person who appeared to be the waiter.

"Is this to your liking, Mr. Okoro?" Miguel asked.

"Yes. It's perfect. Thank you Miguel."

"Maravilloso. Wonderful." Miguel appeared honestly excited that they were pleased. "If you should need anything, this is my friend Carlos and he will find me en un minuto, in a minute, ok? Ok." Tyus and Symphony giggled at Miguel's animated personality.

Carlos proceeded to gently place the napkin in Symphony's lap before popping the bottle of champagne and pouring water. Symphony closed her eyes inhaling deeply, digesting the fresh clean breeze from the crystalized ocean. The sun had begun to set, leaving splendid streaks of orange and yellow across the lively waves. Tyus observed her, the stunning view paled in comparison to his Sweetpea.

"Symphony, is this to your liking?" Tyus echoed Miguel's words.

She paused, deeply digesting her surroundings and *him*.

"Resplendent." She whispered, bright eyes capturing his orbs as they amorously smiled. Love silently capering between them but Tyus quickly shifted his head before he said something he didn't think she was ready for.

Symphony and Tyus dined in silence, delighting in

succulent flavors of honey buttered prawns, lobster tails, filet mignon, and a creamy garlic parmesan pasta that Symphony was willing to lick off of the floor if any dripped from her fork.

"Oh my God, Ty. This shit is - OMG!" She squealed, doing a little shimmy in her chair.

"I can't even lie, Sweetpea. This shit is fire." He chortled.

Carlos cleared their plates offering dessert options. Chocolate pie, strawberry cheesecake, and Pastel de tres leches - they opted for all three and a second bottle of champagne. After they devoured the desserts, Symphony made a mental note of what food she would be ordering for the duration of their trip. Carlos tapped Tyus on the shoulder, whispering something in his ear as she savored the last piece of tres leches cake and took a sip of champagne.

"Can I have this dance, beautiful?" Tyus asked, standing with his hand extended towards her.

"Bae, there's no music-"

She ate her words as the lovely chords of a saxophone resounded against the midnight air. A handsome young man, no older than eighteen dressed in a tuxedo appeared from behind the sheer white drape effortlessly playing Kenny G "Songbird."

Symphony's dewy slate orbs glistened against the moonlight. *Who the fuck am I? Why do I keep crying?* She internally debated as she joyously clutched Tyus' hand. He firmly enfolded her, resting his lips against her neck. Intoxicated by more than the champagne, they swayed to the tranquil sounds of the music co-mingling with the ocean waves. They were enthralled, hypnotized, cast under each other's spell -

his inhale indistinguishable from her exhale. They swayed and kissed and caressed and danced and kissed some more. The fruitiness of the champagne seductively lingered on their tongues.

Symphony closed her eyes tight, praying that this wasn't a dream. *My dear, that's love.* She carefully considered Syncere's words by way of Dr. Jacky. *Could this be love?* She mused, squeezing her eyes tighter, shuddering from the touch of his fingertips against her bare back. Her heart fiercely pounded, unconsciously she audibly gasped, clasping her chest overwhelmed by the moment.

"Baby? Are you ok?" Tyus momentarily disconnected to observe her.

Symphony nodded. "Yes. Bae, can we - um, can we go?" She breathlessly stuttered, lustfully eyeing him settling on the presentation of his manhood against the linen pants. Tyus was familiar with the wanton gaze.

"Let's." Tyus eagerly uttered.

He hurriedly signed the receipts to ensure Carlos and the Kenny G songbird dude received their tips before ushering Symphony towards the lobby. Aching dick and throbbing puss, Tyus and Symphony peered around the lobby desperately searching for Miguel, shit, anybody who could quickly get them back to their suite. Miguel wasn't playing about being available in a minute, he appeared out of nowhere - *un minuto.* No words were exchanged. Tyus simply nodded and Miguel took the hint. The savory stench of desire seeping from their pores. It also may have been the way Symphony was attached to Tyus' waist practically unbuttoning his shirt as they meandered through the resort.

Their insatiable behavior in the golf cart was no different. Unable to keep their hands off of each other - fondling, kissing, touching, feeling. The three minute ride seemed like a lifetime.

"Adios Miguel." They both shouted, jumping out of the golf cart before it was safely parked. They raced up the one flight of stairs to their suite like some horny teenagers. Tyus pressed Symphony against the door with hungry feverish kisses. One hand explored her thighs while the other fumbled to unlock the door with the code.

"Shit! What the fuck is the code, baby?" He inquired with Symphony's tongue halfway down his throat.

"Birthday. Backwards." She panted as his finger slipped into her naked jewel.

"What the hell?" Tyus was disoriented at the realization that she didn't have on any damn panties. He calmed, knowing they would be completely locked out of the room if he got the code wrong a third time.

"Listen! 8-6-2-2-1-0!" Symphony whispered through a moan. "My birthday - October 22, 1986 backwards."

Click. The door was disarmed. "We are changing that shit tomorrow." Tyus bantered.

They crossed the threshold greeted by a beautifully illuminated room. The same luminaries that lit the pathway to the cabana circled the jacuzzi tub that was filled with bubbles. Red rose petals lined the walkway to the king size bed and floating candles emblazoned the pool on the private balcony. It was gorgeous and romantic as fuck.

"Damn! Miguel came through." Tyus whispered.

Symphony momentarily paused her pursuit to bask in

the loveliness. She gazed at him with *I love you* lingering on her lips. But she acquiesced. Unsure and honestly petrified that he didn't share the sentiment.

"Symphony." The bass-filled tenor of his voice when he spoke her name created an instant flood in her unclothed treasure. "Stop." He embraced her from behind and whispered against her ear. "Whatever bullshit is swirling in your head - stop." She smiled.

"Alexa, play Beyonce 1+1." He requested. As the intro beat reverberated through the room, Tyus trailed a single finger down the curve of her face, caressed the nape of her neck, untying the halter dress. Symphony slowly pulled the pins from her bun, releasing her curly auburn brown mane. The dress eased down her quivering body, her nipples hard as diamonds. Pooled at her feet, she pushed the dress aside, diminishing the miniscule gap between them. Tyus surveyed her naked frame. His dick jerked beneath his pants like a caged animal, impatient, antsy to be released.

Symphony unbuttoned the white linen shirt exposing his honey caramel chest. His white linen pants hung low at the waist directing a path towards the bulge that continued to grow with every touch from her. She could see the ombre beast distended against the linen fabric ready for her to give him permission to unleash. Symphony slowly unzipped his pants, steadily disrobing his sexy ass frame. She tugged on the pants, pulling them down as her body followed, dropping into a squat coming face to face with the released beast.

The curved ombre monster delightfully glistened in the amber lights. Even after the amazing meal, Symphony was hungry, famished, ready to binge...on him. She caressed his manhood with both hands, always astonished by the fact that two hands were required to effectively manage his lengthy circumference. Symphony teased him, planting soft kisses from the tip down the base on repeat. He desired to grab her head and guide her where he wanted, shit... critically needed her to be. But his Sweetpea was in complete control, enfolding every inch of him.

Symphony flattened her tongue and licked from the base to the tip like his dick was a caramel lollipop before taking his girth into her sweltering mouth. Tyus flinched, regaining his stance so he wouldn't go out like a punk. Slow, steady, salacious strokes up and down his shaft. Her velvety lips and savory mouth covered the entirety of the massive monster. Symphony welcomed the immense intrusion against her tongue. She moaned, slurping to the rhythmic sounds flooding the background. The delightful taste of his manhood fulfilled her gluttony.

"Shit Symphony. Goddamn baby." Tyus moaned - loudly. The neighbors, shit the entire resort, was about to know her name. Symphony was savage, unrelenting. Twisting, turning, sucking, licking. Her mouth suctioned around his mass, then she wiggled her tongue against his pulsating veins while caressing his balls. Tyus fucking lost it. Firmly grabbing her hair, encouraging the rhythm as she gripped his ass.

Damn ma! Shit! Tyus mused. "Symphony. Baby. This shit is lethal. Baby, I'm -" He exhaled, tossing his head back trying to gather his thoughts.

"Mmmhmmm." She sang against the swell of his dick.

"Sweetpea. Baby. I'm coming." He grunted. "You gotta get up."

"Mmmhmmm." Symphony continued the beautifully debilitating thrashing of his dick.

Tyus' grip on her hair grew tighter and tighter and tighter until he released - literally.

"Ah shit! Baby. Sweetpea! Fuck!" He couldn't gather a coherent sentence as Symphony indulged, shit, delighted in his syrupy juices. Tyus was weak, allowing her to nudge him onto the bed. She climbed the length of his body, trailing soft kisses up his shivering flesh. Tyus clutched the back of her head, bringing her lips to his. Exchanging lustful, wanton, carnal kisses, he stealthily guided his dick into her sodden treasure, snatching every iota of her breath away. Their bodies were exquisitely entangled - flesh of his flesh, blood of her blood. Symphony didn't have to question if this was making love. She felt Tyus' presence tingle through her limbs, fingers, and toes. He was willful, deliberate, swimming in her ocean searching for a precious treasure.

"Ty. Bae. Oh my God. You feel so...so...so ...baby." Symphony breathlessly panted, overwhelmed by his unspoken love.

Tyus was hushed as he repositioned them, never disengaging from her jewel. He was on an animalistic mission. Whatever he craved and desired was buried in the depths of her pussy and Tyus was relentless in his chase, refusing to liberate until he depleted every drop of oxygen from her body. His pleasing pound elevated to a beautiful bludgeoning of her puss as he whispered lascivious questions and commands.

"Is this my pussy, Symphony?"

"Yes, baby. All yours. Shit. Ty."

"You sure about that? Huh? I can't fucking hear you." He hammered, filling her puss to capacity.

"Yes, Ty. Fuck. What's the code?" She hissed, ready to tap out. "I need a fucking safe word." Symphony screamed as he mercilessly bashed into her gem. The gushing sound of the collective juices adding to the melodious tunes.

"What code? Shit." He furrowed in confusion, blurting the first thing that came to mind. "Birthday. Shit. Birthday backwards. Goddamnit, Symphony." Tyus grunted, heavily thrusting, reaching the tip of his climax.

"Birthday. Fuck! Birthday backwards." Symphony howled, climaxing as she clawed her nails into his shoulders, certain she drew blood.

Tyus stroked once more reaching his pinnacle, grunting into the folds of her salty yet sweet neck. He readjusted them again to prevent the smothering of his heaviness. Labored breathing, Symphony laid against his chest. His heart pounded at the most beautiful pace. She was intoxicated by the rhythm like a lullaby.

"Symphony." Tyus muttered, as she jolted from her reverie, shifting her head to look at him. He stared deeply, intense.

"Yes, bae?" Symphony whispered, trailing her fingertips across his dewy chest.

"I don't want to scare you." He stroked a loose tendril from her face.

"I won't be scared. I promise." Symphony had no idea what she was consenting to but she didn't care. She trusted him. Loved him.

"I love you, Symphony." Tyus held her gaze, firmly

caressing just in case she recoiled. But she didn't. She melted further into his chest with tears in her eyes.

"Ty, be careful with me." She blinked, unleashing the tears. "I've never been in love before. I might be bad at it. I may be a *dangerously in love* kinda chick. So you gotta be careful with me." She cried, tears staining his chest. "I love you, Ty. I think I always have. I just -"

Tyus hushed her, resting a finger against her lips.

"It's just *I love you*. No conditions or explanation necessary. Those three simple words pack enough power, baby. I'm dangerously in love with you too, Symphony."

He planted multiple kisses against her forehead and thumbed away her tears. She incoherently chuckled.

"What's so funny right now?" He curiously asked.

"You're not saying you love me because I had all your dick in my mouth are you?" She boisterously cackled as he tackled her.

"Your ass is crazy." Tyus tickled as she squirmed until she straddled him. He rested his hands around her waist. "But I love your crazy ass."

14

Tyus and Symphony spent their last night in Cabo similar to the first. This time with a moonlight picnic on the beach. Symphony's white spaghetti strap maxi dress flowed with the gust of wind as she admired the full moon illuminating the thunderous ocean. The high winds caused dangerously active waves so the couple wasn't permitted to get too close to the ocean. Symphony was enamored and pacified by the calming sounds enfolding her arms around her body, deeply inhaling the fresh breeze.

"Bae, do we have to leave?" She pouted, peering over the Libra symbol tattoo on her shoulder to gaze at Tyus. He was perched on the plush red blanket with a picnic basket filled with some of their favorite resort dishes and a bottle of champagne. Symphony admired his handsome chiseled face and the sage green sparkle around his eyes under the stars. She sexily grinned, prompting him to move in her direction.

Tyus ambled behind Symphony, caressing her waist,

nestling in the folds of her rose-scented neck. "We definitely have to go home baby, but we can make a plan to come back soon. I promise."

"You make a lot of promises Mr. Okoro." She turned to face him with her arms firmly embracing his neck. Placing a finger against his lips before he could protest the statement. "And you've kept every single one."

They lustfully blushed, inhaling the freshness of the midnight breeze and each other. Symphony and Tyus had the time of their lives in Mexico. Some highly active days renting ATVs and jet skis, romantic nighttime boat rides and many leisurely moments of lovemaking. It was beyond Symphony's imagination. Tyus was so much more than she could fathom - the man she loved. *But will our love feel the same once we're home? Once we're back to the regular grind.* She pondered as they delighted in the honey butter shrimp that she'd devoured on several occasions during their trip.

"Symphony." Tyus spoke, his voice immediately breaking her trance. "Stop, babe."

"Stop what, Ty?" She furrowed. "Why do you always say that?"

"I say that because worry is impressed all over that pretty ass face of yours. Stop wondering about our fate after this trip, baby. When I said I love you, I meant that shit. I love you under this beautiful moonlight in Mexico and I'm going to love you next week in Haven. So stop, Sweetpea. Let's enjoy our last night in paradise." He leaned over kissing against her forehead.

"Ugh, why do you know me so well?" Symphony whined. "This just feels really good, Ty. Shit, almost too good. I get nervous when my life is not overwhelmed with drama. It's this strange feeling of being steady yet unstable, bracing for some shit to blow up."

"Ok negative Nancy." Tyus laughed. "I don't want to hear any more of that shit. We're good, Symphony. I promise."

"Cross your heart and hope to die?" She sexily laughed.

"I can do better than that." Tyus gave a sneaky smile reaching into the picnic basket, revealing a medium-sized burgundy and gold box with a matching bow.

"Ty. Bae. What is this?" Symphony questioned, those damn tears welling again. *Cry baby. Ugh!* She mused silently grunting in frustration.

"If you open it, you'll find out." Tyus moved the picnic basket, diminishing the space between them.

"Come closer." He instructed as she rested between his legs with her back leaning against his chest.

Symphony's hands trembled as she slowly opened the box.

"Baby, relax, it's not an engagement ring." He chortled. "Not yet." Tyus winked. Symphony's moon-stricken eyes bulged as he chuckled.

She continued to unwrap the box revealing a beautiful platinum necklace with a charm shaped like a flower. The tears streamed down her beautifully flushed cheeks, salting the corners of her lips. The gifts from inconsequential people meant nothing to her. But Tyus was more consequential than she had words to describe so this gift was priceless.

Tyus thumbed away her tears, placing two fingers under her chin, guiding their mouths into a sweet kiss.

"It's a lotus symbol." He spoke against her lips, their foreheads still enmeshed. "It's a symbol of life and renewal." Tyus removed the necklace to dress her long neck with the exquisite symbol.

"The uniqueness of the flower, the way it appears to be actively blooming like a spiritual awakening. When I saw this, I immediately thought of you, Symphony." He paused, positioning the charm in the center of her neck. Her heart ferociously thumped against his fingertips.

"Symphony, you're so full of life, but like this lotus, you're still blooming, growing, developing. Baby, in those moments when you think you're not a priority, when you lose sight of your greatness.... Those times when the tremors hold you hostage, think of this necklace as your calm, your peace-" Tyus paused, strumming a finger down the bridge of her nose. "- an extension of me, Sweetpea."

Symphony was hushed, overwhelmed with emotions. She delicately placed her fingertips against the necklace before tenderly kissing Tyus.

"It's kind of like our soul connection, huh?" She lovingly gazed.

"Exactly like that, babe." Tyus was absolutely enamored as he trailed kisses along her neck.

They lovingly lazed for countless hours with the rambunctious waves and full emblazoned moon offering the most splendid backdrop for their impassioned night of love-making on the beach.

SAD AND SOMBER couldn't describe how Symphony felt when she and Tyus left Mexico. They were already making plans to come back for his birthday in June. But nothing could express her dispirited sentiment when Symphony and Tyus departed each other during the layover in Dallas. Tyus was flying to Atlanta for meetings and Symphony was going back home. He would only be gone overnight but she was downright despondent and depressed; scowling and sleeping the entire flight home alone.

Thankfully, an Uber was available as soon as she grabbed her luggage. It was after 10 pm and she was exhausted. Symphony willed herself not to fall asleep in the car. No desire to be taken hostage by the Uber driver who appeared harmless but you never know. She giggled at her sleepy delirium as the glow from her phone prevented her dozing. It was Tyus.

Bae: Hey Sweetpea. I landed. You ok?

Sweetpea: Yeah bae. I'm in the Uber. I'll be home in about 10 minutes.

The phone rang.

"Hey Bae." Symphony answered, sounding like she lost her best friend. "Are you at the hotel?"

"Stop sounding like that babe. I'll be back tomorrow." Tyus yawned. "Yeah, I just walked in my room."

"I know. I just want to be back in paradise for a few more days with you." She paused. "I know you're tired because I'm exhausted too and will be collapsing in my bed in about five minutes. Go to sleep, Ty. Get some rest. We'll talk in the morning."

"Alright, Sweetpea. Text me when you make it in the house. I love you." Tyus declared.

The butterfly-goosebump tingle resurfaced every time she heard those three words from him in that bold baritone tenor. It was like a divine foreign language that she was desperate to fully comprehend. "I love you too, Ty. Goodnight."

Symphony pulled her suitcase from the trunk of the car, schlepping to the side door to enter her house. She deactivated and reactivated the alarm once she entered the mudroom. Dropping all her belongings on the bench, Symphony sent a quick text to Tyus - *I'm here. I love you.* And Syncere - *Pri I'm home. Exhausted. Getting under the damn bed.* She was so tired she was practically seeing double.

"I just want to sleep." Symphony mumbled to herself. She hit the kitchen light switch, prepared to grab a bottle of water before crawling up the steps to her bedroom.

"Good evening, daughter." The soft yet throaty voice of Malynda delivered a menacing chill down Symphony's spine. Her mother was quaintly perched at the glass top kitchen table with wrinkled hands folded atop a picture frame.

"Shit!" Symphony screeched. "What the hell are you doing here Malynda? How did you get in my house?" She didn't move from her position near the kitchen exit because she had no clue what state of mind her mother was in.

"You continue to disrespect your mother with that foul mouth, daughter." Malynda tsked. "And this was my house well before you came along, little girl."

Symphony observed her mother as she cautiously footed

further into the kitchen. Malynda appeared lucid, well as sane as she could be. She looked like she stepped right out of a 1970s publication of Jet Magazine. Bell bottom jeans, knee high block heel boots, sheer off the shoulder floral print ruffle blouse too thin for the winter chill, and dangling peace symbol earrings. Symphony couldn't deny her mother's beauty; always likening her to 70's bombshell Jane Kennedy.

She leered into the matching almond-shaped greyish brown eyes that were passed down from her grandmother's lineage, button nose, full lips, and thick coffee brown naturally wavy hair. The only distinct difference between them was their skin color and hair texture thanks to Symphony's European father. It was like looking into a mirror and Symphony prayed that her reflection, her life, would be starkly contradictory to her mother's. Malynda's angel face concealed the evil and hate that resided inside.

"I'm going to ask you one more time before I call the police. Why are you here and how did you get in *my* house?" Symphony remained calm but still cautious.

"I remember this picture like it was yesterday." Malynda held up the tarnished picture frame. "Your grandmother insisted on having a picture of the two of us for her wall of James women. I despised this yellow dress she made me wear to match yours. Look at you smiling so damn big. That grin always reminded me of your father." Malynda stared at the picture with a look of disdain.

"You're not the only one who despises that picture. The look on your face right now is the exact look you had that day. Displeasure. Indignation. I was what, maybe three or four years old, and elated to be dressed like my doll-faced mother for a pretty picture. But you - the pained guise; like you loathed being near me. No smile, no life in your expression. You wouldn't even touch me. Look at that -" Symphony closed the distance between them, snatching the picture from her mother's grasp as she pointed. "I am literally clutching your fingertips just to be close to you." Silent tears fell from her exhausted yet ignited eyes.

"Why did you hate me, Malynda?" Symphony cried. For the first time she demonstrated vulnerability, sorrow, and heartsickness in her mother's presence..

"I didn't hate you, daughter." Malynda rolled her eyes still settled at the kitchen table. Symphony was sitting directly across from her mother. As much as it pained her, it was beyond time for Symphony and Malynda to have a truthful conversation.

"Well what would you call it if not hate? You never hugged me, kissed me, you barely talked to me. You made me call you Malynda instead of mom since the day I uttered my first words. Why do you think me and Syncere call our grandmother, G-ma? Because we were almost seven years old before we realized she wasn't our mama but our grandma. What mother looks at her child with such derision and disgust?" Symphony's voice cracked.

"I killed myself trying to be what I thought you wanted - smart like you, athletic like you, but nothing was ever good enough for Malynda Neolla James. You didn't show me any attention until G-ma and Poppa did. That was the only time you cared enough about me to even voice my name. Daughter... that's all you've ever called me. Oh, let me not forget, I got a little more attention when you dressed me up to go see the random white man that I eventually learned was Joel Pederson, my father. But then you screamed and yelled at me every time he made us go away." Symphony's grey orbs grew fiery red as her mother just sat there - emotionless.

"I deserve an explanation, Malynda. Why do you hate me?" She questioned again, howling.

"I did not want you, Symphony." Malynda shouted. Her first time showing any signals of life. "Joel wanted me to get an abortion but my mother and father made me keep you. They said I was too far along in my pregnancy and it would be murder. Daddy constantly told me God wouldn't be pleased." She strangely grunted. "Having you meant I couldn't have Joel. And I wanted Joel. He loved me but rejected me because of you." Malynda matter-of-factly stated without flinching.

"He used you. You were his fake ass Queen of Sheeba. He used your pretty black face for his personal fantasies. Joel was never going to put you on Broadway or in a movie. But you fell for that shit." Symphony noticed a familiar rage brewing in her mother's eyes.

"He could fuck his pretty black mistress and then go to his beautiful home in the suburbs with the white picket fence and blonde hair blue eyed wife and kids. Of course he didn't want your brown-skinned, kinky-hair baby. Why would he?" Symphony angrily smirked while aggressively wiping her tears. Nostrils flaring, she pointlessly endeavored to cease the madness brewing in her spirit.

"How the hell did you get in here, Malynda? You seem to forget the restraining order applies to G-ma's permanent *and* secondary address." Symphony threatened.

When Malynda showed up at the hospital a few years ago after their grandmother's second stroke, Symphony and Syncere got a restraining order against her. Symphony never wanted to have her mother arrested but she would for G-ma's protection.

"The basement. I still have a key and that's the one door that you neglected to secure." Malynda gloated. "And don't you dare talk to me about Joel. You know nothing about him. He loved me. He would still be loving me if it wasn't for you."

Symphony stood from her seat. She'd heard enough of this nonsense.

"You're an idiot. Why would I expect a woman with diagnosed mental disease to make any damn sense?" Symphony motioned towards the door, encouraging her mother to leave.

"Get out of my house. Now Malynda... before I personally remove you!" Symphony shouted, throwing the water bottle against the wall.

Malynda slowly rose, staring at Symphony as she unhurriedly padded across the kitchen stopping at the archway. "Aren't you the least bit curious as to why I came here in the first place? Why I've been calling you, daughter?" Malynda remained eerily calm. Symphony didn't know if it was medication or just plain crazy.

"You can exit from the basement, the front door, the damn window. I don't give a shit but you need to get out of here, Malynda." Symphony firmly nudged her mother towards the door.

"You're acting like you really wanted me as your mother. You and Syncere had all of the attention from momma and daddy. You were fine and well taken care of. Your life was good." Malynda refused to move any further.

Symphony's dewy eyes were aching from tiredness and wrath.

"You're right about one thing. G-ma and Poppa were all I had. The only people me and Syncere could count on, since you and Aunt Maleyna were piss poor mothers. I thank God for them and owe G-ma and Poppa my life. But you have memories of a false past. I don't share those memories. My pain, my hurt, my abandonment are real. I needed my mother in my life even if I didn't have a father. I needed you to want me, Malynda." Symphony's pain was undeniable, vehement sobs echoing against the aged walls.

"Please leave. I'm begging you." Symphony leaned against the foyer table, lifeless. She'd reached her capacity, unable to consume anymore of Malynda's presence. She opened the front door for her mother to exit as Malynda turned to face her daughter.

"This is for you." Malynda handed Symphony an envelope. "Since you never let me tell you why I came in the first place."

"Fine! Why, Malynda? Why did you come?" Symphony acquiesced.

"Your father. Joel. He's dying." Malynda dryly blurted. "Read the letter, daughter." She casually strolled away and almost disappeared into the night as if she was a ghost.

Symphony stood in the doorway stunned, unmovable, staring out into the darkness still tightly gripping the envelope. She blinked rapidly, quaking from her stupefied stance, peering around to look for Malynda but she was gone.

Stepping back into her house, Symphony dizzily glanced around the place she called *home* her entire life. Gazing at the pictures on the wall, some matured images and some newer memoirs. This dwelling held so many joyous and traumatic memories. Symphony's emotions bartered between happy and sad as she aimlessly footed into the kitchen. The picture of her and her mother laid against the kitchen table. Trailing her finger along the antique gold frame, she glared at a blissful and carefree version of herself before her heart was blemished and broken by the aloof woman who coldly stared back at her.

Symphony lifted the solid frame from the table absently gawking at the distorted portrait. She still had the envelope in her hand, finally reading six simple words that encompassed a lifetime of grueling agony. *To My Daughter, From Your Father.* Symphony released a thunderous bellow, slamming the framed photograph against the glass top table, shattering them both, broken pieces scattered across the floor cutting Symphony's arm and toe. She didn't flinch, bleeding as the matching orbs of the photo's likeness glared back at her, unblemished.

15

Tyus called Symphony as soon as he awakened the next morning. His day was filled with consecutive meetings while in Atlanta before his 6pm flight that evening. Tyus wouldn't normally pack business into one day like this but he desperately wanted to get back to the two most important people in his life, Symphony and TJ. Tyus hadn't seen TJ since Thanksgiving so he was long overdue. He and Symphony promised TJ that he could pick their date night activity when they returned from Mexico. TJ had already called five times with different ideas ranging from Dave and Buster's to bowling.

Tyus called Symphony again but she didn't answer or respond to his text but it was very early in the morning so he figured she was sound asleep. Footing across the room to the bathroom, he started the shower before retrieving his clothes from the closet to get his day started. The sooner it was over, the sooner he could get home.

Tyus grabbed coffee from Starbucks and was hopping in his rental car by 7:30am, attempting to avoid the Atlanta rush hour traffic. Still no response from Symphony. He left her a voicemail. *"Hey Sweetpea. Did you decide not to go to work today? Call me baby. I wanted to hear your voice before my day got busy. I love you. Call me."*

Tyus arrived at his first site on time. He was back to back all day when he had a moment to breathe for lunch around 1pm. He glanced at his phone, still nothing from Symphony. Tyus called again. No answer. He didn't want to worry her but he decided to call Syncere.

"Hey Tyus." Syncere answered. "I'm in the doctor's office for some tests so I can't talk long. What's up?"

"Hey Syn. Is everything ok with you and the babies?" Tyus asked before adding any unnecessary stress.

"Yeah, we're good. It's just routine after what happened before. The doctor and King are taking every precaution." She laughed.

"Well good. Hey, have you heard from Symphony? I called her a few times and she's not answering." Tyus was trying not to sound nervous.

"She's probably knocked out. Last night she texted me that she was about to get under the bed because she was so tired. I told her to take another day to recuperate since you wore her out." Syncere chuckled.

"Shit, she wore my ass out. I'm struggling through these meetings today." Tyus chortled. "You're probably right though. I'm sure she'll call when she wakes up." He ended the call.

Although Syncere didn't seem worried, something still

didn't feel right. Symphony would've called him if she changed her plans about going to work. Tyus mused over every possibility. *She could be asleep or something could have happened once she walked in the house.* The pit of his stomach churned. Tyus followed his instinct, calling his assistant, instructing her to cancel his meetings and book him on the next available flight.

He arrived back in St. Louis a little before six o'clock in the evening. He powered up his phone. No response from Symphony. His concern escalated into fear. Tyus requested his car from the valet service app before he departed the plane so that it would be ready by the time he reached the garage. He sprinted through the airport. His truck was being pulled around just as he arrived at the valet. Tyus called her again. Nothing.

"Goddammit Symphony, where are you?" He whispered. "Please God let her be alright." Tyus mumbled those words for the duration of his drive.

Thirty minutes later he pulled his SUV into her driveway. Symphony's car was parked in the carport. He peered inside the car but everything looked normal. Tyus unlocked the side door to the house and entered through the mudroom. Her backpack and suitcase were on the bench which was not abnormal either since she was so tired and probably didn't feel like carrying the bags upstairs. Tyus was feeling more at ease thinking maybe she took that strong ass melatonin she sometimes used to help her sleep until he stepped further into the kitchen.

Shattered pieces of glass sprinkled across the floor, the kitchen table completely broken, chairs turned upside down, broken picture frames in the living room, the front door closed but unlocked, and tiny red drops resembling blood on the tile floor and carpeted steps.

"Symphony, baby!" Tyus screamed, carefully navigating the broken glass. "Symphony, where are you?" He dashed up the steps two at a time, panicking. Tyus could hear the television from her bedroom but Symphony hadn't responded.

He opened the door, the gloomy room was pitch-dark because of the blackout curtains. Dimmed illumination occasionally beamed from the television shedding light on the empty bottles of wine and vodka on the nightstand, the same red drops on the floor. Tyus gasped as the visual of Symphony's lifeless legs on the floor peeked beyond the foot of the bed. He rushed across the room, her half-naked body passed out.

"Symphony, baby. Wake up, Sweetpea. Please, baby." Tyus scooped her up from the floor as if she was light as a feather, resting her on the disheveled bed. He checked for a pulse. Thankfully, it was strong. He lightly tapped her face, encouraging her to waken.

"Sweetpea, baby it's Ty. Can you hear me? Symphony please wake up?" Externally, Tyus appeared controlled but internally, he was hysterical, terrified.

"Ty." Symphony groggily responded before she started coughing. "You're back." She slurred drunkenly. Tyus could smell the alcohol seeping from her pores. He didn't have time to be pissed, she needed to awaken and fast.

Tyus carried her to the shower, tenderly settling her on the seat then turned on a low stream of the cold water. He used the handheld shower head to gently dampen her skin.

"Ty, bae, it's so cold." Symphony shivered as she began to come to life. She peered at Tyus' misty eyes, coming to some realization of what was happening.

"Ty. I'm sorry." She sobbed.

"It's ok, baby. I'm just thankful you're alive. That you are safe." He kissed against her forehead, his clothes getting drenched in the process but he didn't care.

Once Symphony was somewhat coherent, Tyus turned off the water, removing her wet bra and panties before draping her in a robe. He perched her zombiesque frame on the vanity chair. Symphony's eyes were transfixed, her voice hushed.

Tyus kneeled in front of her and inspected her body trying to determine if she was hurt.

"Symphony, did somebody hurt you? Did somebody break in here? The door was unlocked." He anxiously probed.

She shook her head no but still no words.

"Did you break the table downstairs?"

She silently nodded yes.

"Baby, why? What happened?" Tyus continued his inquiry.

Symphony's glorious grey orbs flooded with tears when she whispered, "Malynda."

That one name carried an enormous amount of tragic heaviness. Tyus discontinued his interrogation for now. Symphony preferred to disclose details at her own time and he would be there when she was ready.

"Baby, stay right here okay. I'm going to start your bath

and change my clothes, okay?" He nodded, encouraging her to do the same. She obliged.

Tyus turned the knob, activating the stream of steaming water and added the lavender oil and bubble bath that sat in the basket on the ledge of the bathtub. Symphony was placid, aphonic tears salting her cheeks as she watched Tyus intently move around the space. He momentarily exited the bathroom removing his wet clothes. Navigating across the bedroom into her closet to find the clothes he left for when he stayed overnight. Tyus paused in the closet, releasing the breath he'd been holding since he saw Symphony passed out on the floor. He blinked rapidly, clearing the mist from his eyes, readying himself to return to her - to take care of her.

Tyus walked back into the bathroom just as the tub was almost full. He grabbed the hairbrush from Symphony's vanity and brushed her curly tresses into a ponytail, then pulled a facial wipe from the dispenser and tenderly cleansed her tear-stained face. Tyus was simply following the exact same routine he'd observed her conduct during bath time over the past several weeks.

"You ready to get in?" He whispered. Symphony remained voiceless, nodding her response. Tyus extended his hand to help her stand so that he could remove the robe. He continued his chivalrous approach offering her aid into the bathtub. Symphony audibly exhaled when her body submerged into the steamy water.

"Is the water too hot, Sweetpea?" He asked. She shook her head no. "Rest for a little bit while I clean up the room, okay?" Tyus kneeled down to kiss against her forehead.

"Symphony, can I hear your voice please? Tell me that you're ok." His eyes pleaded.

"I'm ok, Ty." Symphony whimpered, her voice raspy and hoarse.

Tyus smiled, elated to hear any sound from her.

"Hey Google, play Jill Scott radio." He instructed, still following her routine. Tyus lit a candle and dimmed the chandelier over her tub. Everything was exactly how she liked it, minus the wine. Tyus gave her everything she needed and things she didn't know she wanted. His thoughtful actions were a testimonial of protection without uttering a word. Symphony laid back on the tub pillow and closed her eyes as Jill Scott's "He Loves Me" resounded through the bathroom.

While Symphony relaxed, Tyus gathered up the bottles from the bedroom into the trash and pulled the sheets off of the bed. A white paper envelope floated through the air before landing on the floor. He picked it up and read the inscription. *To My Daughter, From Your Father.*

"Shit!" Tyus yelped, glancing towards the door, hoping she didn't hear him. The envelope was still sealed so Symphony hadn't read whatever bullshit her father had to say in the letter. Tyus placed the envelope on the nightstand, bracing himself for the reckoning that would follow once she decided to read the contents. The vibration in his pocket broke his daze.

"What's up, bro?" Tyus asked King.

"What's up, dawg? Hey, have you heard from Symphony? Syncere was trying to call her but it kept going to voicemail. The doctor gave Princess some different medication and it knocked her out, but I promised I would keep trying to reach Symphony."

"Yeah, I'm at her house now. Her phone is dead." Tyus stepped out into the hallway. "Man, please don't say anything to Syncere, let Symphony talk to her. But some shit went down with Symphony and her mother last night or this morning. I'm honestly not sure."

"What the fuck? Is she alright?" King shouted.

"Man, she scared the shit out of me but she's good now. She's taking a bath." Tyus peeked into the bedroom. Symphony was lightly humming to the music which was a good sign.

"I guess just tell Syncere you talked to me and her prima is good. I'll make sure Symphony calls her in the morning."

"Alright man. Let me know if you need anything. I can't leave Princess, but I can get Titan or Lennox over there." King declared.

"Thanks bro. I think I'm good right now but I'll let you know." Tyus walked back into the bedroom and finished changing the bed linen before he walked into the bathroom. The mature doors squeaked, she shuddered, looking up at him and then giving a miniature smile, but it was better than nothing.

"You good, baby? You ready to get cleaned up?" Tyus leaned against the doorframe.

"Yeah." Symphony laid back resting on the pillow again.

Tyus strolled across the bathroom, sliding the vanity chair close to the bathtub. He clutched the sponge adding the citrus scented body wash before gently caressing her skin. Tyus delicately sponged her neck then journeyed to her breasts as she continued to relax under his spell. He cleaned one arm, then the other before sponging her stomach. Gingerly massaging the sponge along the folds of her private lips. She gasped, melting further into the comforts of the warm water. Tyus continued down her satiny smooth legs, making his final stop at her perfect toes. He navigated up the length of her frame repeating his actions in reverse. Symphony lifted from the bath pillow, allowing him to caress against her back with the sponge. She deeply exhaled, the earlier angst, agitation, and rage dispelled.

Tyus attentively ensured she was clean from head to toe. Extending his hand to help her out of the bathtub, Symphony stepped onto the mat, her naked frame on display. He cherished her body, every smooth layer and bodacious curve, passionately drying every inch of thickalicious skin. Tyus was always calming his manhood in Symphony's presence and tonight was no different. But this was not the time for that. He lotioned her, rubbing, grazing, gliding his hands over her right arm noticing the cut on her forearm. Symphony flinched as they locked eyes.

"I'm sorry." He mouthed breathily.

Tyus' mind was reeling, wondering what the fuck happened between Symphony and Malynda. He didn't give a damn if the culprit was her mother or her father, he was ready to kill whoever the mutherfucker was that caused her this level of distress.

Symphony stepped into the grey cotton nightgown then ambled over to the sink. She bandaged her arm, applied deodorant, brushed her teeth, and finished cleansing her face, staring at her tormented reflection in the mirror. Tyus leaned against the doorframe attentively observing. He saun-tered across the bathroom nestling behind her, capturing her waist and snuggling into the folds of her neck. He inhaled, intoxicated by the fruity aroma. Symphony closed her eyes, reaching up and fondling her fingers through his hair as he gazed at her in the mirror. Tyus couldn't imagine inhabiting a world that didn't include Symphony.

"I love you." Tyus uttered, closing his eyes, tightly nestled against her.

They jointly ambled into the bedroom where Tyus had a serving tray with water, tea, and soup on the nightstand. He had already folded back the cover and encouraged Symphony to lay down. She slid into the bed, crawling into a fetal position as he blanketed her.

"Sweetpea, can you try to eat something please?" Tyus pleaded.

"I'm not hungry, Ty." She remained motionless. "Can you just lay with me?"

He obliged.

Tyus and Symphony reveled in a soundless tender-hearted enmeshment for what seemed like eternity but only a few minutes depleted.

"Ty." Symphony spoke.

"Yes."

"I wasn't trying to hurt myself. I promise I wasn't." She turned to find his eyes.

Tyus cupped her chin. "What were you trying to do, Symphony?"

"I was angry and slammed the picture frame on the table. The glass shattered and cut my arm and foot." Symphony's lip quivered, unsuccessfully quelling the tears that blemished her face. She cuddled against Tyus as he massaged from her nape down her spine on repeat.

"It's ok, Sweetpea. Just get some rest for now." Tyus kissed against the fluff of her curls.

"Can you promise me we will talk tomorrow and you'll tell me everything?" He

questioned and she nodded.

"Including what's in the envelope." He continued.

She glared at him before nodding again.

"Talk, babe." He demanded.

"Yes. I promise. We'll talk about everything."

Symphony held Tyus so tight, their limbs delightfully enmeshed, his start indistinguishable from her finish.

16

Sleep escaped Tyus for the majority of the night. Every time Symphony so much as whimpered in her sleep, he reacted. Extremely concerned, he laid awake staring at the ceiling as the walnut colored blades of the ceiling fan aimlessly circled. Flashes of Symphony's limp body sprawled on the floor invaded his psyche. He could still smell the stench of alcohol seeping from her pores as he cleansed her body. *What if I didn't leave early? How long was she laying there? What if she...* Tyus shuddered, refusing to fathom the universe without her.

As if she heard his inner thoughts, Symphony cuddled against his chest, finding respite in his caress. Tyus kissed her temple, inhaling the scent of lavender and honey. Fear and love laced his handsome face as he stared at her. Full pouty lips, glowing amber skin, long lashes, and the softest lyrical snore. Symphony's external allure conflicted with the wretched desolation and misery that plagued her inside. The room was dusk, the illumination from his cell phone interrupted his uneasy gaze. The cutest toothless face filled the screen.

Tyus whispered, "What's up lil man? It's early. Are you ok?"

"Hi dad. Yeah, I'm good. Where are you?" TJ sighed, appearing sad on the screen. "I miss you, dad."

"I miss you too, man. Hold on a minute." Tyus gently placed Symphony against the pillow, easing out of the bed. "I'm back home, TJ. I have to take care of a few things today but I promise to pick you up for dinner, ok?"

"Can we go to the burger place with the root beer floats? Oops!" TJ covered his snaggletooth grin with his tiny hand. He giggled, guilty of revealing a secret.

Tyus laughed. "Let me guess, Grammy and Pop-Pop let you have root beer?" TJ nodded. "Yes, we can go to Freddy's. Is your mom around?" TJ didn't answer but just started moving through the house with the phone.

"Tyus Anthony Ramos Okoro Jr! Who are you talking to on my phone at this hour?" Tyus chuckled, hearing Gia's Spanish accent surface as she fussed at TJ.

"Tyus, hey." Gia appeared on the screen. "Did this boy really call you this early?"

"Daddy said I could call him at any time." TJ pouted.

"Hey Gia. He's right. TJ knows he can call me whenever. I wanted to get him tonight if that's cool." Tyus confirmed.

"Yeah, that's fine. I didn't know you were back. Is everything ok? You look exhausted." Gia asked with TJ sitting on her lap.

Tyus leaned against the wall in a dark corner of the room

peering at Symphony as she shuffled searching the bed for his presence. "Yeah. I'm good. Um, I gotta go. I'll be there no later than five. Bye lil man. Be ready ok?" He nodded, grinning.

"Ty." Symphony's voice was raspy. She furrowed, pinching against her temple in pain. Her head was throbbing, vision blurred as she scanned the room for him. *Maybe I was dreaming?* She mused, slowly lifting from the bed missing his embrace.

"Are you ok, Sweetpea?" Tyus whispered from the corner.

She smiled, thankful that her dream was actually a reality. Symphony's movements were unhurried, now feeling the effects of her drunkenness and heartache.

"I'd be better if you weren't so far away." She lazily smiled.

Tyus obliged. Stealthily sauntering towards her. She bit the corner of her bottom lip admiring his shirtless Herculean frame. He did the same, sexily grinning at his troubled beauty.

"Good morning, gorgeous." Tyus kissed against her lips, handing her the bottle of water and Tylenol from the nightstand.

"Good morning, bae." She returned the kiss. "Did you sleep ok?" He nodded.

"You? How'd you sleep?" He asked. She nodded, but no real response. "You need to eat. I'll order breakfast." He cuddled against her backside.

"I can fix something." Symphony laid her head against his shoulder, still reeling from the headache.

"Um, but you can't. The kitchen is in no condition for cooking." Tyus teased, but his voice was serious.

"Oh yeah. I guess I forgot.. Hurricane Symphony." She joked, a vain attempt to lighten the mood. But she recognized that Tyus was ready for an explanation.

"You get dressed and I'll take care of the rest. Meet me downstairs when you're ready." He cupped her chin, encouraging eye contact to ensure she understood his words. Tyus needed her to not only be ready for breakfast but prepared to tell him the truth.

Symphony stared at Tyus until he disappeared from the room. She grabbed the robe from the foot of the bed, draping her thick frame. Footing into the bathroom, she cleansed her skin and brushed her teeth, surveying the curves of her face, the bend of her button nose. She shuddered from the reflection. Her mother's pedigree was always ever present but Symphony wondered about the other aspects of her genealogy for the first time in a long time.

———————————

TYUS STOOD at the archway separating the living room and kitchen observing the mess. He huffed, preparing himself to clean up the glass. Carefully disposing of the larger pieces of glass, Tyus swept then vacuumed the tile floor until there were no physical signs of the commotion.

Symphony dressed in leggings and an oversized sweatshirt. Steadily trekking down the steps, not ready to see the evidence of her breakdown. She adorned a miniscule smile, pleasantly surprised to see that Tyus had cleaned the entire kitchen but the dreadful image of Malynda placidly seated at the kitchen table circulated repeatedly through her head. *Your father. Joel. He's dying.* She dwelled, shaking as tears formed in the corner of her eyes.

"Symphony." Tyus had been silently observing her from the mudroom doorway. The anguish and trepidation evident with every heaving rise and fall of her chest.

"Baby, come here please." He requested and she complied, quickly accepting his open arm invitation. Symphony cried silent tears as Tyus embraced her standing in the middle of the kitchen.

"She finally admitted it." Symphony whispered.

"Who admitted what, Sweetpea?" He questioned, ushering her towards the kitchen island to sit on the bar stool. Tyus stood between her legs, never relinquishing his hold of her waist.

"Malynda. She admitted that she never wanted me because my father - Joel, didn't want me. G-ma and Poppa made her keep the baby... keep me." Symphony sighed, leaning her back against the island as Tyus thumbed away her tears.

"Joel is dying." Symphony blurted. "Those words just... casually rolled off Malynda's tongue like it was nothing. Like I was a stranger holding a conversation with her on a random street."

"Does she expect you to see him? Attend the funeral?" His eyes furrowed.

Symphony shrugged her shoulders. "I don't know. You *never* know with Malynda."

"Did you two have a fight? Is that why the table is broken? Did you hurt her, Symphony?" Tyus interrogated. He'd been worried that Symphony may have done something she would regret, given her violent past with her mother. But he'd already settled that he would contentedly find a resolution for whatever she'd done. Life or death. That's how much Tyus loved her.

"No. Nothing like that. We argued. I screamed. She settled in that chair emotionless. Staring at me. Eerily calling me *daughter*." Symphony absently glared at the kitchen chairs Tyus lined up against the wall.

"I... malfunctioned -" She stiffly chuckled. "- after Malynda left. I broke the table after she gave me the letter."

The buzz of the doorbell and Symphony's phone sounded off simultaneously. *Prima.* She mouthed. Tyus motioned his head to the phone, encouraging her to answer as he walked towards the front door.

"Hey Prima." Symphony answered, her smile actually reached her eyes when she heard her cousin's voice.

"Hey Pri." Syncere smiled. "Are you ok? Tyus was worried about you when he called me yesterday. I didn't get a chance to call him back because the doctor gave me some strong ass medicine."

"Medicine? What happened?" Symphony was concerned.

"Nothing happened. My feet were bothering me again so the doctor ran some tests. She gave me something for anxiety and it knocked me out."

"Pri, I'm sorry I wasn't there." Symphony cried for more reasons than Syncere could comprehend at the time.

"Symphony, it's ok. I'm fine. Baby boy and baby girl are doing great. No reason to cry." Syncere paused. "I'm about to be on my way. Somethings going on with you."

"No Syncere. You will stay your wobbly bed-ridden ass at Cartwright Castle." Symphony teased. "I had a rough couple of days but I'm good now. Ty is here and we're about to have breakfast. I promise I'll come over tonight and we'll talk."

Syncere was satisfied with that response so Symphony ended the call as Tyus continued to plate their breakfast. Bacon, egg, and cheese croissant sandwiches, fruit, and coffee.

"Thank you, Ty. For everything." She sexily smiled, leaning over to kiss him.

"My pleasure, Sweetpea. Can you promise me something?" She nodded, blowing to cool the hot coffee.

"If this ever happens again, can you pick up a phone and call me, Syncere, Ledia, anybody, before you pick up a bottle of alcohol. You scared the shit out of me, Symphony." Tyus exhaled deeply, finally able to release, admitting his distress.

"I know Malynda said some fucked up shit, and if I ever get the unfortunate chance to meet her, we will have words. But she is not worth your life, baby. You have me, Syncere, G-ma - so much to live for Symphony. So many people who love the shit outta you." Dewy eyed, he passionately caressed her face.

"I'm so sorry, bae. Please forgive me. I didn't mean to scare you and I promise it won't happen again." The vehement tears resurfaced, salting the corners of her mouth.

"She's not worth it. She's never been worth my tears and I know that now."

"Ty, baby, I love you. Can you please forgive me?" Symphony licked against his lips, splitting his mouth with her tongue, tasting the hazelnut coffee flavor. She continued in a whisper against his lips, "Please, bae. Please forgive me."

Symphony snaked her arms around his waist, fingering the band of the basketball shorts. She gently clutched the girth of his dick in the palms of her hands. His veins were swollen, pulsing and perfect. Tyus' manhood expanded with every firm stroke, each gentle caress, every sweet nibble along his Adam's apple.

Although only a few days depleted, Mexico seemed like a lifetime ago. Tyus was desperate for her and Symphony yearned for him. Thankfully, he was still shirtless. She journeyed her tongue down his chest, lavishly sucking and licking his nipples.

"Shit, Symphony!" Tyus yelped, dropping into the neighboring bar stool.

Symphony slid off of her stool into a squat, happily greeting his deliciously ombre dick. She possessed an uninhibited hunger for Tyus. Loving every moment of his manhood on her palate, Symphony feasted. Licking, supping, devouring, absorbing every single inch of the dick.

"Symphony. Fuck, baby!" Tyus moaned. He didn't bother informing her of his impending climax because he was certain she wouldn't cease.

Once her greed was satisfied, Tyus effortlessly lifted her from the squatted position onto the kitchen island. He practically ripped the leggings from her flesh, critically needing to indwell the sodden walls of her succulent pussy. Meter by glorious centimeter, she welcomed the encroachment of his girth. Her treasure unconsciously contracted, adhering to every stroke as he delved deeper like a moth to a flame. He slowly slithered completely out of her, just to reacquaint her puss with his dick at a measured, systematic pace. Traversing in and out on repeat. He teased her, exiting and entering at a slothful frequency. She was deranged. Insane in the membrane.

"Ty! Oh my God. Baby, please." Symphony implored, painfully gripping the edge of the island top.

Tyus remained speechless. The bass-filled melodic tones of his groans echoing throughout the kitchen as he continued to explore the adventures of her treasure. Gaining momentum, he dove dick first into the depths of her precious treasure. Drilling against her g-spot, Symphony beautifully bellowed. The pleasure and pain synchronized in agreement, dispatching tingles from the crown of her head to the tips of her toes. She was breathless. Oxygen dwindling. This heavenly harassment of her pussy was intentional, studied. Symphony didn't understand the meaning but she was desperately willing to learn.

Tyus was focused, his sparkling honeyed eyes misty with adoration and rapture for her.

"Damn, I love you, Symphony. I am so fucking in love with you. Please don't ever do that shit again. Baby, I can't lose -" Tyus' thought trailed off, enthralled as he neared the pinnacle.

"Bae, I love you so much. I'm so sorry." Symphony whimpered. "Ah! Ty, please." She wasn't opposed to begging.

Tyus lifted her leg over his shoulder plummeting into her sultry infinite core.

"Aaah! Bae. Shit. Shit. Fuck. Shit!" She extended that final *shit* for about sixty seconds until her orgasm began to cease. Tyus tunneled through her puss one last time before releasing a thunderous howl of his own.

Symphony's body was lethargic and damn near comatose. Semi-conscious, she deflated, laying motionless against Tyus' shoulder. Her fluttering chest was the only indication of life. Tyus wasn't concerned since she'd blacked out before. He secured her with one hand while he fixed his shorts with the other. Carrying her bridal style, he climbed the steps to the bedroom. Resting her on the bed, he removed the clothes since the leggings were ripped and Symphony preferred to sleep naked.

Footing across the room to the bathroom, he glanced at the clock. It was already after two o'clock. Tyus and Symphony talked, nibbled their food, and made love for most of the morning and afternoon until she blacked out. He entered the bedroom with a hot towel to wash her body. She flinched, but never awakened as he cleansed every morsel of his sex from her frame.

Tyus took a shower and laid with Symphony for a little while dozing off to sleep. Thankfully, he set the alarm on his phone so he wouldn't be late picking up TJ. When Tyus made a promise to his son, he never disappointed. He nudged Symphony, but no reaction. She was exhausted mentally and physically and they still hadn't discussed the letter from her father that was still resting on the nightstand. Tyus wouldn't dare open the letter without her permission;

however, he did contemplate taking it with him so she wouldn't read it alone. He was not convinced that this was her last traumatic episode.

"Symphony. Baby, I gotta go." He whispered in her ear. "I need to pick up TJ."

She tussled a little then whimpered, "ok."

"Sweetpea, did you hear me? I'm leaving to pick up TJ." He repeated. "I'll call you later. I love you."

"I love you too, Ty." Symphony breathily confirmed. Tyus was unaware if she was alert or dreaming.

He opened the nightstand drawer to find a pen and sheet of paper. Scribbling a quick note and sending a text message explaining why he left just in case she didn't remember. Before leaving, he retrieved the partially eaten breakfast sandwich and fruit cup from the kitchen, bringing it to her room with specific instructions in the note to eat. Tyus secured the covers over her body, still mellowed from the splendid lovemaking. He kissed her cheek, whispering more loving sentiments, then hesitantly exited the bedroom.

17

Symphony didn't wake up until after six o'clock. She stirred, examining the darkened room searching for his Herculean frame. The room was empty but the ache streaming through her hands and thighs were evidence of Tyus' presence.

"Ty." She called out for him but no answer. Symphony peered at the nightstand greeted by a piece of paper and food on a serving tray. She retrieved the note and bottle of water, then leaned against the tufted headboard.

Hey Sleeping Beauty. I didn't want to wake you but I had to pick up TJ at five. He's staying with me tonight. We would love to have you join our Uno game. :) Call me when you wake up. And eat something. I love you.

Symphony smiled as her phone illuminated.

Prima: Hey! Are you still coming over? King made his famous homemade pizzas. #delish

Prima: Ha! Yes. I just woke up. Give me 30 minutes.

Prima: Ok. I can't promise that I'll wait for you to eat. LOL

Symphony laughed and it felt good. She noticed a text from Tyus.

Bae: Do as I asked Sweetpea. Don't text me. Call. Love you.

She simply shook her head because Tyus knew her too well. Exiting the bed, she instructed Google to call Bae. The phone rang twice before Tyus answered fussing at TJ in the background.

"Hey baby. Did you sleep good?" Tyus' smile could be felt through the phone.

"Why are you fussing at my lil buddy?" She retorted, giggling. "Yes. Too good. I blacked out again, didn't I?"

Tyus lustfully chuckled. "Just a little bit. I guess I have that effect on you." He teased.

"I wish I could lie but you do, bae." Symphony affirmed, nibbling her lip just thinking about what Tyus does to her body.

"Are you joining us tonight? I would prefer that you not be alone."

"I'm going to see Syncere. I need to tell her about Malynda... and Joel I guess. More importantly, I need to find out what's going on with these tests she had the other day. I'm going to stay there tonight." She paused. "Is that cool?"

"Of course I want you here, but I'd rather you stay there than be alone in your house. So yeah, baby, it's cool." Tyus sighed. "Um, what are you going to do about the letter?"

Symphony remained silent for a few seconds too long but Tyus allowed her time to process.

"I think it's something I need to do with Syncere. She just -"

Tyus interrupted. "Gets it." He paused. "No need to explain, Sweetpea. That's your cousin, your best friend - shit, basically your sister. She knows things that I can't begin to understand. I think it's best for you to share this with your prima."

"Dad, you have to draw like 100 cards by now. Are you going to pay attention?" TJ's pouting was apparent through the phone.

"Ty, babe, go ahead. I would hate for you to lose a game of Uno because of me." Symphony laughed. "Tell TJ I said hi and I hope to see him soon."

"Will do. I love you, baby." Tyus exclaimed.

"I love you. I'll text you when I get there." She ended the call, then secured her house, making a mental note to get a new lock on that damn basement door.

———

"Prima!" Syncere squealed, pulling Symphony into a tight squeeze. "I've missed you. Are you good?"

"I missed you too, Pri. Yeah, I'm better." She stepped into the house with a duffle bag. "Can I stay tonight? I need you to help me with something." Symphony requested.

"Of course. Anything. Do you want to talk now or eat first? King just put the pizzas in the oven." Syncere was practically salivating.

"Let's eat first because I know your ass is starving." They guffawed, walking hand in hand through the two-story foyer into the great room.

"Prima!" King greeted.

"Primo!" Symphony chortled.

"You good, baby girl?" King searched Symphony's eyes for reassurance as he extended his fist for a bump. She nodded.

King presented beautifully baked pizzas, toasted ravioli, and salad for dinner. They laughed and feasted until Symphony and Syncere disappeared into the guest room.

"What's up, Symphony? What's going on with you?" Syncere was propped against the headboard, caressing her bulging belly.

"I should be asking you the same thing, Syncere. Is everything ok with you and the babies? Why are you rubbing your stomach like that?" Symphony questioned, concerned.

"I'm fine. Thing one and thing two are fine." Syncere laughed. "You would rub your stomach too if you had a foot pressing on your bladder and another one kicking your spine."

"Oh, damn. I guess you have a point." Symphony said, shaking her head. "I ain't never doing that shit."

"For Tyus you will." Syncere winked. "Now what's going on?"

"We need to call G-ma first." Symphony dialed their grandmother via the Facebook Portal device they recently bought so G-ma could video chat.

"Hi G-ma." The cousins chimed in unison.

"Hi, my girly girls. You both look beautiful. I like talking on this lil thing." G-ma giggled. "Symphony James, I haven't heard from you. I was worried."

"I'm sorry, G-ma.. I just had a lot going on after Mexico."

"Yes, I understand. My Malynda can be a lot to handle." G-ma tsked, rolling her eyes.

"What!?" Symphony questioned.

"What does that mean, G-ma?" Syncere nervously inquired.

"That means I know Malynda James paid Symphony a visit the other night."

"How? Did she come up there?" *I'll kill here.* Symphony mused angrily.

"No. She knows better. Lyndi called me yesterday. She actually spoke like she had some sense for about 10 minutes." G-ma shook her head laughing. She'd resolved a long time ago that her daughter's mental stability - or instability was beyond her control.

"Did she tell you she basically broke into the house?" Symphony hissed.

"Broke into your house!? What the hell? I mean heck." Syncere corrected.

"Now you know my daughter only gives one side of the story. She ain't never gonna tell on herself. Everything is always somebody else's fault." G-ma sighed. "She did tell me about Joel Pederson."

"Joel Pederson?" Syncere parroted, brows slapping together in confusion.

"Syncere!" Symphony shouted. "Can you please stop repeating everything?" She pinched her temple, vainly endeavoring to cease the migraine forming.

"What should I do, G-ma?" Symphony desperately questioned. A single tear salting the corner of her mouth.

"Follow your heart, Symphony. You always have and it hasn't led you astray. Now, I can't guarantee you that talking to him will bring you any closure so you have to decide if a meeting with him will help you heal or do harm. In his condition, you may not be able to get what you're seeking. Whatever that may be." G-ma shrugged.

"Yeah, I hear you and I understand. I just don't know if I want the second time I've seen my father in my entire life to be on his deathbed." Symphony cried as Syncere caressed her shoulders. "I'm just so pissed! Typical Malynda! She flies in like a storm leaving so much destruction in her path."

G-ma tossed up her hand, pausing any further ranting. "But only if you let her, baby girl. Only if you let her." She leaned closer to the screen to ensure Symphony was listening.

"I realized a long time ago that despite my daughters' destructive paths, I was a good mother. I did all that I could for Lyndi and Leyna." G-ma peered at Syncere at the mention of her mother MaLeyna. Unlike Malynda, Syncere's mother stayed away, still struggling with addiction. Unbeknownst to Syncere, King had eyes in the streets to make sure it stayed that way as long as MaLeyna James had no plans for rehabilitation.

"I prayed daily asking God where I went wrong, but he gave me another perspective. He showed me what I did right?" G-ma smiled. "And that was with my sweet girls - Symphony and Syncere. You are my gifts from God. My reassurance that I've been a good mother and grandmother. You both are everything I hoped Lyndi and Leyna would've been. But -" Tears stained her face as she sighed. "I taught you to listen to your heart and be confident in your decisions. That's all you can do now, Symphony."

Symphony and Syncere nestled in the bed silently sobbing once they ended the call with G-ma. King peeked into the room; always in protector mode. Syncere nodded, reassuring him that everything was ok as Symphony laid against her stomach crying. They sat in familiar silence. Comforting one another as the cousins had done since they were little girls.

"Joel is dying. He may already be dead." Symphony's whisper broke the silence. "That's what Malynda came to tell me after she broke into my damn house."

"Wow. I'm sorry Prima." Syncere kissed against her cousin's cheek. "That shit still hurts even if he wasn't around. An unknown piece of you is gone forever."

"He left me a letter. What could he possibly have to say to me after all this time? It's funny how people faced with death finally find a conscience. I guess that line between heaven and hell gets really real when you are knocking on death's door."

"Yeah. Like G-ma always said, do you want a visit from the death angel or death devil - take your pick?" They chuckled, recalling their grandmother's threat every time they stepped out of line.

"Can you read it for me, Prima? The letter - can you read it?" Symphony requested.

"Of course." Syncere whispered.

Symphony slowly relented her weakened frame from the

bed, retrieving the letter from her purse. She handed it to Syncere, leering at the words *To My Daughter From Your Father*. She stood in the bay window with her arms crossed, seemingly embracing herself, staring at nothing while considering everything.

"Ready?" Syncere asked. Symphony nodded.

Dear Symphony, If you are receiving this letter, I'm either dying or dead. Eight months ago, I was healthy and vibrant - living the best life I've lived in years. And now cancer has rapidly invaded my body. Maybe it's a punishment for the things I did. The way I treated you. Karma. I don't know but here I am writing this letter to my only daughter. A girl, a woman I've never known. I will never know. I could make excuses - blame Lyndi, blame my departed wife, my boys, but...I'm the only one to blame. You did nothing wrong.

I'm weak and don't have much time. So there is not much to say to you, Symphony, other than I'm sorry. Your father, Joel Simon Pederson.

The envelope included a tattered photo of Joel playing the clarinet. The inscription read - *New York Symphony Orchestra, October 22, 1986.*

Symphony didn't make a sound. Inaudibly weeping.

"There's a picture, Pri." Syncere extended her arm, encouraging Symphony to view the photo. Symphony crawled back into the bed crossing one leg over the other. She unhurriedly captured the photo. Staring.

"He played in the New York Symphony... on the day I was born." Symphony cried at the realization. Always wondering the origin of her name, the picture filled one of the many gaps of her story. She clutched the photograph, x-raying every detail. Her steamy tears stained the blush colored pillow until she fell asleep. Syncere blanketed her cousin when Symphony's phone vibrated on the nightstand. A picture of Symphony and Tyus on the beach in Mexico filled the screen.

"Hey Tyus. It's Syncere. She's asleep." Syncere's gruff voice yawned.

"Is she ok?"

"She will be. We talked to G-ma and read the letter."

"How'd that go?" He nervously probed, desperately desiring to be with her.

"She cried a bit but did pretty good. No violent outbursts. No drinking." Syncere gazed at her cousin, tears now clouding her eyes. "Thank you, Tyus. I'm so thankful for you and the way you love my cousin. She told me what happened. How you found her. I would be completely lost if something happened to my prima."

"It's my pleasure. I do love her, Syncere. The shit is driving me crazy... I love that woman so much." Tyus rubbed his nape, pacing the hardwood floors. "Should I come over? I can take TJ to my parents."

"No. Let her sleep. I'm sure she'll call you in the morning. You and TJ should come for breakfast. I would love to meet him." Syncere grinned.

"It's a deal. Call me if she needs anything. Ok?"

———

SYMPHONY JOLTED FROM HER SLEEP, blinking away the haze disrupting her vision. The glowing shine from the sun peeked through the sheer curtains that accentuated the beautiful blush and grey decor. Symphony audibly stretched, screeching as she arched her body from the mattress. The delectable savory aroma of bacon and pancakes tickled her nose. She smiled, thankful that her cousin had a husband who loved to cook. Reluctant to uncouple from the bed, Symphony grabbed her phone and slowly sauntered into the bathroom, deciding to shower before joining Syncere and King for breakfast. She perched on the toilet to check her messages first.

Bae: Good morning, beautiful. TJ and I are getting pancakes. Text me when you wake up.

Symphony pouted, wishing Tyus would've called so she could join them for breakfast.

Sweetpea: Good morning Bae. I'm up. You should've called me. :(

The three dots immediately illuminated then ceased just as fast as they appeared. *Hmm!* She mused, wondering why Tyus didn't finish his text message. Certain that she would connect with Tyus soon, Symphony queued music, adjusted the shower temperature and undressed. Her melodic voice resounded as she sang along word for word with "Love of My Life."

Unbeknownst to Symphony, Tyus and TJ had just arrived at Cartwright Castle. Once he got TJ acquainted with Syncere, he snuck into the guest bedroom to surprise his Sweetpea. Holding a beautiful bouquet of yellow and orange roses, Tyus quietly chuckled, hearing Symphony spit Common's rap lyrics from "Love of My Life" effort-lessly. This was clearly her jam. He knocked on the cracked bathroom door as he pushed it open, joining in on the lyrics.

Y'all know how I met her. We broke up and got back together. To get her back I had to sweat her.

"Ty! Bae!" She screeched, clutching her imaginary pearls. "You scared me to death! What are you doing here? I thought you were getting pancakes with TJ?" She probed.

"I'm sorry, baby. I would've called but I decided to come and see you instead." Symphony didn't realize it until his glorious body with that sexy ass smile appeared, but he was exactly what she needed in that moment. He continued. "I'm sorry. I shouldn't have just come in like this." His voice filled with contrition.

"Bae, you're fine. You just scared me, that's all. Are those for me?" She peered at the vibrant roses.

"Only you, beautiful. You ok?" Smiling, he laid the roses on the counter before sexily strolling towards her. Tyus snaked his arm around her waist, snatching her breath away with a hungry kiss before she could respond. Nestling and nibbling against her neck as he untied the robe. Reaching under the plush heavy fabric, he palmed the curve of her naked ass.

"I missed you, my love." Tyus bit his bottom lip exam-ining her magnificent body.

"Ah, baby. I missed you too." She breathily exhaled. "Wh - where is TJ?" She stuttered, chilled from the cool breeze against her body and his fondling fingertips.

"Entertaining Uncle King and Auntie Syn." Tyus

responded before tickling her nipple with his scorching tongue.

"Babe! TJ is here? We can't - not while he's - *shit!*" She panted as Tyus stroked a plump fingertip down the saturated folds of her private lips. "- not while he's in the other room, bae."

"You're about to cum in a minute anyway, Sweetpea. That's all I want... for now." He muttered, slipping the blunt tips of two fingers into her waterlogged pussy. Symphony didn't hesitate, shamelessly grinding on his fingers. She needed this release and he was acutely aware of her yearning. The weight of his imposing body inadvertently nudged her against the countertop. One thick, curvy leg tangled in his arm as he sensually plunged into the depths of her puss. Symphony's lips parted, searing to be sucked and pacified. The minty toothpaste flavor penetrated their palates. She passionately clutched his cheeks, endearing his lips with languid, yet powerful kisses.

"Ahh, Ty! I want to fucking scream!" She longingly whimpered. His effort was intense, unrelenting as he rocked to the pace of her pulsating treasure. "Bae! I'm -" A gasp seized her ability to breathe.

"Cumming, baby - " Ty sexily whispered, completing her declaration. And that's exactly what Symphony did. She came with a force that rendered her weak in the knees. Tyus apprehended her before she faltered, planting her firmly on her feet.

"Get your shower and meet me in the kitchen, love." He casually kissed her lips, washed his hands, and leisurely sauntered away as if moments ago he didn't savagely dismantle her pussy.

Symphony stared at him until he disappeared from her sight. She quickly showered, still reeling from the wantonly critical climax. After a tumultuous night, she actually felt weightless, tranquil. She hadn't made any decisions about Joel or Malynda, for that matter. Finally trusting her intuition, she decided to do as her G-ma instructed and follow her heart. Symphony sauntered into the kitchen glowing, looking properly satisfied.

"Ms. Symphony!" TJ jumped off the bar stool and straight into Symphony's arms. "You smell like peaches." He giggled.

"Hey buddy!" She squealed, tightly squeezing the snaggletooth cutie. "It's been too long. How have you been?"

"Great!" TJ exclaimed in his best Tony the Tiger voice. Everyone guffawed at this kid's animation.

"Boy, get over here and finish your breakfast." Tyus chortled. He stood, offering Symphony a seat at the kitchen table, planting a sweet kiss to her temple before she rested.

King prepared pancakes, bacon, eggs, and hashbrowns. Syncere leered enviously as everyone enjoyed a mimosa and cream tequila spiked coffee. The miniature comedian kept them entertained until mid-afternoon when he conked out on the couch. Symphony and Syncere didn't whisper a word about the letter, Malynda, nothing. They simply enjoyed each other's company until Syncere cuddled up next to TJ for a nap.

The day quickly relinquished to night as the full moon gleamed through the floor to ceiling window. Tyus convinced Symphony to stay at his house until he arranged for the basement door to be secured properly. He wasn't certain about Malynda's mental stability and was damn sure not going to take a chance.

TJ was elated to pick dinner, spaghetti and meatballs, and a movie. With Tyus leaned against the corner of the sectional, Symphony nestled against his chest while TJ rested his head in her lap. Long legs spread across his dad's, attentively watching the animated film, *Soul*, for the fifth time.

Symphony gazed at the handsome twin faces and simply smiled. She had no dream that this could be her life. No dream that she actually wanted this life - but she did. Disappointed that she'd wasted precious time on situationships and inconsequential people but thankful that Tyus aggressively, yet lovingly influenced her to get her shit together. He loved her unconditionally. Protected her at all costs. From the moment she flirted with Tyus over a year ago, settling for a one night stand, she'd been incapable of shaking the command he had over her.

"Ms. Symphony?" TJ planted his big sleepy eyes on her, disrupting her daze. She lifted her brow in recognition. "If you love my dad, does that mean you love me too?" He yawned, watching the credits roll on the screen, completely oblivious to the criticality of his question.

Tyus peered at Symphony, anticipation residing in his eyes.

"How could I love Tyus number one and not love Tyus number two?" She tickled his feet, causing a fit of giggles to echo throughout the room. TJ climbed across his dad to embrace Symphony. Tyus' heart catapulted across the room overwhelmed with emotions. And Symphony's heart wasn't far behind, pounding fiercely as she reluctantly freed TJ, hopelessly concealing her tears.

"It's time for bed, lil man." Tyus scooped up TJ, tossing him over his shoulder. He powered off the television and turned to Symphony, "you too, pretty lady. I'll meet you in the room." He winked. TJ waved at Symphony, sleepily bouncing against his dad's broad shoulder.

She obeyed Tyus' instructions and retired to the bedroom. Symphony disrobed in front of the full length mirror examining her naked frame. The curves of her bodacious body remained unchanged but there was something different about her face. Her grey irises glistened again. The curve of her lips was genuine. Symphony was happy.

Tyus greeted her, enmeshing his half-naked body against her back. His growing erection pressed against her ass.

"You are so fucking beautiful." He coddled her neck, massaging his fingertips down the length of her body. "I'm never going to let anybody hurt you, Symphony. You can trust that."

They lovingly beheld each other's gaze reflected in the mirror. Heartbeats in sync, singing the same rhythmical melody.

"Make love to me, Ty." It was more of a statement than a question as she silently cried. Tears of pure joy.

"My pleasure." His reverberating baritone was confident and assured as he captivated her, making sweet love into the wee hours of the morning.

18

Tyus squinted, slowly opening one eye to be greeted by tiny little toes. "Lil man, what are you doing in my bed? I told you to knock before entering when Ms. Symphony is here." Tyus groggily declared.

"*My* Symphony is not here." TJ nonchalantly stated as he rose to jump on the bed.

My Symphony. Tyus mused, brows slamming together in confusion. Then TJ's words registered.

He roused, grabbing TJ by the waist mid jump. "What do you mean she's not here? Where did she go?" His voice trembled, concerned.

"I don't know, dad. She cooked me pancakes and then she left." TJ hopped off the bed, picking up a piece of paper from the floor. "Oh, this is for you, dad." He handed over the paper and darted out of the room as quickly as he appeared.

Tyus didn't immediately pay attention to the paper.

Snatching his phone from the nightstand, he pressed the icon to auto dial Symphony. No answer. Straight to voicemail. *"Sweetpea, where are you? I'm worried, baby. Please call me."* He paused, nervously holding the phone. *"I love you, Symphony."*

"Where the fuck are you, baby?" Tyus whispered, perched on the edge of the bed. He rubbed a hand down his face, angrily glaring at the disrespectful sun leering through the window.

Tyus retrieved the wrinkled paper from the nightstand. Shaking his head at the syrup-ridden fingertips imprinted on the yellow note paper.

Bae, I'm sorry I left you this morning, but I had to follow my heart. I have to finish this, Ty. For me...for us. I love you, babe. I'll be back soon.

"Fuck!" Tyus shouted.

"You said a BIG bad word, dad." TJ's little voice giggled from behind the lounge chair in the dark corner of the bedroom. "Mommy says there are little bad words and big bad words. That was a big one."

"I'm sorry lil man. I will try not to say big bad words." Tyus re-read Symphony's note. "TJ, can you do me a favor and get yourself dressed... quickly? Don't forget your underwear this time, ok?" TJ nodded, then ran to his room.

Tyus hit the auto-dial again on speaker phone as he quickly dressed in a black sweat suit and black *Timbs*. He tried her phone one more time but no answer.

While waiting for TJ to get ready, Tyus replayed last night's conversation with Symphony. Repeatedly tasting her succulent sweet juices on his palate, he made love to her like a delicate flower. Soft, sweet, pleasing. Declaring his undying adoration for her through every lick, suck, nibble, and stroke. After satisfying his gluttony, Tyus rested between Symphony's curvaceous legs, head nestled against her pillowy stomach. She endeared him, massaging her fingers through the thick coils of his hair as she confessed.

"I talked to the great oracle today." She chuckled. "My G-ma. About Joel Pederson. I keep thinking if he's dead already, then I'm no closer to getting answers than I was months ago. But G-ma asked, what if he's not? What if he can offer me something that could... heal my heart?"

Shit! Tyus scrambled to get TJ bundled in his coat, hat, and gloves to weather the Missouri frost. They rode in silence other than TJ's periodic spelling words outburst. Tyus pulled into the school drop-off line and hurriedly exited the passenger seat, vainly attempting to remain calm. He and TJ exchanged their choreographed hand gesture ending with a unison *pow* sound. Observing TJ enter the school building, Tyus dialed Syncere. Before *hello* could fully escape her tongue, he interjected.

"Syn, what did the letter say?" Tyus sternly spoke into the car speakers.

"Hey Ty. Um, the letter. Symphony's letter?" Syncere questioned, fighting grogginess.

"My bad, Syn. I didn't mean to wake you but Symphony left early this morning before I woke up. She just left a note saying she had to follow her heart." He sighed, aggressively fisting the steering wheel. "I think she's going to see her father, Syn. She can't do that shit alone."

"Oh my God, Ty. No. She can't. You have to find her."

Syncere paused, tightly clenching her eyes trying to envision the logo on the envelope. "Um, there was a rose on the envelope. Um...something with a P. Uh...Penrose, I think. Prim-"

"Primrose Garden?" Tyus probed.

"Yes! That's it. Primrose Garden. The envelope had a rose logo for Primrose Garden Nursing Home." She shouted. "That's not that far from Haven. Maybe 40 minutes. Let me call King. We'll meet you there?"

"No. No, Syn. You are on bedrest for a reason. King and Symphony ain't kicking my ass for dragging you out." Tyus chuckled. "If it's ok with you, let me be there for her this time."

Syncere smiled, tears welling in her eyes. "You've always been there for her, Tyus. Even when her silly ass didn't want to recognize it." She giggled through her sobs. "Thank you, Tyus."

"For what?" He furrowed.

"For seeing the real Symphony. The one I've known and loved for my entire life. You've protected her in ways that I couldn't. Thank you for fighting for her heart. Even through all of the complicated and messy layers." Syncere smiled, sighing as she wiped her tears away. "Please text me when you find her. Ok?"

"I got you." Tyus ended the call. While he was talking to Syncere, he plugged in Primrose Gardens in the GPS. She was right, since it was still early, the drive was about 35 minutes. All of this time Symphony's father had been less than an hour away from her. He guessed Malynda was trying to inform her of Joel's impending demise, given her incessant calls and texts over the past few months. Symphony opted not to respond. Tyus silently prayed that she wouldn't regret this decision to see her father. Dead or alive, hopefully this is what she needs to begin the healing process.

TYUS PULLED into the parking lot of the Primrose Gardens Nursing Home. Spotting the black Audi Coupe, he parked next to Symphony's car. It was a beautiful facility surrounded by acres of green grass. The floor to ceiling stained-glass windows with etchings of roses were stunning. Tyus walked through the automatic entry doors pleasantly greeted by the receptionist. He peered around, spotting a waterfall, a large fish tank, and residents in wheelchairs scattered throughout the foyer enjoying an ice cream social.

Tyus surveyed the room, searching for Symphony when his eyes landed on a strangely familiar set of beautiful grey orbs, salt and pepper curly shoulder length hair, and a long black and red floral print dress that draped the floor. *Malynda James.* Tyus pondered, recognizing the powerful ancestry of G-ma Neolla James. Malynda gave him a glimpse of his Sweetpea in about twenty years - hopefully, a bit saner.

"Sir, how can I help you?" The receptionist questioned with a smile. He shuttered, forgetting that she was even there.

"Yes. Forgive me. Actually I see who I'm looking for. Thank you." Tyus smiled and nodded as he walked away.

Malynda was perched in a plush lounge chair facing the

waterfall. The impression on her face was placid. She was completely motionless. If he didn't notice the rise and fall of her chest, Tyus would've thought she was lifeless.

"Excuse me, ma'am. Are you Ms. Malynda James?" He questioned, slowly strolling towards her. Malynda blinked from her reverie before leisurely turning in the swivel chair to connect the voice with a face. And what a handsome face it was, given the blush across Malynda's fuchsia painted lips.

"Why yes, I am, handsome. And you are?" She strived for a sexy grin, but it was just... weird.

"I'm Tyus. Tyus Okoro. Symphony's -"

"Gentleman caller." Malynda sang in that annoyingly cynical tone.

"Um, no ma'am. I'm her boyfriend. Her man." Tyus closed the distance between them, taking the seat directly across from her.

"My daughter always did have a weakness for beautiful men. Much like her mother I suppose." She snickered. "You came for her? How sweet." Malynda's inflection was laced with the perfect combination of nice and nasty.

"Yes, I did. But first, we need to talk?" Tyus' inflection, on the hand, was filled with the perfect mix of *don't fuck with me and mine*. Malynda was hushed, simply nodding her understanding.

"Ms. James -"

"Please, call me Malynda." She blushed. "You, handsome, can even call me Lyndi."

"Ms. James. I will make this real quick and easy." He paused, clenching his jaws, trying his best not to call this woman a bitch. "Stay away from Symphony. I'm only going to ask you once, otherwise I can make your life miserable. I understand that you are her mother and I will respect you as such. But you are a cancer to her soul. Venom. Detrimental to the condition of her heart. And I simply can't allow that. The damage you have caused over the past thirty plus years will take more than a lifetime for me to repair. But, I will move heaven and earth for that woman to ensure she's loved, protected, and adored like she deserves. Even if that means making her mother's life a living hell."

"Is that a threat, handsome?" Malynda muttered.

"It's a promise. And I don't bullshit commitments." Tyus grimly smirked.

"What could you possibly do to me, young man, that I haven't already done to myself?" She inquired. Expression stoic.

"I suggest you don't test me, Ms. James." Tyus leered. Malynda held his ogle in an intense stare down. She was unperturbed, seemingly dismissing his warning.

Since Malynda's untimely resurfacing, Tyus leveraged his investigation skills and uncovered some interesting facts about Malynda.

"That lovely, expensive little facility you live in by the lake - it's funded by Mr. Pederson, correct? Once he's gone, where will you live? How will you maintain? Oh, that's right. You have a pretty hefty insurance policy on him. A forged insurance policy, nonetheless." His smirking escalated to complete pleasure as Malynda began to squirm.

A few weeks ago, one of Tyus' business partners emailed him a report on Malynda and Joel. Joel had been funding Malynda's living expenses for the past seven years.

They'd rekindled a secret affair after his wife died. Possibly before.

"One phone call from me and the money's gone and you go straight to jail - or wherever the courts send people in your condition. Or I could just show the police the footage of you breaking into Symphony's house. What's your pleasure?" Tyus paused, fire brewing in his eyes, anticipating her response. She had none. "Please leave Ms. James. And do not come back."

Finally, a sign of life beat against Malynda's beautiful face. She was crying. Real tears. "You're too late. My Joel is already dead." She matter-of-factly declared, standing to her full height before slowly sauntering away. And just like that, Malynda James vanished.

SUITE 1218. Tyus stalked outside of the room that the nurse directed him to for Joel Pederson. He deeply exhaled, preparing himself for whatever he was about to face. Turning the corner to enter, he labored in the threshold, watching her. The room was bright with a large picture window and photos covering the wall above the hospital bed where Joel laid. Hands rested at his abdomen, dressed in a light grey button down shirt, blanketed from the waist down. He looked peaceful, as if he simply fell asleep. Symphony rested in a chair next to the bed with her back facing the door. She was fixed, unstirred.

"Symphony." Tyus whispered. His soothing timber always calmed her spirit.

She gasped, standing from her seat as she cracked a slight smile. Symphony didn't turn to face him, but she knew he would come. Secretly hoped that he would find her because she really couldn't - shouldn't do this alone. Symphony arrived at Primrose Garden a little before 7am. Joel died just an hour before. It was now after 10am - hours had passed and she just sat there. Watching him. Discerning every miniscule detail - pale yellow and navy blue striped walls, pencil sketches of music notes and various instruments in wooden frames, bi-focal reading glasses on the nightstand.

Joel's lifeless pale body, thinning sandy brown hair, lines settled under his eyes and the corners of his lips, the arc of his face and pointy chin that mirrored hers. The countless pictures of mysterious family members. Smiling. Joyous. Grandparents, brothers, aunts, uncles - people she would never acquaint. Unattainable memories.

"Sweetpea, baby, are you ok?" Tyus dismantled the gap between them, enfolding his arms around her waist, his chest pressed against her back. Symphony sighed, resting her head against his shoulder. The visible tremble of her hand suddenly dissipated in response to his soothing caress. Tyus nestled in the fold of her neck, inhaling the natural scent that calmed his spirit.

"He died this morning. Not long before I arrived." She whispered, gaze fixed on nothing while pondering everything. "I have two brothers. They already left. Joel told them about me." Symphony chuckled. "Can you believe that?

They all knew about me and just went on with their happy lily white lives."

Tyus circled around now standing in front of her. Blocking the traumatic visual. He cupped her chin, encouraging her to look at him. "Symphony, baby, don't do this. Let's go. Let me take you home." The routine glisten of her grey irises was replaced with redness and pain. He lovingly regarded the rawness stalking in the depths of her eyes. Contemplating how he can fix this.

A knock at the door halted his musing. "Excuse me sir, ma'am. My condolences for your loss. The funeral home is ready to take him now." The petite nurse dressed in scrubs covered with puppies softly whispered. "Ma'am, will you be finalizing arrangements for your father?" She questioned.

Symphony's entire body jerked as if she was hit with the force of a bullet. *Father?* Suddenly, an eerily calming sensation covered her flesh. She smiled at the woman, picking up her purse from the chair.

"No." Symphony matter-of-factly exclaimed. She quickly ambled out of the room, never looking back, liberating herself of the ghost of Joel Pederson. Tyus immediately followed her, praying that Symphony didn't run into Malynda since he didn't actually see her leave the building.

Symphony moved expeditiously through the hallway, into the foyer, darting through senior citizens enjoying ice cream and live music. Well, an old lady singing songs and playing the xylophone. Tyus glanced around, noticing Malynda tucked in a far corner, concealed under a hat. He threateningly leered at her. She nodded her understanding.

Symphony ran out of the front door, deeply inhaling,

then exhaling the fresh crisp air, releasing the breath she didn't realize she was holding.

"Baby, are ok. Symphony? Talk to me." Tyus demanded, caressing the small of her back as she continued to intake breaths deeply.

She nodded. "Get me out of here Ty. I want to go home. It's finished." Symphony took one final inhale, filling her rosy cheeks as she audibly released. He stroked a finger down the bridge of her nose as they shared an adoring blush.

Tyus snuggled her against his sturdy frame as they sauntered to the car. He kissed her before opening the passenger door for her to enter. Securing the seat belt, he kissed against her forehead and she leaned into him and smiled. That was all the evidence he needed to know that it was finished and she was going to be ok.

Tyus hurried to the driver's seat, preparing to call his brother Titan and friend Lennox to pick up Symphony's car. Pulling the phone from his back pocket, Tyus noticed that he'd missed several phone calls and texts from Titan and King. He hopped in the car and hit the button to dial his brother. Symphony comforted against the headrest, almost dozing off to sleep just that fast.

"What's up bro?" Tyus spoke into the car speaker.

"Man, where are you? Where is Symphony?" Titan shouted.

"I'm taking care of some business. With Symphony." He paused to look at her. She was still disengaged from the conversation. "What's going on, T?"

"Um, it's Syncere. She's at the hospital." Titan's tone was concerning.

Symphony jolted from her sleepiness. "Syncere? Titan, what's wrong? What happened?" She panted, nervously anticipating his response.

"I was with King at a site this morning and Syn called crying. She'd called 911 because she was in pain and... bleeding." Titan whispered his last word.

"Oh my God. Oh my God. Please, no. Please God." Symphony pleaded silently as tears quickly flooded her face. Tyus gathered the necessary details from Titan and hauled ass out the parking lot. The Infiniti's tires screeched through the streets momentarily disrupting the quaint serene neighborhood.

MIDDAY TRAFFIC ADDED an additional half-hour to the forty minute commute to the hospital. Symphony practically had an asthma attack, panic attack, and passenger road rage all at the same damn time. Tyus caressed her hand unsuccessfully attempting to keep her calm as she screamed for drivers to *get the fuck out of the way*. To make matters worse, they were unable to reach King after multiple attempts.

Symphony debated every sane and insane reason for his silence. She shuddered, endeavoring to rebuke the traumatic thoughts infiltrating her mind. Tyus abruptly stopped the car in front of the emergency room entrance, thankfully disturbing her heart wrenching trance.

"Go, go, go." Tyus shouted and Symphony obeyed. She

dashed through the automatic doors searching the waiting room but no King. Thankfully, she knew one of the ER nurses and was able to get some details about her cousin's whereabouts. Symphony's mind went blank and she felt dizzy when she heard him say, *"emergency cesarean."*

After the momentary daze, she bolted through a few sets of double doors reaching the elevator bank. Symphony knew exactly where a patient in Syncere's condition would be. She texted the location to Tyus before entering the elevator. Thankfully, the car was empty. Aggressively pressing the number seven, praying that it would move faster. Of course in the middle of an emergency, it stopped on three different floors before reaching her destination.

Symphony ran to the maternity waiting room, circling around until her eyes landed on King. Normally a gigantic figure, King looked small, defeated, as he perched in a corner, face resting in both hands.

"King." Symphony whimpered.

His head popped up in response. King peered at Symphony, fresh tears swelling in the corners of his eyes. She quickly sat next to him, gently placing her hand against his shoulder.

"I was only gone for two hours. She said she would be ok. I only left her for two hours." King's speech was broken, breathless. "My Princess was crying, she was in so much pain. Terrified. The paramedics let me keep talking to her, then nothing. I screamed her name. I screamed, *Princess.* But no words. I couldn't help her, Prima. I couldn't-" He audibly sobbed. The vehement pain was palpable. Fucking heart-breaking.

"They won't let me see her. I need to hear her voice, Symphony. I need to kiss her and take care of her. I'm her King and she's my Princess. I can't lose -"

Symphony angrily interrupted. "No! Don't! We will not do that. Prima is a fighter. Do you hear me?" She didn't wait for a response.

"I'm going to see what information I can get. Syncere is going to be fine. And my two peas - " Symphony paused, blinking back the newest collection of tears debuting as her voice croaked. "Our two peas in a pod are going to be kicking and screaming and driving us insane." She laughed and so did King.

"For Syncere Cartwright?" The voice of a tall Black man still dressed in the disposable covering worn during surgery called out, quickly gaining their attention. Moments later, Syncere's obstetrician Dr. Cynthia Ingler appeared as well.

"King." Dr. Ingler simply greeted. "They're resting." She spoke quickly, attempting to quell the terror strained across King and Symphony's faces. Before the doctor continued, Tyus joined them in the waiting room. He lifted his brows to Symphony, praying for a positive response in return. She nodded.

"They?" King stated simply to ensure he heard correctly.

"Yes, King. They." Dr. Ingler smiled. "Baby girl was first weighing five pounds three ounces and 11 minutes later, baby boy at six pounds even."

King loudly sighed, his head tossed back between his shoulder blades. Smiling towards the ceiling, he whispered a word of thanks before continuing.

"My Princess - when can I see her? Syncere. When can I see my wife?" King probed.

"You know I always give it to you straight, King. Syncere had a rough time in surgery. We had to heavily medicate her to address the increased blood pressure and heart rate to ensure we could safely and quickly retrieve the babies while also keeping her safe - alive. She scared me, King, but your wife is a tough cookie. Syncere is stable but she's going to be in a lot of pain and groggy when she wakes up. So you must be patient. Ok?"

Dr. Ingler spoke briefly with the tall gentleman behind her. "Dr. Chapman here will take you to see her. The Cartwright babies are in the nursery. Buzz the nurse if you would like them brought to the room." She patted King on the arm and walked away.

"King, go. I'll talk to the nurse." Symphony instructed as King speedily disappeared down the hall. Once he was out of view, Symphony turned to Tyus, collapsing her forehead against the center of his firm chest and wept.

Nearing the end of a long gloomy grey December day, the maternity floor's waiting room reached its capacity filled with family and friends eagerly anticipating a peek of the newest additions to the James - Cartwright family. Syncere slept for hours as her vitals stabilized throughout the day. Her first words when she awakened were *King* and *twins*. Symphony chuckled, watching Syncere literally transition from practically comatose to fully alert mommy mode within an hour.

The maternity suite's oversized door crept open as the nurse entered with a big smile, pushing the wide mobile crib. All of the James women, including G-ma's, grey orbs glistened with delight at the sight of the twins snuggled together. Syncere trembled with anticipation, the gratification of motherhood outweighing the post-operation pain streaking through her pelvis.

"Mommy, Daddy, meet your beautiful babies." The nurse scooped out both babies effortlessly, laying them against Syncere's naked flesh.

"Oh my God. You are perfect." Syncere whispered, planting kisses against their tiny temples. The twins squirmed and cooed at the sound of their mother's voice. There was not a dry eye in the room.

Symphony stalked from across the room surveying the blessings before her. Although it still riled her to even consider the parents God chose for her, Symphony was thankful for the love and family she had right before her eyes. Her chest began to rapidly heave, overwhelmed with joyfulness. Grateful. In less than 24 hours, she'd experienced the beauty and tranquility of both life and death. Feeling orphaned in one moment and cherished in the next. The emotional juxtaposition of gaining peace through the death of a man she loathed and the new lives she adored.

"Prima." Syncere raspily called out. "Come and meet your peas." The cousins locked mirrored orbs with a smile.

Symphony cleaned her hands then extended her arms to welcome the tiny baby boy with a face identical to his father swaddled in a blue blanket and matching hat covering his head.

"Meet your nephew, King Elias Cartwright, Jr." King proudly announced his namesake.

Syncere followed suit, transferring the baby girl into her

cousin's other arm. Symphony admired the tiny cutie adorned with those James women eyes, swaddled in a yellow blanket and hat concealing her curly chocolate brown hair.

"Meet your niece, Empress Symphony Neolla Cartwright." Syncere sang. Symphony was surprised. Honored. The floodgate of tears discharged at the realization of her and G-ma's namesake.

It was now after midnight but Symphony couldn't bring herself to leave the hospital. G-ma was reluctant to leave but acquiesced at Syncere's insistence. Thankfully, Aminah had arrived and volunteered to get G-ma home safely. Syncere laid against King's chest in the hospital bed. He looked like a giant, his massive feet dangling off the side with no care. Symphony smiled, still watching them. King Jr. cradled against his mother's breast and baby Empress cuddled in the arc of her daddy's chest. They were beautiful. Their love was breathtaking. And Symphony was enamored, yet terrified. Was this the desires of her heart - love, marriage, and babies?

"Symphony." Tyus' exhausted baritone was gruff yet reassuring. "Sweetpea, you need to get some rest."

"I can't take my eyes off of them." She adoringly grinned, quickly eyeing Tyus.

"They are pretty spectacular - King Jr. and Empress that is." He softly cackled.

Tyus perched behind her, caressing her shoulders as he kissed against her neck. He unequivocally loved and cherished Symphony. Her protector. His beloved. Tyus envisioned a similar future with her but wavered on Symphony's sentiments.

"I remember Syncere telling me that she prayed for love,

marriage, and babies for her Prima. Prayed that somebody would come into her cousin's life to protect her, offer love without requisites. Guard the condition of her heart." Tyus lovingly squeezed Symphony's waist, turning her around to face him.

"Let me see how I'm faring against this wish list. Love, and without conditions - check. Protection, guarding your heart - check, check. Now for marriage and babies...." Tyus stroked her cheek, cupping her chin for the softest, sweetest kiss that calmed her trembling hands, sending a vibration between her thighs.

"I love you, Symphony. More than you probably even realize. That night I found you on the floor, I prayed that you were unharmed, alive. I knew then that you were mine. My responsibility. My Sweetpea. Your heart belonged to only me."

Symphony cried, digesting the sincerity and authenticity of his words. She swallowed, loudly exhaling, attempting to quell her nervousness. Subconsciously, she reached for her lotus flower necklace for comfort as she often did. It was gone. Symphony gasped, peering around, searching for it on the floor.

"Are you looking for this?" Tyus held up the lotus flower necklace gently wrapped around his pointer finger. Sexily grinning, waiting for her to notice the sparkle of the stunning yellow halo diamond ring dangling from the chain.

"Ty!" Symphony shouted, then quickly covered her mouth since they were still in the hospital room. "Ty. What are you doing?" She whispered.

"I'm not doing anything right now, Sweetpea. I know

you're not ready." Sadness and understanding lingered in Tyus' honey brown eyes.

"Bae, I love you." Symphony interjected, caressing his cheeks to assure him of her feelings. "I -"

"Shhh. I know you love me, Sweetpea. I've never doubted that. Even through all of your crazy shit." He laughed. "I just want you to know my intentions, Symphony. I want to give you the desires of your heart - known and unknown. But in your time. When you're ready. The meaning of the lotus flower necklace remains the same. Your symbol of life, renewal, calm, and peace. And adding this ring signifies commitment...from me."

"Because you don't bullshit commitments." Symphony giggled, as Tyus wiped the tears from her reddened cheeks. "I love you Ty and I can't imagine what my life would be if I didn't meet this beautifully caramel man who literally swept me off my feet. I would probably be in jail for killing some-body." She laughed as they transitioned to the lounge chair. Symphony laid across Tyus' lap fondling the necklace and ring as she continued.

"But I found myself when I found you, bae. I'm finally comprehending Symphony because you love me as I am. I've spent so much time pretending, concealing my pain with anger. My *boss bitch* behavior. The meaningless situation-ships." She smirked, rolling her eyes. "I'm on a journey, Ty. My heart is finally healing. I want to make sure my heart is whole for me... before I can commit to being whole for you. Because I too don't bullshit commitments."

Tyus smiled. Fathoming her words and the sincerity and veracity that resided within them.

"Baby, that's perfect. You're perfect." Tyus gently kissed her lips, capturing her tongue. Their mouths clinging passionately, sensually - with love.

"You promise you won't give up on me, bae." She whimpered with their temples enmeshed. Her silent tears stained his face.

"Nah Sweetpea, I'm stuck with your crazy ass forever." He affirmed. "Just the way I like it."

Tyus and Symphony snuggled in the hospital lounge chair, a glimpse of their future life across the room. They smiled. Gaze Affixed. Lovingly yoked. Tyus caressed her back as she gently stroked the curves of his face. Adoringly kindred, her start was his finish, his beginning - her end. Exchanging tranquil inhales and exhales until they drifted asleep.

EPILOGUE

"**S**weetpea, are you feeling ok? I wasn't expecting you to be asleep." Tyus nestled behind Symphony in the king size bed. She shuffled closer to him, groggily stretching her curvy frame.

"Hey bae. I had a headache so I took a nap." Symphony yawned. "The Cartwright Clan were here earlier helping me unpack and keeping me company." She laughed, referring to Syncere and her toddler twins, Emi and King Jr.

Tyus was hushed for a long moment. "That's good." He dryly murmured.

Symphony raised an eyebrow. Tyus was different, a little distant. He'd been that way for the last few days. She turned, eyeing him closely as he laid on his back, hands propped behind his head staring at the ceiling.

"Ty, bae, are you ok?" She stroked a finger down his handsome face.

"I'm good." His tone remained short, brittle.

"Ty -"

"Symphony, don't ask me what's wrong again when you already know. I don't want to talk about it." He jolted up, then perched on the edge of the bed.

"Finish getting some rest." Tyus stood from the bed, attempting to walk away but she grabbed his arm.

"Tyus, babe, please don't do that. Just talk to me please." Symphony whined.

"We've been talking about this and your position is clear. You are ready to be everything but my wife." Tyus hissed, ambling across the room to change his clothes.

Almost two years had passed since Tyus declared his love for Symphony. She still wore the lotus charm necklace that housed the beautiful yellow diamond ring symbolizing his commitment and intention for their relationship. But Symphony was still hesitant although she and Tyus were making other steps towards lifelong promises. There was no doubt that she absolutely loved and adored him, but she was sometimes still haunted by the trauma of her past. Therapy helped deal with her emotions about her mother and father, but her struggles were still very real and present. Thankfully, Malynda hadn't surfaced since that fateful day in the nursing home.

"Ty, I thought we agreed that we wouldn't rush. You said you wouldn't give up on me." Tears began to bubble in Symphony's gorgeous grey eyes. Her curly mane scattered across the mustard yellow wall length headboard.

Tyus furrowed, rubbing a hand down his face before turning to address her.

"Do you really think I'm giving up on you, Sweetpea?

When I'm practically begging you to take this next step in our journey. You're right - I did say I wouldn't rush but our circumstances have changed and they require immediate attention, not the leisurely consideration you've been giving for the past two years." Tyus repositioned on the bed, gently enfolded her foot between his hands, caressing and massaging the achiness away. Even in his dismay, he always lovingly regarded Symphony. "Honestly, Symphony, I had no dream that two years would lapse and we would still be here... not together as husband and wife."

"Babe, we have such an amazing life. What is a piece of paper going to change?" She shyly shrugged, endeavoring not to be dismissive.

"Symphony! Please don't attempt to dilute the sanctity of marriage into just a piece of paper." Tyus snapped. He glared at her, angry mistiness swelling in his eyes because she just didn't seem to understand his plight.

"Do you remember when I said you make it hard to love you?" Symphony nodded, wiping away a single crocodile tear. "I recant that statement, baby. I cannot comprehend feeling this kind of love with anybody other than you. And in my opinion marriage solidifies that."

Tyus repositioned her legs to cradle around his waist, drawing her closer into his frame. "Have I not given you everything your heart desires? Hmm?" Tyus trailed a finger down the bridge of her nose to her pouty lips allowing no time for a response.

"Love, compassion, understanding. A family, a home. You wanted a new house in Haven. Well you're sitting in your brand new house with your G-ma and cousin not far away. Just like you requested. Symphony, you can ask me for anything and baby it's yours." He paused, now massaging her curvy thighs. "You wanna know the desires of my heart?"

"Ty, don't -" She pleaded, praying that he would end this conversation. Symphony was vastly aware of his desires, but still deeply fearful of abandonment and heartbreak.

"I want an Okoro Crew. A family bearing my name. Not an Okoro - James Crew. I want all of you, Sweetpea. I want love, babies, and marriage. I want Mrs. Tyus Anthony Okoro."

"We are not traditional types of people, Ty. Our bond, this love, is stronger than people who carry the same last name." She rebutted.

"No, we are not traditional and that's why we've been doing shit the way we want to do it since day one. That will never change. But making a commitment to each other, to a higher power, to our families and children is important to me. And you know I don't-"

"I know, Ty. You don't bullshit commitments." She interjected, smiling, but Tyus wasn't amused.

He kissed her temple, lingering there for several sweet moments. Anguish laced the folds of his handsome face.

"I want you and everything that's in our future to carry my family name. I just don't understand why that's so hard for you to comprehend."

The rise and fall of her chest contradicted the breathlessness commanding her body. Tyus' adoringly dewy gaze and sentimental words penetrated her heart in a different way.

He'd always been acutely attuned with the desires of her heart, but rarely expressive about his own. Today, Tyus was free of ambiguity about his ambitions.

"I'm going to finish unpacking my office and order some dinner. Rest, baby." He cupped her chin, encouraging her lips to his. Tyus peered into Symphony's eyes for what felt like an eternity, delicately kissing her before ambling out of the room.

Symphony eyed him until his glorious frame disappeared. Angst and tribulation weighed him down - and she was unnecessarily the cause. She reminisced on Tyus' words the first day they met in front of Davenport Realty almost three years ago. *Hello gorgeous. There is only one Tyus Sweetpea.*" Symphony softly chuckled through her tears. He was right. There'd only been one man for her - *him.*

Symphony hurriedly shuffled to the other side of the massive mattress to retrieve her phone. She pressed the screen to dial G-ma and Syncere on video chat. The group call rang three times before a response.

"Hi, girly girl."

"Hey, Prima."

Syncere and G-ma sang in unity.

"I messed up with Ty... again. But I have an idea and I need your help." Symphony cried.

TWO WEEKS PASSED since Tyus and Symphony's disagreement and the tension was stout. She'd fruitlessly attempted to resurface the conversation but Tyus hurriedly shut her down. In his words, *it's your show Sweetpea, I'm done with it.* Unbeknownst to her, Tyus awakened multiple nights just to simply observe her. He wanted her. Not just in his bed, or in their home but as his wife. Tyus was disheartened and invigorated by her all in the same breath. And it pissed him off. Their movie nights became strained, dinners grew silent and Symphony's alarm for her relationship escalated every second.

It was a warm and breezy day in June and Symphony was preparing her gorgeous new home to welcome guests for their new beginnings party and to celebrate Tyus and Titan's birthday. The beautiful two story house with grey stone and black shutters was just a block from her cousin's. Over the past two years the couple spent so much time at each other's homes that they decided to build an abode together.

Symphony surprised Tyus with a golf outing for his birthday with his father, his brother Titan, King, Nicolas and Lennox the morning of the party. Tyus was hesitant to leave her with the final touches for the party but she was insistent that her crew could handle it. His only directive was to be back at the house by 4pm. Syncere and Aminah scrambled throughout the house overseeing the decorations while G-ma, King's mother Lorna and Tyus' mother Racine were supervising the kitchen. But actually, they were nibbling, critiquing the food and in the damn way.

The chef was busy preparing the Italian themed menu

for 50 guests. Chicken parmesan, shrimp scampi, gnocchi, fettuccine alfredo, mixed vegetables, salad and a host of delicious hors d'oeuvres. The backyard had been transformed into an all white extravaganza with splashes of deep orange, sapphire and yellow. White shimmery satin cloth draped the tables accented with fresh roses and gold candelabras in the center. The vivid roses meticulously arranged to construct the flower wall was the focal point of the backyard positioned under the pergola.

Symphony peeked out of the window of her master suite to see several guests arriving dressed in various shades of yellow. Hostesses greeted them with their choice of Toussaint Winery's red blend wine or prosecco, and passed hors d'oeuvres.

"Prima, he's here." Syncere squealed, announcing Tyus' arrival home.

Symphony audibly exhaled, clutching her stomach as the butterflies and goosebumps collided. "Ok. I'm ready." She could hear his beautiful baritone echoing from the hallway.

Tyus entered his master bedroom suite welcomed by a trail of white roses leading him to his Sweetpea perched in the bay window seat. Symphony was stunning in a white strapless flowy A-line silhouette with sheer chiffon overlay. Her wild curly mane was tamed into a high bun decorated with a glistening rhinestone comb resembling the lotus flower charm. Diamond stud earrings lead the trail down her lengthy neck to the timeless necklace Tyus gifted her during their vacation in Mexico. Tyus' honeyed eyes widened at the sight of her beauty. He was rendered breathless.

"Sweetpea, baby, you are exquisite." He closed the distance between them, desperately needing to be closer to her. "You did all of this for my birthday?" Tyus kissed against her temple, placing his hands atop of hers, still resting against her stomach attempting to settle the flutter.

"Anything for you, bae." She sexily smiled. "Can we talk?" He nodded in agreement.

"Ty, I love you and I'm sorry for my bullshit. For the past two years, you've done nothing but love me without rules or conditions and I've taken that for granted. I've taken you for granted. You've given me a life that I couldn't even imagine in my wildest dreams. Pleasing me has always been your priority even when I didn't deserve it. And I want to return the favor, bae." Symphony's alluring grey orbs were dewy with tears.

"Baby, what's going on?" Tyus nervously questioned as a knock on the door disrupted his gaze into her glorious grey eyes.

TJ's cute face was ushered into the room by Syncere. He was handsomely dressed in off-white shorts, a yellow button-down shirt, and saddle tan loafers. He'd grown a couple inches and a few teeth over the past two years. TJ waved, grinning up at his dad as Symphony welcomed him into their coupling. He was holding a black velvet box that he handed to Symphony.

"Remember when TJ asked me if I loved his dad, does that mean I loved him too?" Symphony cupped TJ's little face, the tears that were previously a threat began to escape.

"TJ, I love your dad with all of my heart and I love you. I

want us to be a family. Would it be ok with you if I officially joined the Okoro Crew?" She smiled.

TJ's brow furrowed in confusion. "Duh, My Symphony! You, Dad, me, and my baby sister True are already in the Okoro Crew." TJ shrugged, giggling as he leaned against Symphony's bulging pregnant belly, planting a sweet kiss.

Symphony and Tyus walked to the beat of their own drum since the inception of their relationship. While Symphony didn't follow the traditional order of love, marriage, and babies, she was gaining the desires of her heart. Tyus was the love of her life. TJ was the best addition to her world that she didn't realize she needed. And in about six weeks, she would welcome a baby girl completing her unconventional family dynamic.

"Tyus, do you still wanna be stuck with me - with us, forever - starting today?" Symphony opened the blinds, revealing the back yard filled with their family and friends willingly waiting to witness their unconditional love.

"Surprise!" She twinkled. "You wanna meet me at the altar since we're going half on baby?"

"You damn right, Sweetpea. You, TJ and baby True are my forever and always." Tyus lovingly proclaimed.

Symphony opened the black box revealing the yellow diamond ring and a matching wedding band for him. Her hands trembled, her breathing labored as she unsuccessfully ventured to speak. Tyus planted his hand against the lotus flower necklace and gently tapped. Symphony instantly calmed.

"I'm ready, Ty. My shattered heart is mended and ready...

for *you,* babe." She happily sobbed, kissing against the palm of Tyus' hand and tightly squeezed TJ, still nestled against her belly. Symphony melted, joyously enmeshed between her two heart beats.

THE END.

LOVE NOTE TO MY READERS

Hey Loves! Thank you so much for reading Pretty Shattered Heart. Symphony is a mess! But I loved all of her messiness. LOL. Symphony and Tyus were layered characters that pushed me to think beyond the happily ever after. I absolutely loved the way Tyus loves Symphony!

I hope you laugh and fall in love with them as much as I did!

Let me and the world know what you think by leaving a review on Amazon or Goodreads.

But what about Aminah? She has a story to share. Will she and Nic figure this thing out or will they continue to camouflage their painful pasts? Stay tuned for Aminah Loveless's story in Pretty Shattered Mind.

BOOKS BY ROBBI RENEE

WWW.LOVENOTESBYROBBIRENEE.COM

French Kiss Christmas

Pretty Shattered Soul

The Love Notes Journal

Join my private ladies only Facebook Group - Love Notes.

Follow me on social media

- Facebook and Instagram @LoveNotesbyRobbiRenee
- Twitter @LoveRobbi.

MEET ROBBI RENEE

Hey Loves! I grew up in St. Louis, Missouri (in the words of Nelly, "I'm from the Lou and I'm proud!) with two incredible parents and two amazing older sisters. Being the baby of the bunch, I always had a vivid imagination and was wise beyond my years - *too grown for my own good* if you ask my mother! My love for talking too much, journaling, various genres of movies, books, and all things Oprah led me to complete a journalism degree, doing everything but being a journalist. I dishonored my childhood dreams of being in some form of entertainment, pursuing every career but anything related to reading, writing, or journalism.

I rekindled my love for reading and writing during the 2020 pandemic where my alter ego, Robbi Renee was born, starting my company, Love Notes by Robbi Renee. I was challenged to write and publish my first novella, French Kiss Christmas, published December 2020.

Robbi Renee draws upon personal experiences with life

and love. My written works are inspired by my adoration for Black love, and stories of romance, heartache, trauma, intuition, and redemption.

Stacey/Robbi Renee enjoys her own Black family love story with her husband and teenage son. Don't miss what's next for Robbi Renee at www.lovenotesbyrobbirenee.com

Made in the USA
Columbia, SC
03 February 2025

53249560R00148